WOODWALKER

WOODWALKER

WOODWALKER

EMILY B. MARTIN

HARPER
VOYAGER
IMPULSE

An Imprint of HarperCollins Publishers

WOODWALKER. Copyright © 2016 by Emily B. Martin. All rights reserved under International and Pan-American Copyright Conventions. By payment of the required fees, you have been granted the nonexclusive, nontransferable right to access and read the text of this e-book on screen. No part of this text may be reproduced, transmitted, downloaded, decompiled, reverse-engineered, or stored in or introduced into any information storage and retrieval system, in any form or by any means, whether electronic or mechanical, now known or hereafter invented, without the express written permission of HarperCollins e-books. For information, address HarperCollins Publishers, 195 Broadway, New York, NY 10007.

EPub Edition MAY 2016 ISBN: 9780062473707

Print Edition ISBN: 9780062473714

10 9 8 7

To Lucy and Amelia.
It wouldn't have happened without you.

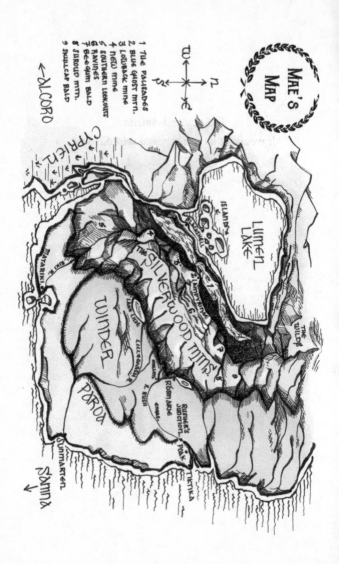

PROLOGUE

King Valien drummed his fingers on the rough table, the scars on his right hand shining pink against his copper skin. Both he and the figure facing him were keeping their hoods up over their heads, and this extra covering coupled with the unsettling news he had just received were making his skin damp with sweat. Before him, the only distinguishing characteristic the shadowed figure bore was a wrought-silver band around one finger, set with a milky pearl.

"Are you sure?" the king pressed quietly. The tavern buzzed with the ambient noise of townsfolk drinking away the day's toils, but he could take no chances that he might be overheard. If there hadn't been a howl-ing storm outside, he would have met his informant far out in the hills, away from sharp-eyed folk all too ready to report his surreptitious meeting back to his council.

"Positively," replied his informant. "I found them in Sunmarten. All three. Queen Mona Alastaire and her brothers. My king, the royals of Lumen Lake are not dead as we assumed. And it's only a matter of time before our enemies find out as well."

The king frowned, his fingers still restless. This changed everything. This threw every power in the eastern world into a startling unknown. His own crown, so recently won, would be among the first to be affected.

"Well," he said evenly, curling his fingers into a fist and staring at the hooded figure. "We must do something about it."

CHAPTER 1

Drowning. Not the method I would have chosen to win the trust of bystanders.

I had been watching the man and woman for the better part of an hour from where I sat on the pier. They worked in tandem, with one diving gracefully into the water just as the other surfaced. They stayed under for an alarmingly long time before reappearing to empty the woven baskets around their necks. He could hold his breath longer than she could, but it was clear she could dive deeper, the shine from her golden hair lost to the gray-green depths. I shivered as I watched; the late April breeze was warm here on the coast, but the water still held on to its winter chill, and the pair were only wearing light clothes. In fact, he was bare-chested, while she wore a dark sleeveless shirt tucked into her trousers. Their pale skin sported a fresh layer of sunburn.

It was unusual, this sight. Most folk in the coastal country of Paroa were fishermen or merchants—the waters were simply too rough and too sparse to support successful diving. Yet here they were, bringing up basketfuls of abalone and sorting them into piles on the shore. A few wary gulls hopped eagerly around their catch.

"Finished, have you?"

I looked up, the sea-beaten fisherman blocking out the sun's glare. He gestured to the net in my hand. "I'll not pay you for idle time, you hear? If you're done, you're done." He tossed me a copper coin. I set down the netting, my fingers red from mending the fibers, and tucked the coin into my pocket. He gathered up his net and made his way back along the pier, passing the two divers and their growing pile of abalone.

I stood, brushing flax off my trousers. The lonely coin I had just garnered from the morning of mean work would not take me far, and that meant I would have to hunt for another job if I wanted anything for lunch. I started back the same way the fisherman had gone.

It was a gusty day, and the water foamed on either side of the pier, covering the stones with salty spray. I walked up the exact center of the pathway toward the two divers, unnerved by the roiling waves. The woman knelt on the rocks, picking over her most recent catch. As I reached her side, I found my way obstructed by a pair of legs tottering under an unruly armful of canvas and oars. I ducked, but the oars stretched wider than the pier, and the idiot carrying them wasn't bothering to use his eyes . . . and the vengeful ocean was just dying for a victim. So it was without further ado that I cracked my head on one of the blades and toppled sideways.

I managed one phrase—*"earth and sky!"*—before plunging into the stinging water.

The power of the current was astonishing, first tossing me into the rocks before dragging me away from the shore like a master hauling on a mule. I flailed under the surface, clawing for some kind of purchase, but I had never learned how to swim, and my efforts did nothing to stop my descent. Air streamed out of my mouth, each bubble a firefly winking away toward the surface.

A slow burn crept through my chest; my mind numbed in horror. I thrashed in the raging water. After everything—every wretched thing I had been through, every indignity, every loss—this was how I was going to die.

Before I could fully give in to my panic, however, the water swirled behind me, and two arms wound up under my armpits, lofting me toward the sunlight.

We broke the surface, and I spluttered like a cat choking on a bone as my rescuer dragged me on my back to the edge of the pier. Two freckled arms reached down from the rocks and hauled me onto solid ground. Golden hair flashed in the sunlight.

The woman diver climbed up the slick rocks, shedding water. The man knelt beside me.

"Take a few deep breaths," he said.

I did, hacking out salt water. The woman dropped down on the man's far side, wringing out her braid.

"Not a swimmer, are you?" she remarked.

I shook my head. Water trickled out of my ears. "How could you tell?"

"Did you swallow any water?" asked the man. The blonde of his beard was darker and redder than his hair, which matched the woman's.

"No." I touched my forehead, my hand shaking slightly. "Am I bleeding?"

"No, but you'll have a bruise. Nothing a balm can't take care of."

I drew in a slow breath, relishing the sensation of air in my lungs. As my fright eased, I looked at the woman. She regarded me with a distant coolness, one eyebrow raised ever so slightly.

I steadied my trembling hand and held it out to her, palm-up. "Thank you. I'm useless in the water. You saved my life."

She looked first at my hand, and then back up at my face, her eyes narrowing just slightly.

"Well," I said, using my outstretched hand to sweep my bedraggled hair over my shoulder. "I suppose I've imposed on you enough. Bless the Light for your skill in the water and regard for a stranger's life." I bent my knees to stand. "Good luck with your abalone."

"Wait," she said.

I paused, looking at her again. She cleared her throat.

"Colm," she said. "Don't you think we ought to see to that bruise? She could have been concussed."

Her brother—of this I was sure, thanks to the golden hair, freckles, and the familial look she shot him—furrowed his brow, but before he could speak, she picked up her tunic and pulled it over her head.

"Come," she commanded, standing. "Let's get you into the tavern. The barman may have something warm you can take. Brandy, perhaps."

"I'm . . . not . . ."

But she dragged me to my feet and steered me back up the pier, wending in and out among the bustle of fishermen. I won't lie—I didn't put up much of a fight. Her brother Colm shrugged on his own shirt and started after us.

"Your abalone," I protested.

"We'll collect more," she said flatly.

The tavern was quiet and dark after the blazing activity on the pier. It wasn't time yet for the boatmen to come plodding in to banish the day's weariness with a tankard, and so the only other person inside was the barman. The golden-haired woman sat me down at a table by the empty fireplace and pulled out the chair across from me.

"What about my brandy?" I asked, raising an eyebrow.

She ignored me and sat down, her wet trousers dripping onto the flagstones. Her brother sank down next to me with an air of unease.

"What's your name?" she asked me.

"Mae," I said. "What's yours?"

"Where do you come from, Mae?"

"What's it matter to you? This town is full of travelers."

"But none, I think, that hail from your homeland. Your accent and careless mannerisms betray you."

"What mannerisms?" I asked, stung.

She gestured impatiently. "You shout a remarkably specific oath—no one within two hundred miles of here says *earth and sky*—you give thanks palm-up, and you take to water as well as a drunken cat. I spent too long tiptoeing around your imbecile king to not recognize someone from the Silverwood Mountains."

"He's not my king."

"Don't lie to me . . ."

"No," I interrupted, crossing my arms. "You're not wrong. I'm from the Silverwood. But Valien's not my king. And if you think I stick out, you should see yourselves. You look like a couple of cornstalks in a bean field. You're not native Sea-folk any more than I am."

She folded her hands on the table, her eyes icy. "So," she said.

"So," I replied. "Thank you for saving my life, and for pretending to buy me a brandy, but I think I'll be on my way."

"What do you mean when you say Valien is not your king?"

"Just what I said. I'm no citizen of his, and I'm not loyal to his council."

"But you're from the Silverwood Mountains."

"Once upon a time, yes, I was."

"Care to elaborate?"

"Not if you're going to keep secrets yourself." I started to rise from my chair, but as I did, she reached into her damp collar and drew out a long silver chain. Dangling at the end was an iridescent pearl as big as my toenail.

"Do you know what this is?" she asked.

"A pearl."

"And where do pearls come from?"

"They're spit up by mussels."

She closed her eyes briefly, holding her breath at my ignorance. "We'll come back to that. I mean *where*— where in the eastern world do we find pearls?"

"Lumen Lake, of course. I'm not an idiot. I lived in the mountains right next door for most of my life."

She closed her fingers around the pendant. "There you have it. We are folk of the lake, Mae. We come from Lumen."

I allowed surprise to register on my face. "Well, what are you doing diving for sea snails in Tiktika, three-hundreddy-some-odd miles from home? I didn't think anyone escaped the Alcoran invasion three years ago. Shouldn't you be dead, or enslaved?"

"Yes," she said quietly, but before she could continue, a spate of shouting filtered through the tavern's speckled window. We turned to peer out onto the docks, where a flurry of activity was broiling. A tussle was drawing a knot of eager bystanders. Some were trying to separate the culprits, but most were egging them on.

"Oh, great Light," the woman spat.

Colm rose from the table. "I'll get him." He headed out into the sunlight. We watched as he waded into the sea of onlookers, reached down, and lifted a figure by the collar. Brushing off riled spectators like mosquitoes, he bore his quarry back toward the tavern. The ragdoll figure in his grip twisted and shouted, his toes barely brushing the ground.

" . . . and I hope you choke on it, you cheating son of a cowbird! I hope your boat springs a leak the next time you . . . Put me down, Colm!"

Colm threw his catch into the remaining chair and sat down again without a word. The newcomer's hair was a darker, dirtier gold than the other two, but he had more freckles than the two of them put together. Perched under his right eye was an old white scar shaped like an upturned smile. Across the table, the woman was glaring at the boy with a look that could have frozen the waves lapping at the pier. A familial look. Another sibling.

"Swear that fisherman started it," he said, meeting her glare with a thrust-out chin. "All morning I helped him haul nets, and then he goes to count out my share of the catch and he . . ."

"Arlen," she interrupted. "Be quiet."

He slouched back into his seat, glowering and nudging his swelling lip with his knuckle. Then he noticed me.

"Who's that?"

"We were in the process of figuring that out," she

said, turning her attention back to me. "Where did we leave off?"

"With you claiming to be Lake-folk when most tales say you should either be dead or diving for pearls under the Alcoran flag," I said.

"Many people did die that day, but obviously we were not among them," she said with a bitter edge to her voice. "We three were the only ones to escape the lake."

"Convenient for you, if not for the rest of your folk."

Arlen slammed his hands on the table, his eyes blazing. "How *dare* you . . ."

"I'm not interested in debating the truths of that day with you," she said, overriding her youngest brother's outburst.

"Then what *are* you interested in?" I asked. "I've given you my thanks, which I'm starting to regret. What say we part ways as unlikely acquaintances and leave it at that?"

"Because I'm not interested in that, either. I'm interested in information. You come from the Silverwood, the lake's eastern neighbor. I saved you from drowning. As repayment, I would appreciate information on the current state of Lumen Lake and the plight of our folk."

"You're Silvern?" Arlen asked, looking me up and down. "Of course you are, now I see it. Colors that dark, you're not fooling anyone . . ."

"Arlen, great Light, if you can't say anything useful, then keep quiet." His sister's eyes didn't leave mine.

I quirked an eyebrow at her. "You speak pretty

boldly for a refugee from a fallen country. And anyway, you're out of luck. My information is more out of date than yours. I haven't been in the mountains in five years, long before the Alcoran invasion."

"Why not?"

"None of your business."

For someone dressed as a displaced vagrant, she certainly could convey a look of authority. I tried to return her icy stare without blinking.

"Why not?" she asked again.

"None of your *damn* business."

Her cool gaze flicked over my own tattered appearance. "You don't look as though you moved away for better opportunities. Family trouble?"

"Hardly."

"Punishment?" Her eyes narrowed. "Exile?"

That was quick. I hadn't anticipated we'd land on the topic so promptly. My hesitation seemed to confirm things for her. She leaned back with the air of someone used to interrogation.

"Exile, then."

"Fine." I waved a hand in irritated concession. "I was banished. I'm not to set foot under the eaves of the Silverwood."

"What for?"

"What does it *matter*?" I spat.

She drew her index finger along her lower lip. "I suppose it doesn't. Perhaps appearances are correct, and you really are just a common criminal."

"I am *not*," I replied forcefully.

She lifted a delicate eyebrow, and I huffed in acquiescence. I'd lost control of the conversation. "I spoke out against the imbecile king."

"Against King Valien?"

"Against Vandalen. Valien was only the prince when I was a citizen. All his father had to do was snap his fingers, and I went from a member of the Royal Guard to someone with no title and no home."

"But Vandalen was killed last year, when he tried to overthrow the Alcoran invaders and claim the Lumeni throne as his own. I heard the news in Sunmarten. Valien's the new king now. Couldn't he reinstate you?"

"I sincerely doubt it. Vandalen's old councilors won't give up the idea of acquiring Lumen Lake, and unless things have changed drastically, Valien won't have any power over them. He'll be nothing more than their puppet until he finds some kind of leverage."

I could almost see the woman arranging her thoughts behind her stormy blue eyes. "You were in the Royal Guard, you say?"

"I was a Woodwalker."

"You're *all* Woodwalkers," Arlen said, his chin on his fist.

"No." I pointed at him, irked. "I can't believe how many people outside the mountains have that misconception. We're not all Woodwalkers. Woodwalker is a title, a rank. We're stewards, charged with protecting the mountains and directing the rest of the scouts. We command the Wood Guard, the highest branch of the Royal Guard . . ."

"All right, enough," he said, waving his hand to cut me off.

His cavalier dismissal to my rank galled me. "Who do you think you are?"

He smirked. "I'm—"

"Arlen!" his sister snapped. At first I thought she might be upset at his attitude, but then I wondered if she was more concerned about *what* he was going to say rather than *how* he was going to say it. Nevertheless, something was kindling in her eyes. She focused her attention on me again. "So then, you know the mountains? I mean to say, you can get through them?"

"Of course I can. Blindfolded."

"Without being caught by the Royal Guard? By the other Woodwalkers, who possess the same skills as you?"

"I imagine so. I know where they range and what sets them on alert."

"Even now, after being away for so long?"

"*Yes.*" The bitterness of my banishment welled up in my voice. "The Silverwood is my home. It's my identity. It's as much a part of me as my own bones. That kind of thing doesn't go away just because some idiot with a crown tells you to get out."

She regarded me. Arlen had a blank expression on his face, but Colm was watching his sister with a shrewd stare.

"Mona," he said quietly.

She turned to him. "It could be time."

"We don't know what we'll find . . ."

"We will *never* know what we'll find," she fired back, her eyes alight. "No news of our folk can get through those wretched mountains, and the passages south are blocked now. We've wasted too much time in caution's shadow."

I looked between the two of them. "What?"

"You're being too quick to trust," he said, glancing at me. "Your desire to free our folk is clouding your judgment."

"When will we have another chance, Colm? When will we be presented with someone who knows the mountains but doesn't answer to their king?"

"Wait," I said again. "What?"

Arlen was catching on. He sat forward. "We're going back?" His eyes were bluer than his sister's, but they burned with the same energy.

"We have a guide," she pressed, staring Colm down. "That's all we've ever needed."

I gripped the table, trying to slow down the momentum this conversation was gaining. "Wait. Wait. Nobody's guiding anybody anywhere."

She whirled on me, and once again I was hit by the full blast of her authority, despite her plain clothes and sunburned skin. "We have had a plan of action since the day we dragged ourselves out of the river that flows away from Lumen Lake, but one thing always stood in our way: we could never get back to our folk. We escaped south through the Cypri waterways, but they're blocked now by the Alcoran ships that ferry the wealth of the lake south to our enemies. The only way back is through the mountains, and no one save the Wood-folk can navigate ten feet under those eaves. You are just the person we have been looking for."

"No," I said flatly, "I'm not."

"Three years we've been wandering unfamiliar lands, and not once have we come across a single Silvern. Your king has closed off the mountains. Nothing flows in or out. You are our first, and likely only, chance."

"I'm sure you think that's true, but why on earth should I agree to this?" I gestured to her. "Every aspect of my upbringing and training tells me you're my enemy, or at least a hostile neighbor, and here you are asking me to lead you among my own folk? What's in it for me?"

"You say you are not loyal to King Valien."

"But I'm still loyal to my folk and my rightful home."

"Exactly. And I think we can both agree that despite the antagonism between the lake and the mountains, we have a common foe in Alcoro. At one time, the mountains were the path of trade between Lumen Lake and the rest of the eastern world. Our wealth flowed through your country. Your silversmiths partnered with our pearl divers to create the most exquisite works under the stars." She held up her pearl pendant again, letting it swing from her fingers. "The Alcorans have changed all of that. They exploit the skills of my folk and funnel our wealth into foreign lands." She leaned forward. "It doesn't have to be that way. If we can retake the lake, we can open up trade again through the mountains. It benefits your folk as well as mine."

"That still doesn't help *me*," I said.

She was still leaning forward on her elbows, her shoulders tense. I got the feeling she was doing some swift thinking.

"Mona," Colm said again, his voice just a bit more desperate.

She flicked her eyes around the empty tavern and then straightened, rolling her shoulders back in a practiced move. "My name is Mona," she said quietly. "Do you recognize that name?"

"It's a typical lake name. Wasn't it the name of the queen who was killed in the invasion?"

She looked at me pointedly. Next to me, Colm rested his bearded chin wearily in his hand.

My slow dawning of realization must have shown plainly on my face. "Wait . . ."

"Yes. I am that queen who should have been killed. I am Mona Alastaire, Queen of Lumen Lake and the Twelve Islands." She held up the pearl pendant again. "This isn't just a pearl. This is an heirloom of my line, one of the first and largest ever found in Lumen, passed down through the monarchy since it began."

"How on earth did you survive the invasion?" I asked.

Her gaze flicked briefly to Colm before settling back on me. "We swam."

"Down the southern waterways?"

"Yes. We ended up in Matariki, for a while, but Alcoro uses it as a port, and we couldn't stay there. We worked our way up through the hills of Winder to the southern borders of the Silverwood, but we couldn't find anyone who could navigate it. We spent a great deal of time trying to find a way through, but what little money we had eventually ran out, and we were forced to return to the coast. We're water-folk, after all, and could earn a meager living diving. We had fairly good luck in Sunmarten for quite some time. Until this fool"—she nodded to Arlen, who huffed a great sigh—"started a drunken brawl in front of half the population at midwinter, shouting that we were the rightful monarchs of Lumen Lake." She gave him a familiar glare.

Her brother somehow managed to look both abashed and smug.

"And nobody confronted you about it?" I asked. "No one's tried to apprehend you?"

"I have come to hope that anyone listening to his ranting assumed he was a drunkard spouting nonsense. But all the same, we fled the town before rumors could spread."

Arlen rolled his eyes. "Almost four months ago this happened, and you'd think I'd been doing it every night since."

"I just pulled you out of a fight!" Colm said.

"At least I wasn't *ranting* this time. And I didn't *start* the brawl."

"At any rate," Mona continued, "no one has approached us, and we've been careful to keep a low profile."

"Working as divers?"

"*You* didn't recognize us," she pointed out. "And you should be more familiar with our folk than anyone on the coast."

I stared at her for a moment, processing her story. This was powerful news for the eastern world— powerful and dangerous. A few seconds of silence ticked by, and then I shook myself.

"That . . . that doesn't change anything," I insisted with forced conviction.

She settled back into her chair again. "I am queen of a very wealthy nation, Mae. From the looks of things, you are penniless as well as homeless."

"That's not true," I retorted. "I have enough copper in my pocket to buy a whole pistachio from the nut vendor."

"Do this for me," she said. "Get me and my brothers successfully through the mountains, and I will make you richer than your paltry king."

"And after?" I said. "What becomes of me afterward?"

"Whatever you like. Stay as a citizen of the lake. Charter a boat to take you south. Perhaps we can even try to parley with King Valien and have your sentence lifted. He may listen if we can reclaim power."

"Why don't I bolt right now and bring this news to the first Alcorans I can find?" I asked. "They'd pay me just as well, I imagine, and they're already in power."

"Because you'd get a dart in your back," Arlen said sharply.

"Because the strength of a Woodwalker is in her integrity."

I swung my gaze to Colm, startled to hear words from my old pledge coming out of his mouth. He gave a slight shrug. "If history books are to be believed. Perhaps the rank no longer upholds that value."

I stared at him, an old, dormant devotion flaring to life somewhere deep inside me. Mona smoothed down a smile, knowing he had driven right through the heart of the issue. Seeing this smugness on her face shook me back to my senses, and I tried to bury that flicker of warmth back in its shell.

"How rich?" I asked.

She smiled and held up her pearl pendant. It shimmered in the dusty sunlight.

"As rich as you need to be. You'll be able to buy an island of pistachios."

"Hang on," Arlen blurted, his brow furrowed in thought. "I'm all for going back and routing out Alcoro, but how do we know we can trust"— he gestured up and down at me—"this? Even if she's not loyal to the Silverwood king, she's still Silvern, hardly our ally. She might leave us in the mountains."

"What on earth would I gain from that?" I asked him. "Risk my own neck by violating my banishment just to leave you? The sentence placed on me if I return is execution. If I'm entering the mountains again, I'd damn well better get something out of it."

"Of course," Mona said coolly. She ignored her youngest brother's scowl and turned to Colm. "But we can't proceed if you're opposed, Colm. I can see you thinking. What do you say?"

He was silent for a moment, his chin resting once again in his hand.

"I'm worried we're being too hasty," he said finally. "I'm not keen to attempt the Silverwood, even with a guide, especially as she's been away from it for so long. What if the king has changed his scout paths? What do we tell him if we're caught? And are we absolutely sure we can succeed if we do reach the lake?" He shook his head. "There's just too much we don't know. But you know I'll follow you anywhere, Mona, and I'm as anxious as you are to free our folk." He lifted his chin off his hand. "I'm not opposed. If you go, I'll go."

She smiled at him. "Good. I'm grateful to you, Colm." She looked back to me. "So it's settled, then."

I shifted. This had all happened very fast. "I suppose."

"Excellent."

"I'll need a day or two to collect supplies and plan our route," I said.

She fluttered a hand. "Of course."

"And money. Unless you want to split the pistachio."

"We have enough to outfit us for a journey. Arlen can go with you to make your purchases. Anything else?"

I looked at her, the deposed queen, her blonde hair frizzing as it dried in its braid. I glanced at her two brothers. Arlen was eager; Colm looked weary.

Drag these three through the Silverwood without alerting the king's scouts to our presence, only to face a hostile force on the far side? Risk the sentence laid on my head for three ousted monarchs with so little chance for success?

My stomach growled, as if trying to add its opinion to my inner debate. It had been some time since I had had enough money for a decent meal. Besides that, Mona had saved my life. But underneath both of these sentiments trickled that deep, dark, dreadful love, the one I had been trying to so hard to wipe away in my exile.

I wanted to see my home again. I wanted to do my rightful job. I was a Woodwalker, and I was desperate.

I pinched the bridge of my nose in my fingers, and then looked toward the bar.

"Brandy," I said. "I think I'll need that brandy."

CHAPTER 2

The supplies I would have preferred to take with me through the mountains were difficult to come by in Tiktika's coastal markets. Fishing tackle and boat materials were available in abundance, but gear for a journey through woods and mountains was in short supply.

I went from stall to stall, with Arlen trailing me, seeking suitable wares that would last us through our journey. Mona had sent him along, I knew, to help carry my purchases, but also to be sure I wasn't going to pocket her money and flee the town. He made a great show of reluctance over every item I selected, painstakingly counting out the necessary coinage.

"We've got cord," he said, leaning against a wooden pillar as I tested the strength of a length of rope.

"We're going to need something heftier to hang our food in the trees each night," I said, coiling it up.

"For bears?"

"Bears, and everything else. Mice, raccoons, skunks . . . few creatures would pass up a convenient bag of fruit."

"Is it true the Wood-folk can communicate using animal calls?"

"Well, sort of. Not in general. But the Wood Guard uses a set of bird calls to signal to each other. Cardinal means *all clear*, towhee means *rally to me*, that kind of thing."

"How is the Wood Guard different from the Royal Guard?"

"There are three branches to the Royal Guard," I said, my gaze passing over a cordwainer selling stiff boots and shoes. "Wood Guard's the highest branch, made up of the scouts and headed by the Woodwalkers. We're stewards rather than soldiers; we keep an eye on the forest and our impact on it. The Armed Guard is the army. Both of us are trained for combat, but the Wood Guard deals more with stealth and sniping than swordplay."

"And the third branch?"

"Oh. The Palace Guard." I snorted a bit as we passed a silk vendor. "We call them the Guard of Last Resort. Friendly rivalry. They protect the palace, and the monarchy, which is important, but we like to think of them as lounging around in pretty uniforms while we do all the dirty work." I drew up short a few stalls down and groaned in envy. "Speaking of."

It was the bowyer, her stall packed with bows of all makes. Reel-mounted Paroan bows crafted for bow-fishing, recurved Winderan bows made of sheep horn. There were even a few clumsy crossbows. Alcoro was the only country currently equipped with crossbows, and they guarded the secrets of their engineering very closely. That didn't stop others from attempting replications. I passed over these newfangled weapons and picked up a bow most familiar to my grip—a short flatbow, though even it was composited with horn, rather than being one solid piece of wood like I was used to.

"May I?" I asked the bowyer. At her nod, I strung the bow and pulled the sinew back to my cheek. It bent with relative ease compared to my old, dense hickory bow, but I could still feel the power in its short limbs.

"Sycamore?" I asked.

The bowyer nodded again. "Ten easterns."

Arlen whistled. "Nope."

I gazed longingly down the sight. "It's got a nice draw."

"We haven't got that much, and even if we did, Mona would kill me. Besides, I'm armed. We won't need a bow."

I sighed and straightened the bow. Ten golden easterns was more money than I'd had in the past six months combined. Too much for a composite sycamore bow, I told myself. And I'd have to buy arrows as well. Resignedly, I unstrung the sinew and set the bow back among its fellows. Still, I brushed the flat limb with a wistful finger.

"What's next?" Arlen asked, probably hoping to distract me from the stall.

I moved reluctantly down the aisle. "Oilcloth."

We moved down the aisle, where I looked over a selection of oilcloth pouches. He hung over my shoulder and continued his questions from before. "Is it true that if you step off any established path, the mountains are bewitched by the king's sorcerers to disorient you?"

"Where on earth did you hear that?"

He shrugged. "It's one of those stories, you know, they tell you as a kid."

"Well, it's nonsense. The king has councilors, but they're not sorcerers. They couldn't bewitch a twig any more than you or I could."

"So no magic?" He squinted, as if unwilling to believe me. "How do you make sense of the mountains? How come nobody else can get through?"

I turned to him with some surprise. "How do you folk hold your breaths for so long? How do you avoid falling prey to cold water? Skill. Preparation. Heritage. Just like you, and every other nation: the Sea-folk's cunning with boats; the Hill-folk's knack with livestock. There's nothing special about us."

"And the Light? Do you revere the Light?"

I shrugged and went back to picking through the oilcloth. "As much as anyone else. Do you?"

"We did, sort of. But Mona's not too keen on it now. Alcoro, you know, they have this whole grand plan they believe is divinely inspired. They invade other nations thinking they're fulfilling the prophecy of the Light, that it's their destiny."

"Yes, I've heard that. That prophet, that . . . what do they call him, the Prism? He was supposed to have carved his prophecy into the rock that the Alcoran capital is built around, right?"

He waved his hand irritably. "It could be set in steel and inlaid with gems, and it would still be wrong. What kind of divine power directs one nation to enslave another? What kind of prophet justifies murdering a monarch for material gain?"

I held up my hands. "I'm just trying to buy oilcloth."

He frowned at the pouches in my hand. "Are you sure you need three of those?"

"Yes. Three silvers."

He handed me the money with pointed resignation. "How much more stuff do we need?"

"Not much. For the next week or so, we'll be traveling up the River Rush, and there will be plenty of traders' towns. It won't be until we leave Rósmarie, the quarry town at the foot of the mountains, that we'll really be on our own. So we don't need to carry as much up front. I do need to replace some of my herbs, though."

We moved down the rows of stalls until we came to the herbalist, surrounded by plants and tinctures of all kinds. I looked through her wares. She carried many exotic products—eucalyptus oil, ginseng, and bright golden packets of powdered turmeric—but these were all expensive, and I could cobble together substitutes from my own medical kit. But my stores of peppermint were low, and I was entirely out of lavender oil. I nudged Arlen, who was leaning against the next stall, fingering a tray of jasper pendants.

"Seven silvers."

"*Seven?* What for?"

"For the medical kit. I can find a lot of herbs in the forest, but not everything. Seven silvers."

He counted out his coins. "Just what kind of injuries are you planning on treating?"

"With you lot, who knows? I imagine you'll get creative. Give me the money."

"What is *that?*" Mona asked later that evening, when we were laying out our wares.

Arlen cradled the jasper pendant in his hands. "For Sorcha," he said wistfully. "To give her when we return, as a token of my love."

She closed her eyes, pained. "You courted her for two weeks before the Alcorans invaded, and yet you wasted a handful of silver buying her a pendant?"

"She loves me."

"She *slapped* you." Mona plucked the money bag off of his belt. "Which I now have the urge to do. Rivers to the sea, be sensible. You don't even know if she's still alive. Don't waste our money."

"We can use it to start fires if our flint gives out," I said, waving the two apart and rolling out my map on the table. Maps of the Silverwood were difficult to come by and usually incomplete, so I had sketched out my own, making the best guesses I could where distances were concerned. Some of my details were vague at best—Lake Lille was out of proportion and the southern reaches of Winder and Paroa were outrageously simplified, but these landmarks had no bearing on our journey. Mona bent over my work. Arlen slunk to his pack, scowling, and stowed the jasper pendant inside.

"You've drawn the islands wrong," Mona said.

"What islands?"

"The *Lumeni* islands," she said, pointing with irritation to my crude rendering of Lumen Lake. "You only drew five, and they're all incorrect."

"How about I redraw them if we *get there*," I said, sliding the map out from under her finger. "Let's focus on what's before us." I traced the River Rush. "We start off heading southwest. We'll hit Rusher's Junction in three days or so, four if we move slowly." I pointed to the town at the head of the great delta that ran out to the sea. "After the junction, we pass from Paroa into Winder. Sea country into hill country. From there it'll be smaller travelers' towns up to Rósmarie—seven, eight days at the most. And then it gets a little trickier." I tapped my finger at the border of the Silverwood. "What used to be Tradeway Road is impassable to outsiders; over the last fifty years or so, the monarchs let the trailhead fall into disrepair, and it's almost impossible to find now. Besides that, it would lead us directly to Lampyrinae, the king's palace, so it's no good to us. I plan on taking us further south, through the center of the forest."

"Is there a path?" Mona asked.

"No. That's the bad news. The good news is that it will be much, much harder for the king's scouts to pick up our trail. At a reasonable pace, we should get through to the Palisades in about two weeks."

"The Palisades?" asked Arlen.

"The big stone escarpment separating the lake from the forest . . ."

"I know what it is," he said, opening up a bag of fruit leathers we had purchased earlier that day. "Where all the waterfalls come down. We have to go down it? Is that even possible?"

"In some places," I said. "We'll have to be careful, though. It may take us a few days."

"Ugh." He dropped his head back against the wall with a thud. "Can't we ride, or at least get a pack-horse?"

"Sure," I said sharply, gathering up my map. "Go out and buy yourself a pack-horse with what coins you have left. She'll be of great use to us while we're traveling light along the road and sleeping in inns. But you can't get a horse through the mountains, not the way we're going. You'd have to hawk her in Rósmarie." He was glaring at me. "Look, I never said this was going to be easy, or fun, but you lot asked me, not the other way around . . ."

"All right, all right," Arlen retorted. "I get it. We walk."

"It can't be worse than escaping the lake," Colm said quietly.

This comment silenced the other two siblings for a moment, lost in some shared memory. I tucked my map into my pack, letting the conversation lapse. When it became clear that none of them were going to start up the logistics again, I cleared my throat.

"Tools, weapons," I said loudly. "What have you got?"

Mona gave a small shake. "An auger, I hope." Before I could ask what she meant, she looked up, focusing her authority once more. "Arlen is the best warrior of the three of us, though he had to trade his sword in Lille."

"I still have the Bird," he said.

"You have what?" I asked.

He loosened a strap on his pack and held up a length of wood that curved sharply at one end. Two pearls were set into the wood, transforming the curve into the beak of a bird's head. "My atlatl. Bird of Prey."

"An *atlatl*?" I stared at the antiquated weapon. "*That's* the weapon you were talking about? Your folk still use *atlatls*?"

His ears reddened. "No, we use swords and bows like the rest of the East—longbows, too, not your stubby little flatbows. But this was the first thing I managed to rip off the wall when ballistae started blasting the lakeshore apart."

"Do you have darts for it?"

"A few."

I waved my hand. "I suppose it could deter a raccoon going after our food." He swelled with indignation, but I turned to Colm. "What about you?"

He shook his head. "I couldn't get to anything in time when we fled the lake. All I've got's a knife."

"Likewise," said Mona, cinching down her pack. "But I doubt any weapon will be much use to us no matter what the scenario, don't you think?"

"Yes," I agreed. "Lighting fires in the Silverwood will draw every scout within ten miles, so hunting is out of the question. Unless something goes very wrong, there should be no need for combat, not that we'd be much good against more than a few opponents, anyway. Folk along the road to Rósmarie are friendly enough, and there's nothing to fight in the Silverwood."

"Nothing to fight?" Arlen asked, somewhat startled. "Bears, and wildcats, and snakes . . ."

"You try to engage a wildcat with your atlatl, see how well that goes. Unless you hit it between the eyes, your dart's going to feel like a bee sting." I shook my head. "Not that it matters. Wildcats aren't going after a full-grown man, and bears are more interested in the jerky in your pocket. Snakes just want you to leave them alone. Unless you go poking around a den, there's nothing to fight."

"Well, there's always Wood-folk, I suppose," Arlen said with a mock sigh. He dug in the bag of fruit again. "What about you? What's your weapon?"

I slid my battered silver compass forward a few inches, my fingers resting on the lid. "One of the few things I managed to smuggle out upon my banishment. The king took my bow along with my rank and title. The bearing's starting to drag a bit, but it won't impact us." I slipped it into the pouch at my belt, worn into the compass' familiar shape. "Other than that, a pocket knife, like you. Listen, stop eating our food!"

"We're going to resupply in three days," he insisted as I snatched the bag of fruit leathers away.

"And the less we have to replace, the better. You haven't won back your pearl beds yet, and I'm not keen on mending nets in every town we cross to earn a few coppers." I cinched my own pack shut. "If we're going to get to the lake without being caught, we're going to need everything on our side—good luck, good fortune, and good sense. Let's try not to sabotage ourselves before we even start."

The journey through Paroa along the River Rush could easily have been downright pleasant. Late April along the delta gave us its best face, bathing us in gentle sun and fragrant breezes. The banks spilled with lilacs and jonquils, and carts laden with colorful goods rumbled past us on their way to the traders' towns along the river. But with each step I took, anxiety gnawed at my insides. I second-guessed myself a hundred times that first day, and I had to force myself to carefully recall my reasoning behind taking up such a dangerous and desperate task.

It wasn't easy.

The king's council had made it perfectly clear what my consequence would be if I violated my banishment—I would be lucky to see the end of a week inside my prison cell. In light of this reality, I nursed the lingering dread that this fool's errand could not possibly be worth the risk.

For most of the morning, I walked just ahead of the three siblings. They were energized by their momentous decision to return to their folk and spent the walk discussing the finer details of their plan. Well, I say discussing—it mostly consisted of Mona making bold assertions, which were then countered by Arlen, who seemed to enjoy being argumentative just for fun. Colm was largely silent, though every now and then he added a quiet word or phrase to the bickering that changed the whole perspective of the conversation.

I didn't join in. They spoke with a confidence I didn't share, as if the journey through the Silverwood was already over and done instead of a looming, shadowed uncertainty. I forced myself to think one step at a time, focusing on the road immediately before us.

"Mae."

I started—I hadn't realized Colm had left his quarreling siblings' sides. "What?"

He fell into place next to me. "I have some extra coin. Do you want to buy new shoes at the next market?"

I flushed at the thought of him evaluating the state of my ragged footwear. "Thank you, but I doubt we'll find the right kind."

"What's the right kind?"

I lifted one foot, hopping on the other to keep pace

with him. "Soft soles. Apparently we're the only culture in the eastern world that doesn't wear hard-soled
shoes."

"Are those the shoes you were banished in? Have
they lasted this long?"

I put my threadbare sole back to the ground. "Oh,
no. They wore out after my second winter. I had to
find a tanner in Cyprien who would make these for
me, and it cost me about a month's worth of work."

"I'm sure there's someone in Rusher's Junction who
would make a pair for you."

"No, I don't want to waste the time." I stepped
around a rut in the road. "I'll be all right, especially
once we're in the forest. Besides, they're helping me."

"Helping you do what?"

I gestured to the track before us. "Justify this whole
questionable journey. If I can get you to the other side
of the mountains, I'm betting I can buy new boots."

"Not quite worth the risk of execution, I would
think."

"Well, they'd be really nice boots. And maybe I'll
get a new pack and bedroll, too." And a solid hedge-
apple flatbow with painted limbs.

I thought I detected a smile, but at that moment,
Mona called for him to explain a point she was making
to Arlen. He fell back once more, leaving me to weave
my way around every rock and divot in the road.

That night found us at a wayside inn built solely for
travelers along the delta. We sat at one of the trestle
tables in the low-ceilinged common room. Colm was

dressing a quartet of yellow jacket stings Arlen had sustained after jabbing his atlatl into a tangle of jessamine. Mona was once again studying the map I had sketched out. She was traveling with her long golden hair braided in a circlet over her head, creating the illusion that she was wearing her reclaimed crown.

"What are the mountains going to be like at this time of year?" she asked, marking our current location with a small dot.

"Damp," I said. "And cool, at least at night. There may even still be snow along the high ridges. We'll probably hit some rain."

"Will there be ice on the Palisades?"

"Hopefully not. But let's focus on getting over the main ridge first. One crisis at a time."

I took a sip of the inn's cloyingly sweet cider as I looked over the common room. The space was full of other travelers, and near the bar, a few rowdy merchants were stirring up an impromptu song and dance. Two had hand drums, one had a battered ukulele. The rest simply beat on the bar as the fattest of the lot danced with the pink-cheeked barmaid. Mona watched absently, her elbows on the table and her fingers clasped under her chin.

"Do you know what I miss most about Lumen at times like this?" she asked no one in particular.

"Dancing," I said.

"No. The singing. I don't suppose you know our traditions at the solstices?"

I shook my head.

"The water is filled with boats," Mona said, her voice far away. "All lit with lanterns, and folk are spread out along all the islands. As the lanterns are lit, song is passed back and forth from boat to boat, shore to shore. The water echoes with music for whole nights." She continued watching the merriment across the room. More travelers were joining in, starting the chorus of a well-known ballad.

"I miss the dancing," I said without thinking.

Mona turned her head to me, her chin still on her hands. "I've heard that your folk dance, though I've never had the chance to see it myself. Line dances, aren't they?"

"And circle dances, and partner dances."

"Are you a good dancer?"

I shrugged. "As good as any, I suppose. It never mattered who was good and who wasn't. Are you a good singer?"

She smiled. "As good as any." She gestured across the table. "Colm has the voice."

"I'm not bad," Arlen said, scratching at his stings. "I sang at their wedding."

"Wedding?" I looked at Colm. "You're married?"

A great shout of laughter rose from the revelers. The barmaid had gone to refill several tankards, so the fat merchant was dancing with the stable boy, whirling him around like a bewildered scarecrow. Colm watched them without mirth.

"I was," he replied.

His comment effectively ended our conversation,

the frolic by the bar seeming suddenly tawdry. With the passing of another ten minutes, our cups and bowls empty, Colm rose from the table and announced he was going to bed. Mona and Arlen followed him. I hung behind, citing my need to stitch up a seam on my pack. This task took me all of sixty seconds, but I sat for at least half an hour, watching the merriment slowly turn sloppy, the fat merchant eventually chinning the ukulele player for changing tunes. As the barmaid began dispersing the brawlers, I tied up my pack and stole up the staircase to our room.

Arlen was snoring, but Colm on the cot beside him was unnaturally still and quiet. I slunk past them and settled down on the empty cot under the window. Clouds scudded across the sliver of a moon, patching out the stars.

Earth and sky, I thought wearily, drawing my cloak up under my chin. This journey was already going to be difficult enough. The last thing I needed to carry with me was *empathy*.

Another full day of walking brought us to Poak, which would have been as unremarkable as the other wayside stops had it not become a haven for wandering artists and performers. Where the other towns had sprung up out of practicality, this one seemed to exist solely for the pleasure of the thing. Garlands of ribbons and fraying bunting were strung haphazardly through the trees, and street vendors hawked a spectrum of colorful goods and services. Piles of sweetgrass baskets teetered around gossiping weavers, some smaller than a hen's egg, others large enough to sit in. Children ran here and there with armfuls of flowers, chiding men and women alike into buying posies for their sweethearts. Some folk sat around firepits, roasting breadfruit over the coals and offering hot bits to potential customers.

We wandered the streets as the afternoon waned, drinking in the sights and sounds. We passed a tattooed woman standing astride a circular pen, taking wagers on how quickly she could subdue the alligator inside. As we continued down the street, a chorus of whoops and cheers rose as she leaped on the beast's back. She gripped its jaws in her hands while it thrashed, her chestnut ringlets flying in wild arcs around her head. Arlen hung back to watch.

"Curious place, Poak," Mona said, eyeing a man selling cages of live cottonmouths. "I'd heard of this little town, but we never ventured this far up the River Rush."

"I was here a few years ago for their Festival of the Light," I said. "One of the fire-breathers almost burned the tavern down."

A girl with ribbons in her hair thrust a fistful of jonquils in Mona's face. "Posy for your husband?"

Mona laughed outright. "No husbands here."

"For your sweetheart, then."

"No sweethearts. Brothers. Not worth a posy, I'm afraid."

The girl didn't miss a beat, twirling to me instead. "Posy for your sweetheart?"

"Sorry," I said to her. "I doubt they'd keep."

She stomped away, disgruntled, her ribbons bouncing as she disappeared into the crowd.

"*Do* you have a sweetheart?" Mona asked.

"Well, as of five years ago. Now, who knows?" The word *sweetheart* seemed far too saccharine to describe the complexity of that relationship. We stopped in front of a cloth merchant, and I fingered a bolt of mossy green cotton. "That all got swept away with everything else."

"Sorry to hear it."

I shrugged. "It was for the best, honestly. His family hated me."

"Scarlet," said the cloth vendor.

"Sorry?" I asked.

She smoothed a bolt of blazing red fabric. "Scarlet's the color for your copper skin. Bring out that auburn hiding in your hair. Brown doesn't suit you."

I looked down at my ragged tunic. "Oh. All my clothes end up brown, in the end."

We moved on to the next stall. A vendor sat surrounded by treated goatskins, stretching one over a circular wooden frame. A drum-maker. I tapped the head of one, sending a shiver through the jingles set into the frame.

"You use a tipper?" I asked the vendor.

"A what?"

"Guess not," I said.

"What's a tipper?" asked Mona as we moved along.

"A beater, you know, a little stick. Folk around here use their fingers, though."

"Do you drum?" Colm asked.

"No. I have a brother who does. My parents are instrument-makers."

Mona glanced at me, cocking her head. "They are?"

"Why so surprised?"

She gave a slight shrug. "I suppose I hadn't thought much about what your family used to do."

Her indifferent tone ruffled me. "They didn't *used to do* anything. They *still* make instruments. What did you think, that I came from a family of vagrants?"

Her eyes slid to a tray of jeweled hairpins, a smile playing on her lips. "I suppose I did."

"I had a life, you know, in the mountains. A home, siblings . . . my oldest brother is a blacksmith, my sister keeps bees . . ."

"Oh, don't get huffy about it. I didn't mean any offense. Look at this brooch, Colm, it's lapis . . ."

"I don't suppose your parents had to do anything, did they?"

It was an unkind comment, and she turned to me with a cold stare. "No, they only had to *run a country*."

We faced each other, the sounds of the market swirling around us. Colm looked intently at the lapis pin. Too late, I realized the subject of their parents might be a touchy one. If I recalled my Lumeni history correctly, they had died when Mona was still a child.

"Sorry," I said quickly. "I didn't mean that."

"It's fine," she said primly, turning back to the trays of jewelry. She offered no apology of her own. "I know perfectly well what you meant. It may be different in the Silverwood, but the Lumeni monarchs have always been actively invested in our country. I suppose it must seem a lavish lifestyle to you, coming from a common family, but there is no room for error, and folk are always watching. My mother's motto was 'No one can *be* perfect, but a queen must *act* perfectly.' "

Which explains a lot about you, I thought. But I bit back any further comments, not wanting to spur an argument so early in our journey—though *common family* rankled to no end. With effort we drifted past the jewelry in silence, moving to a stall selling talismans and trinkets meant to serve as household tokens of the Light—cut glass prisms, mirrored pendants, and etched lanterns.

"Silly things," said Mona with a hint of disdain.

There was a puffing sound behind us, and Arlen hurried to join us, red-cheeked in victory. "I won twelve silvers betting on that gator woman!"

"Lovely, Arlen, I'm so glad you're using our money wisely." She held out her palm. "Give it to me before you throw it away on something else."

"I earned it; it's *mine*."

"You didn't earn it, and it's *ours*. Hand it over."

"There's a cockfight in ten minutes . . ."

"Absolutely not."

We moved steadily down the street, coming to a cluster of people underneath a palmetto tree. Someone was shouting in their midst. Just as we approached the crowd, I grabbed Mona's arm.

"Stop."

She made to shake off my hand, but she paused as the shouting from underneath the palmetto drifted toward us.

"... prosperity for the Seventh King means prosperity for the East and beyond, my friends! The Prophecy of the Prism is a blessing to all peoples, handed to the country of Alcoro so that it may be spread throughout every culture. My friends, do not think of the Light as a distant afterthought! It is the source of all life, shining not just down, but up and through and around us in every way. One only needs to hear the words the Prism carved into the stone of my city: *'We are creatures of the Light, and we know it is perfect . . .'"*

"Away, away," I muttered, pushing them back down the street. I doubted a run-of-the-mill Alcoran advocate would think anything of Mona and her brothers, particularly if the rumors of their survival had not left Sunmarten, but there was no sense in risking it. If he recognized them as Lake-folk instead of especially pale travelers, we would have uncomfortable questions to answer.

"I can't believe an entire nation can be so deluded," Mona said through clenched teeth. "How dare they use the words *prosperity* and *blessing* to describe what they're doing?"

"I think they truly believe they're doing the right thing," I said as we hurried past the drum-maker.

"That's even more alarming! Murdering innocent folk, usurping a monarchy, enslaving a people . . . *no*, Arlen!" She dragged him away from the alligator pen, where the tattooed woman was tying a blindfold over her eyes to a roar of eager voices. "We're going back to the inn!"

"Ah, Mona, there's a shimmy dancer performing later—they say she can play a whole tune with the bells on her hips . . ."

"No." Her cheeks flushed with indignation. "I've had enough of this tawdry town. We still have two days of walking before Rusher's Junction, and I want to be on the road as quickly as possible tomorrow morning. I will not spend the evening among proselytizing Alcorans when our folk are still slaves to their appalling Seventh King."

For the first time that day, I found myself agreeing with Mona.

After an uneventful two days, we came to the riverside town of Rusher's Junction. This bustling hub exuded a different kind of energy than eccentric Poak. The streets buzzed with carts, livestock, craftsmen, and merchants, all wrapped up in business transactions. All the main roads of Paroa and Winder converged here; a teetering signpost pointed travelers down the crisscrossing causeways, back to Tiktika, up the river to Rósmarie, southwest to the Leithwash and on to Sunmarten, and eventually to Matariki. An overgrown track meandered halfheartedly northward, leading the foolish and reckless to what used to be Tradeway Road through the Silverwood. We swerved away from this intersection, however, seeking out lodging in one of the inns. Our plan was to take a day to bulk up our supplies for the more sparsely settled road ahead through the hill country of Winder.

We clustered in the common room, savoring the meal doled out from the kitchens. I had been away from the native tastes and smells of my homeland long enough that anything warm could be palatable, but a full meal with bread and meat and wine was a rare luxury. Arlen, too, was enjoying himself, having spent much of our journey so far complaining about my stingy limitations on our food supply. Mona and Colm kept their composure as a lifetime of nobility would have trained them, eating slowly and quietly, but even they seemed to be enjoying the meal. Mona had unwound her hair from its braid over her head, and it rippled loose and silky down her back. Two mustachioed men in the far corner kept tossing glances her way as she moved, her golden curtain glinting in the firelight. I eyed them a few times, hoping their interest was purely superficial.

The monarchs' conversation had again lit upon the minutiae of their strategy to reclaim Lumen. Mona was insisting on solidifying their plan to the point that Alcoro would be unable to ever penetrate the Cypri waterways again, and for once Arlen was wholeheartedly agreeing with her. But Colm was unsure that this was at all possible.

"Alcoro is desperate and misguided, Mona, and those things fuel aggression. Even if we could drive them out of the southern waterways, Cyprien doesn't have the military to repel them for long."

"But the only reason they invaded Cyprien in the first place was to gain better access to our trade, to cut out the middleman," Arlen countered. "If they aren't on the receiving end of our wealth, they have no reason to keep their paws in Cyprien."

Colm shook his head. "Alcoro is a nation with no worthwhile resources of its own. King Celeno . . ."

" . . . is a simpleton and a murderer," Mona said icily.

"And he is frantic. You know what their prophecy supposedly says. You heard the man in Poak. They think the wealth and might of their nation will be realized under the Seventh King. Celeno is the Seventh King of Alcoro, and *everyone* expects him to lead them to some grand prosperity. But their wealth of turquoise dried up two generations ago, and what coffee they produce is offset by the greater exports from Samna. The only thing they have left is their military power. What else can he use to force their prophecy to come true? They won't give up Cyprien. Not while there's still trade to be controlled in the waterways."

"I know you're a student of history, Colm," Mona said, "but I think if there was ever a time to shake off Alcoro's influence in the East, it's now. If Celeno turns his attention elsewhere—and, let's face it, almost any nation has a stronger military than Lumen—if he turns elsewhere and gets killed in the process, the Alcorans' belief in this stupid prophecy will die with him. They'll be hit with the fact that everything they've believed in for centuries is a lie, and their might will collapse." She ran her hand through her hair, idly flashing it in the firelight.

The two men in the corner watched. I watched them.

"Maybe you should keep your voices down," I suggested quietly.

Arlen was checking over his darts for warp. He had propped up the Bird on his tankard, as if letting it preside over the conversation. "Drive them out and keep them out," he said without acknowledging my comment. He rested a dart on his finger. "All the better for us if they fall."

"They *won't* fall," Colm insisted. "They'll only get more ruthless. And if they do fall, it's not all the better for us. They've controlled trade in Cyprien for over fifty years now. Without a clear path to the south and the Silverwood still closed to us, who will we trade with? We *need* their merchants in the waterways."

"I refuse to barter with a nation that has so directly undermined our own," Mona said with venom. "I don't care if Cyprien ferries our wealth in skin canoes—I will not trade with Alcoro ever again. I would think you would feel the same way, Colm, after what they did."

"Of course I do," he said fiercely. "But there's a difference between following my heart and following my head."

"Are you saying—" Mona started before I finally cut in, hoping to steer the conversation to safer ground.

"I've been there, you know."

Mona glanced at me with raised eyebrows. "You've been to Alcoro? When?"

"Four years ago, a few months before the invasion. It was my first winter after I was exiled, and I wandered west, hoping it would be warmer than Winder."

"What's it like?" asked Arlen, hefting a dart in the Bird's beak, its pearls winking. "Dry, isn't it?"

"Inland it is," I said. "Canyon country. And, turns out, stupid cold in the winter. The coast is wetter and milder, enough for their coffee plantations. But they're wary of strangers, and I had no skills they would pay me for, so I had to come back east. I wintered in the Cypri swamps instead."

"Did you ever get to their capital?" One of his darts rolled off the table and clattered across the floor. "Oh, rivers to the sea . . ."

"Callais? No, I never did," I said, watching him retrieve the dart. "I've heard it's a sight, though, towers and spires up and down the canyon walls. Perhaps when I get my payout after you strip their flag from your boats I'll go back and hawk my pearls in the city."

Mona's eyes narrowed at my gibe, but I stretched and yawned to cut her off, rising from the table before she could make a retort. "I don't know about you lot, but I'm going to bed. All this diplomacy is wearing me down."

I made my way across the common room, heading

for the door leading to the courtyard and bath house out back. The night was breezy, and I decided to put off wetting my hair until a warmer evening presented itself. Instead I crossed the courtyard to visit the latrine. Next to the door sat a heavy stone urn of ash and a short-handled shovel used to neutralize the smell. The barest sliver of a moon was waning in the sky, but it shed no light into the courtyard. As a result, I was taken by surprise when I stepped out of the latrine and found my way barred by two dark figures. I pulled up short.

It was the merchants from the corner of the inn who had been eyeing Mona's hair. And, probably, taking notes on their plans for revolution. I stood before them, aware that my knife was tucked into my pack in our room.

"Hi," I said.

"I will not waste words," said the figure on the right. He had a slight accent, flattening the *o* in *words* to *werds*. "So tell me the truth the first time. The three golden-haired travelers who were sharing your table. They're Lake-folk, are they not?"

I eyed him. He was a head taller than me, at least, though this was not a particularly impressive feat given my own height. His mustache curled up at the ends.

"What would Lake-folk be doing this far east?" I asked.

"Yes or no?"

"I don't know. I'm not traveling with them. We just shared idle conversation."

"I'm not a fool. You entered with them and paid for a room with them."

Well, damn. "What makes you think they're Lake-folk? The hair? There are plenty of fair heads around here, from the Winderan hills."

"Sandy heads, perhaps, and tanned skin, but those three are pale as the moon and covered with freckles. An unusual sight. And who else would use an atlatl set with pearls? Who else says *rivers to the sea*?"

I mentally swore to kick Arlen in the shins as soon as possible.

The mustachioed man reached out and closed his fist on my collar. Circling one finger was a thick ring set with a veined stone. Turquoise.

"If they were not Lake-folk, you would have said so right away. I told you to give me the truth the first time. They are spearfishing swimmers from Lumen, and what's more, there are three of them, a woman and two men, one bearded. I think"—he gave me a shake—"that if I checked the woman's blouse, I'd find a certain pearl pendant tucked down the front. We've heard the rumors in Sunmarten."

"Oh?"

"The Alastaires are alive, are they not?"

"Oh."

I jerked my chin forward and bit the flesh of his fist with as much force as I could. He released me, swearing. His partner lunged toward me, but I gripped his forearm and guided his momentum through the latrine door. He crashed into the far wall just as the first wound his fingers around the knot of hair at the back of my head. I pressed my hand on top of his and folded the other into a spear, driving my fingers into the hollow of his throat. He rasped but didn't release his grip, so I swung my foot—hard soles would have been useful here—catching him forcefully between the legs. He reeled, howling, and I took the opportunity to fling him after his partner, slamming the door of the latrine shut behind him. I wedged the urn of ashes against the door and swung the shovel at the latch, denting it out of place. I tossed the shovel aside with a clang and lurched toward the door leading back to the inn.

Mona and her brothers were gone from their table, so I clattered across the common room for the staircase, my heart thudding in my chest. The Alcorans had underestimated me—likely based on my size and the fact that I carried no weapons—but they wouldn't make the same mistake twice. My curls bounced around my shoulders, and the back of my head hurt where he had yanked my hair loose. I took the stairs two at a time and arrived at the room we had rented, throwing open the door.

The room was dark, but all three heads jerked up at my sudden entrance.

"Up, up!" I sang breathlessly. "Everybody up! Come on, be quick."

Mona sat up as I began throwing loose items into my pack. "What's wrong?"

"Two Alcorans spotted you downstairs. Let's go, shake a leg."

Colm and Arlen sat up as well. "Alcorans?" Arlen repeated. "How do you know?"

"Turquoise and mustaches and the accent and *don't ask stupid questions.*" I dragged his cloak off his cot and threw it at him in a bundle.

Mona and Colm were on their feet. "How did they know who we were?"

"Your *careless mannerisms,* believe it or not. Also the Bird." I slung my pack onto my back. "Get up, Arlen, or I'll jam the stupid thing—"

"Where are they now?" Mona asked, cinching down her own pack.

"Using the toilet." I headed back for the door. The other three scurried after me in various stages of readiness.

"Wait," Mona said, grabbing my arm on the landing. "Where are we going? What are you planning to do? We haven't restocked our supplies . . ."

"Let's work on getting out the door," I said anxiously. "One crisis at a time."

We hurried down the stairs and into the night. The evening was still early, and the inns were bright and spilling with people enjoying the hospitality of the town. We turned up the main road toward the signpost intersection.

"Put your hoods up," I said as we moved.

"Where are we going?" Mona demanded. "We can't hide from them on the road just because our heads are covered."

"I know," I said grimly as the signpost loomed in front of us. "I don't think we can take the road to Rósmarie, not if folk are spreading rumors that you're alive, and certainly not if we're being actively followed. Let's get off the main road, and then we'll consider our options."

We hurried into the grass at the edge of the intersection. The ground immediately bumped and buckled into clumps of tussock and rock. The light and sound from the town drifted away behind us; before us, the slim moon perched over the rising hills. When we had moved out of earshot of the road, I stopped.

"So Rósmarie is out of the question," I said, furiously reworking our route in my head.

"Did they know *for certain* it was us?" Mona asked, slightly out of breath. "Or did they think we were just displaced Lake-folk?"

"They were pretty sure it was you. They heard rumors you were alive in Sunmarten."

The moon still shed no light, so I could only imagine the poisonous look Mona was directing at Arlen.

"What?" he protested.

"They may decide to send word back to one of their ships," said Colm before his sister and brother could get into further argument. "They may not attempt to pursue us themselves."

"True, but there could easily be more of them back at the junction," I said. "They might send a few runners back to their ships and a few on the roads leading toward the mountains, anticipating we may try to attempt a crossing. They could probably piece together that I'm Silvern if they really put their minds to it."

"So Tradeway Road is still not an option," Mona said.

"Right. Which means we'll have to leave the roadways." I turned, peering into the darkness. The only way to tell where the sky ended and the land began was the abrupt disappearance of stars. "We can cut a straight line across Winder and hit the eaves of the forest north of Lake Rósmarie."

"How long will that take?" asked Colm.

"Four, five days, maybe."

"Why not just make an arc and head back for Rósmarie?" asked Arlen. "If they don't find us on the road, they might not try to pursue us all the way."

"Because," I said carefully, "I think we just encountered a big problem, bigger than a few merchants sniffing for us along the road."

"Which is?" Mona asked.

"I don't think there's any question they'll send word to King Celeno that they saw you, undoubtedly living and breathing, in Rusher's Junction, dressed for travel in the company of someone who looked suspiciously Silvern. They're not simpletons, despite what you say about their king. They'll piece together that you're heading back to the lake. And if they can act before we get there—"

"—who knows what could happen," Mona finished in the dark, her voice grave. "They could send ships and soldiers armed for war."

"Or alert the Silverwood to our presence," I said. "They could do a number of things, none of which would work out well for us. I think our days just got numbered. I think we've got to get to the lake before word can travel up the Cypri waterways that you're alive and heading for Lumen."

The three monarchs were silent before me. A chilly spring breeze shivered down the grassy slopes, prickling our skin.

"How does our route change?" Mona finally asked.

"It cuts down the time it will take to get to the mountains," I said. "But it lengthens the amount of time we'll spend working through them. We'll hit the ravines east of Lampyrinae, and the way will be steeper. But arcing back to Rósmarie and continuing on our original route would take even longer."

Mona drew in a deep breath and exhaled slowly. "I suppose it's the best we can do. All right. So what do we do for tonight?"

"Let's move further away. Put some of these hills between us and the road. Then we can settle down and make camp."

"What about provisions?"

"We'll think about that in the morning," I said wearily, turning northwest. "One crisis at a time."

CHAPTER 3

We picked our way across the pathless foothills until close to midnight, risking twisted ankles when the alternative could be twisting at the end of a rope. I pushed them hard before making a haphazard camp under an overhanging rock. I rose before the others the next morning to gather kindling and fill my cooking pot at a nearby gurgle of water. I wouldn't have bothered with a breakfast fire, but we had a few satchels of tea left in our packs, and I figured we might as well brew them before we reached the Silverwood. Still, I hurried the siblings through breakfast, dousing the fire and scattering the ashes while they were still nursing their cups.

We shouldered our packs and headed further into the hills, our pace quicker now that we could see the tussocks under our feet. I walked in front with my silver compass clutched in my palm, using the undulating hills as landmarks. The hills of Winder were craggy and deceptively steep, obscuring the views of what lay before and behind us—a blessing and a curse. Broad-winged birds wheeled far above us in the open sky, diving every now and then for prey hidden in the waving grasses. Aside from these, we didn't see another soul until late afternoon.

I had been glancing back at the clouds swirling up behind us, noting with a sinking feeling that we would probably spend our first full night camping in the rain. Focused on this concern, I led the siblings up another hill only to screech to a halt at the edge of a flock of curly-haired sheep. They startled, swirling this way and that, bleating plaintively. We edged to one side, looking for a way around, when two dogs came tearing amongst them, barking and growling. We shrank together as they crouched in front of us, their teeth bared and their hackles raised. Arlen grappled for his atlatl, cinched under the strap of his pack, but in another moment, the shepherd materialized at the edge of his flock, weaving among his sheep. He let out a shrill whistle as he jogged up the hill toward us. The dogs looked back at him, their bodies still taut with aggression.

"Put that away," I whispered to Arlen. He slipped his atlatl back over his shoulder as the man reached his dogs. He was one of the Hill-folk, tall and sinewy, with a scraggly earth-colored beard. Clutched in one hand was a crooked staff.

I cleared my throat. "Good afternoon to you, sir."

He eyed us sharply. "Travelers, are you?"

I nodded. "That's right. Not hustlers." Livestock theft would be a common concern out here in the hills. "Our apologies—we didn't mean to startle your flock."

He looked down at his dogs, still bristling at us. "Easy, Itho. Easy, Peg."

Instantly, their hackles went down and their ears jumped forward. They plopped their rumps on the ground and gazed up at him, thumping the grass with their brushy tails.

"If you're heading to Rósmarie, you're four miles off the road," he said, gesturing with his staff.

"Thank you. We're not lost."

"No? Well, you'll not get anywhere on this route, unless you're heading for the mountains." He chuckled at the absurdity of this comment. Without waiting for a reply from us, he nodded to the sky over our shoulders. "You'd best find a low spot to shelter. Lightning likes to strike the tallest target it can find. Out here, that's you and me."

Mona was gazing at the flock. "You have a barn, I wager?"

He looked her up and down. "I do. But I hardly know anything about you beyond your word, and I don't fancy waking up to find my lambs have disappeared."

She opened the pouch at her belt. "We can pay you for a roof for the night and a few provisions." She produced a handful of silver, the last of our unspent coins.

"Mona, we'll be fine for the night," I said. "We can shelter in the lee of a hill . . ."

"I'll not sleep out in the open in a thunderstorm," she said firmly. "We won't have any use for money from here on out, and we don't have enough food to make it through . . ."

"I'll set snares," I said quickly, trying to override her, but the man perked up at her words.

"'Through'?" the shepherd repeated. "Through what? Not through the mountains?"

She held out her hand filled with silver. "Yes, through the mountains. Don't ask why; it's our own business. Will you grant us shelter and food?"

He stared at the four of us. "Almost fifty years I've lived in the shadow of the mountains, and I've yet to come across a person who's made it more'n a quarter mile in. Folk try, of course, looking to trade with the king, but if they don't get chased out by the Wood-folk, they get swallowed up in the trees." He shook his head and plucked a few coins out of her palm. "But as you say, it's none of my business. I can't say I would advise it, but you certainly can't attempt it if you've got no food. I'll see what Halle can spare you from the pantry."

"You're very generous. I will not forget it."

He gave her a funny look before turning and beckoning us through his flock. When he got a few paces away, I hissed at her, "Try to act less like a queen."

She gave me a withering glare just as he called over his shoulder, "Name's Topher."

We introduced ourselves to him as we followed him down the slope. Now assured we weren't a threat, his dogs bounded joyfully around his knees, their tongues lolling. When we reached the far side of his flock, he quipped a command and the pair shot back through the sheep. Topher let out a series of whistles, directing the dogs this way and that, gathering his flock into an orderly knot. We watched in awe, amazed at the effective way the dogs followed his cryptic commands. With the flock ambling along at our heels, he led us down a well-worn track into the hollow of the hills beyond.

His house was built in traditional Winderan fashion, its stacked sod walls covered with stucco and set partially into the hillside. The grassy roof sloped down to a porch overlooking a pleasant, meandering creek. Downstream stood the barn, opening onto a pasture dotted with gamboling lambs. He directed his flock into the pasture with the help of his dogs and staff before leading us up the creek to the house. The deep-set door opened into a plain but well-kept interior, the earthen walls covered with fresh plaster.

"Guests, Halle," Topher announced as we filed through the door. There was a sharp word from the kitchen, and we passed over the threshold to find a plump woman holding a wriggling lamb, spooning milk into its mouth.

"Oh, dear," she said, her brow furrowed at her husband. "Of all nights . . ."

"Is this a bad time?" Mona asked.

"Well, there wasn't going to be any supper tonight. I haven't got the oven lit . . ."

"Travelers, Halle. Different customs. It's the dark of the Light," Topher explained, nodding to the moonless sky. "Fasting night."

"You fast during every new moon?" Arlen asked.

"And feast during the full. Diligence and joy." He unlatched the door to the pantry.

"I could mix up a pone," Halle said, setting the lamb on the floor. "There's buttermilk in the stream house . . ."

"No, no," I said. "There's no need. A roof and a few provisions are more than enough. Please don't let us impose on you."

Halle rose from the table and joined her husband in the pantry, and together they pulled out several wheels of white cheese, a packet of jerky, a bag of apple leathers, and three jars of bread-and-butter pickles. While they deliberated, the little lamb tottered around the kitchen, milling about with the two dogs as if it was one of them.

"If you don't mind me asking, why do you have a lamb in the house?" Arlen said with amusement.

"Runt of the season," said Halle, laying out a square of linen to wrap the cheese. "She's almost ready to go out to pasture, though I hate giving her up. She thinks she's in charge of Peg and Itho."

I heard the smallest of huffs from Mona, and I shot her a glance, surprised at her contempt. But she wasn't looking at the lamb. She had just brushed against an elegant prism hanging in the deep-silled window, making the lantern light slide over its cut surfaces.

She glared at it as if it had insulted her. I looked back to the Hill-folk, but they gave no indication they had noticed.

One of the dogs sniffed around my ankles, its tail sweeping the air. I edged away. I had never understood other cultures' unnatural desire for keeping animals in their homes. Fortunately, Topher and Halle made quick work of tying up our parcels. We waved aside her insistence on fetching a jar of milk from the stream house and instead accepted a loaf of bread and comb of clover honey for our supper.

"Not very hospitable," she fretted, fussing over the twine on the cheese.

"It's more than enough," I said. "You're very kind."

Thunder rumbled outside. Topher lit a lantern, tucked a bundle of blankets under his arm, and beckoned to us. "Best get to the barn before the sky opens up." Laden with our provisions, we followed him back along the creek. The wind was picking up, cool and electric, sending shivers through the grassy banks, and the first fat drops began to fall just as we passed through the barn doors.

Unlike the sod house, the barn was built of wood, though the gaps in the siding emphasized the scarcity of Winderan timber. The biggest holes were patched with cob and plaster. As we entered, a few rusty chickens chattered in surprise, scattering under our feet. Topher hung the lantern on a peg, nodding to a row of empty stalls.

"Clean hay. Roof shouldn't leak. Pull the gate if you

don't want the hens bothering you. Watch out for the cockerel; he flogs. Anything else you need?"

"I don't suppose you can give us any news of the Silverwood?" asked Mona, setting down her pack.

"News? No news. Place is as closed up as a tomb. Only thing I can say is the new king doesn't seem to enjoy shooting trespassers as much as the old one." He ran his hand along one of the thick wooden beams holding up the hayloft. "We used to have to be very sly about timbering. Swarm of folk, men and women, would go out in the night, fell a single tree, and drag it away to chop. Next night we'd do the same thing in a different spot. Now we can get away with felling a few at a time, and processing them right there. Kids have even started mushrooming around the eaves. Hard to say whether the new king is soft or folk are just huddled up in the very heights of the mountains, cut off from everything else."

Arlen glanced at me, probably hoping to see how I reacted to this information, but I just slid my pack from my shoulders and rested it against a stall. *Probably both*, I thought, though *soft* was certainly the wrong adjective to describe King Valien.

A smoky gray cat jumped onto the gate, purring adamantly. Topher scratched its ears. "I know we've established it's none of my business, but I do have to warn you—if it's trade you're looking for, you can count it out. The Wood-folk aren't interested in what outsiders have to offer."

"We're not merchants," Mona assured him.

"Well, I'm baffled as to what other errand you could have in the mountains." He shrugged and started back for the door. "Keep that jerky away from Mouser." He gestured to the cat, which was sniffing Arlen's pack hopefully. With that, he stepped out into the pattering rain and dragged the door closed behind him.

"Nice man," I said, unclasping my cloak.

"Even though he and his folk timber your border?" Arlen asked, moving his pack away from Mouser.

"Not exactly my border, is it? Regardless, though, not too long ago, timbering was part of Silvern industry. My folk regulated which trees could be felled, and we planted new ones in their places. But that practice was halted during the Silent War with your folk. Our monarchs started getting twitchy about allowing foreigners in the mountains." I shrugged, unwrapping the loaf of bread. "But Winder's a big country, and their scrubby little copses don't provide the timber these folk need. If the Silverwood monarchs had any sense, they'd start up the industry again. At least then they could make sure it was done responsibly." I pinched off a piece of bread. "That's what I've learned roaming these hills for the last five years, anyway. I can't believe I forgot about the Hill-folk's fast. Spend a few months on the coast and you forget other folk's customs."

"A bit superstitious, if you ask me," Arlen said, tearing off a piece of bread. "What does it matter if you exhibit your diligence and your joy? The Light isn't some kind of overseer, demanding sacrifice."

"I don't think that's quite how they see it," I said. "I

think it's more in celebration. It's their way of showing reverence. Every culture has something like it. Don't you have some special place where you see the Light? Some way you revere it?"

"No," he said, kicking off his boots. "Why bother?"

"But we do, Arlen," Colm said quietly. "At sunset, when the light hits the waterfalls on the Palisades. Why do you think we turn and face the cliffs at the end of each day?"

He shrugged. "Because they're pretty, I suppose."

Mona spread one of the blankets over the hay, and we settled down around the jar of honey. "Honestly, I'm ready to be done with it all. I'm not even so sure the Light actually exists anymore."

I looked at her in surprise. "How could it not exist? The sun, the moon, the stars . . ."

"I'm not saying *light* doesn't exist." She dipped a piece of bread delicately into the honey. "I just have a hard time believing there is one Light, one source that inspires all things. It seems like something convenient each culture has latched on to to aggrandize what they hold close to their hearts."

"That's quite a cynical point of view."

"Is it? Think for a moment, Mae, what belief in the Light led Alcoro to do to my country. All the nonsense with the petroglyphs, and the Seventh King . . . it's made fools of an entire nation and slaves of another. Why would the Light pick one people out to go forth and conquer all others?"

"I'm not saying they have things right," I said. "But

I think their extreme interpretation is a bad reason to stop revering the Light. If anything, it's reason to search for the *real* meaning of the Light."

"Perhaps. But perhaps not."

"But think about . . . *Aah!*" Mouser rubbed against my elbow just as I unstopped my waterskin. Water slopped over my boots. "I hate these floppy Winderan waterskins. What I'd give for a wooden canteen." I waved my hands at the cat, now winding around my ankles like a furry snake. "Shoo, go on!"

Mona smirked. "Not a cat person?"

"Cats belong in the wild," I said, lifting my hand out of its reach as it sought to arch its back into my palm. "Along with other animals."

"Don't your folk keep livestock?" Arlen asked, offering his fingers for the cat to sniff.

"Some. Enough. Turkeys, bees, grouse, quail, hogs. But almost every family hunts and forages a little, too. Remember, we don't have your rolling lakeshore for sheep or goats."

"But you don't trade." Mona shook her head. "Such odd, isolated folk. So closed up."

"Guess what, though? Nobody's tried to invade us."

Her face grew darker than the thunderstorm. "Don't you dare speak to me like that. You've got no right."

"I have just as much right as you. I'm not your subject, Mona. Don't treat me like one."

She gave me a patronizing look. "Oh, Mae. I don't."

Galled, I ripped off a heel of bread, gathered up my

bedroll, and stalked away to another stall, unwilling to spend more time in her company than was necessary. The barn groaned against the gusting wind. Outside, the curly-haired sheep huddled together under the overhang, shaking water off their floppy ears. I spread out my bedroll and lay down, listening to the rain lash against the side of the barn. At least, I did until the stupid cat slithered its way over and wound into a ball at my shoulder, drowning out every other noise with its infernal purring.

I was roused by the rusty screech of the cockerel the following morning. Mouser had wandered off sometime during the night, though he had left a layer of gray fur on my shoulder. I sat up, brushing off my clothes. Arlen was still snoring, so I crept quietly past the siblings' stall, slipping out through the barn doors to wash my face in the creek.

I was surprised to see that I wasn't the first one awake. Mona was down by the stream house with Halle. Her golden hair hung wet down her back, and she was holding a crate while Halle rearranged jars of milk inside it. Halle was speaking to her; Mona was frowning. As I approached, she glanced my way and cleared her throat, overriding the hillwoman.

"My thanks, Halle." Mona handed her the crate. Halle set it back inside the stream house, nodded good morning to me, and headed back to the house, drying a jar of milk on her apron.

"What was that about?" I asked.

"Oh, nothing. Just conversation." She waved her hand idly. "She offered us breakfast."

Halle seemed determined to make up for the lack of a hot meal the evening before, ushering us to her table for a breakfast of eggs, buttery grits, blueberry preserves, and steaming biscuits as high as my fist. She turned down the offer of our last few coins, insisting she was only showing the hospitality we had missed the night before. The lamb pranced around the kitchen, bleating and kicking its heels as Halle got its milk ready. The prism sparkled in the morning light, sending shards of rainbows dancing across the table. When one flickered against Mona's glass of milk, I saw her edge it away, her mouth twisted in annoyance.

With breakfast finished, we cleared the table and thanked Topher and Halle for their kindness. The lamb followed us out the door, frolicking in the dewy grass. With a final goodbye, we shouldered our packs and headed back out into the misty hills.

"Well," Mona said as the sod house disappeared behind the first rise. "That's a weight off our chests, if not our backs." She hoisted her pack. "We'll have to eat these wheels of cheese first—they're *heavy*."

I mused over the provisions Topher and Halle had given us. "We'll want to eat the pickles first, so we can use the jars later for game."

"What game?" Arlen asked. "I thought we couldn't hunt in the Silverwood."

"We can't. We're going to have to set snares when

we get to the forest. We'll camp far enough away from the eaves that our smoke won't be suspicious."

"What?" Mona said with genuine surprise. "You're still going to set snares?"

"Of course." I glanced at her. "You didn't think a few wheels of cheese and some jerky would get us all the way to the lake, did you?"

I hadn't meant to sound condescending, but she bristled, anyway. "And you think you can set enough snares to provision us instead? What do you plan on catching? Elk?"

"We can forage the eaves, too," I said with irritation. "If we're smart about rationing, we'll have enough to get down the Palisades."

"What can we forage?" Arlen asked. "Nuts? Berries?"

"Wrong season," I said, checking our bearing on my compass. "Greens, mostly. Nodding onions, maybe ramps. Morels if we're lucky."

"Those things won't travel all squashed down in our packs," Mona said with a sniff.

"Which is why we need the *jars*," I said, unable to keep the smugness out of my voice.

She huffed in indignation, straining against her pack as the incline grew steeper. "You could at least *act* grateful," she said. "If it was up to you, we'd have spent the night soaking wet, with no extra food to show for it. At least I got us *something*."

"I am grateful. But that doesn't change the fact that they didn't give us enough to get all the way through."

She gave a small *tsk*. "I suppose it's your cultural inclination to look down on outside help."

I turned to face her as we moved closer to the crest of the hill. "*I beg your pardon? I have nothing against outside help. I'm perfectly willing to let you throw your money away on luxuries if you're so inclined.*"

"I hardly call a roof in a thunderstorm a *luxury*."

"You wouldn't, would you?" I shot back, leaning around Colm as he strove to place himself between her and me. "Try to keep in mind, *Your Majesty*, that you're going to get wet on this journey, guaranteed. You're going to be hungry. You might even get a bee sting. If you don't think the suffering is worth the trip, we can turn around and find a cozy inn in Rósmarie until King Celeno's soldiers find us."

"Don't," she said icily, "talk to me about suffering."

I opened my mouth to reply, but as we took the last few steps to the crest of the hill, the words died in my throat. The land dropped away before us, and for the first time, we were greeted by the rippling slopes of the mountains soaring into the sky. They buckled and swelled like the folds of a blanket thrown on the floor, fading blue in the distance. The sight stopped me in my tracks. My heart jumped like a fish leaping from the water. For the briefest moment, all the weariness of the past five years slipped away, leaving a breathless joy in its wake.

The others stopped, too, to catch their breaths after the climb. Colm looked between me and the mountains. "How long since you've seen them?" he asked.

I shook myself. "Seen them? Not that long, I suppose. I was in Rósmarie a few months ago." I drew in a deep breath. "But they always catch me off-guard, for some reason, no matter how often I travel this way."

"Why don't you just stay in Rósmarie?" Arlen asked, more interested in adjusting his pack straps than taking in the sweeping sight before us. "If seeing the mountains is so important to you, why not settle down in one of the border towns?"

"I tried, for a while," I said, absently turning my compass in my palm. "I worked in the marble quarries for a few months until they hired someone stronger than me. There's not much other industry in Rósmarie, so I had to leave to find other work. Besides," I said, my eyes sliding from one familiar peak to the next, "it's not always easy being right at the border, knowing I can't go back home."

"Well, the sooner we reach them, the sooner you can," Mona said in a dignified voice. She eyed the mountains with detachment, her chin in the air. "Which direction are we heading?"

I turned away from her on the pretense of finding a landmark with my compass. This bubble of peace that had swelled inside me at the sight of my home wouldn't last, and I didn't want her bursting it any sooner than necessary.

We camped that evening in a brushy copse that housed an elusive whippoorwill, which crooned unconcernedly until nearly dawn. None of us slept well as a result, which made for a touchy trek the following day. The treeless hills became monotonous, and at every rise, the mountains never seemed to grow any closer. The next night brought a spattering of rain, and we sheltered in a tumble of boulders, trying to coax ourselves to sleep. But finally, the following afternoon, we started up the long, gentle rise leading us to the foot of the mountains. Trees sprouted up here and there, soon tangling together into thickets before melding into a solid wall.

We had reached the forest eaves.

A creek rushed out to greet us, widening into a pool that held promise for rock bass. Salamanders squiggled around the muddy banks, which were pockmarked with animal prints. Encouraged, I left the trio to fish the waters and wove along the edge of the forest, hunting for signs of game. I twisted a handful of cord snares and set them across favorable runs. On my way back, I came across a stretch of wild carrots still tender enough to eat, and I gathered them in my cloak with handfuls of dandelion greens and onions. These plus a chance patch of chanterelles, combined with the dozen or so rock bass the siblings hooked, made for an exceptionally good meal. We sat contentedly around our fire, the prickly atmosphere from the previous days dissolved by our progress and full stomachs.

Luck was with us. The following morning, my snares yielded a great deal of game, and we spent the day smoking rabbit, squirrel, and grouse to carry with us. I lamented the loss of the furs and bones, but I didn't have the time to spend tanning and didn't want to carry them on my back over the mountains. I scattered them throughout the woods, silently thanking each creature for its life and apologizing for the waste of its gifts.

I sat skinning a rabbit as the light waned, the last of my catch to prepare. Colm was sitting in front of the medical kit, tying bundles of spicebush and sweet birch twigs together, the kit laid out in neat rows before him. Mona, I noticed, sat a fair distance away, sorting the food we had prepared into pouches. I had already teased her for her aversion to the cleaning of my game when her folk made their livings prying cysts out of mussels, to which she had been too dignified to respond. She had braided her hair back over her head again, donning her crown once more.

"I don't know."

I craned my neck to look over my shoulder, where Arlen was facing the rising slopes, his atlatl clutched loosely in his hand. "What don't you know?"

He gestured to the forest. "I just don't know. I don't like it. It's so closed in. I already feel like an ant in a wad of grass. How on earth do you tell which way is which?"

"That's why we carry compasses," I said. "But you learn its patterns, after a while."

"I'm just used to being able to see the sky."

I looked up. The stars were peeking out of the royal blue ceiling, the sun long gone behind the mountains.

"We stargaze from the trees and the balds." I dropped my gaze into the darkening east. "Summer's almost here. There's its star."

Colm bundled up the medical kit. "The Summer Pearl," he said. "We usually can't see it in Lumen until early in the morning, when it clears the tops of the mountains."

"We call him Suitor Firefly," I said. "He heralds the start of firefly season. His mate has been waiting in the sky for him to come calling." I pointed up, following the familiar arc of stars to the brightest one.

Colm looked up at the arc. "We call that the Goose. He stole a string of pearls from the lake and trails it behind him."

"We say it's a bear being chased by fireflies," I said.

"Why would a bear be chased by fireflies?" asked Mona.

"Why would a goose steal pearls?" I retorted.

"It's creepy," continued Arlen, ignoring our discussion. He turned away from the forest and strode to the fireside, sitting down out of the smoke. "And don't try to tell me your folk don't agree."

"Why do you say that?" I asked.

He settled back on his elbows. "You've got all kinds of names. I've seen your map. Skullcap Bald. Shroud Mountain. Ghost Mountain."

"*Blue* Ghost Mountain," I corrected him. "Fireflies."

"Fireflies aren't blue."

I stared at him. "Yes, they are."

"They're yellow."

"Some of them are. And some are blue. The blue ghosts. You've never seen the blue ghosts?" My hands went idle, amazed that this fundamental part of my culture could be alien to him. "They don't blink. They glow blue, steadily, and they float." I illustrated with my hand. "Blue Ghost Mountain sees thousands of them, every spring and summer, and when they swarm . . ." I felt an old familiar rush, remembering this yearly event, more magical than anything else in the world. "They're like a river of light, silent, just flowing through the forest. They light up the trees, their glow is so strong. We stop everything when they begin swarming, and we sit in the branches above where they're flying, and we play music and dance." I watched his face, his expression unimpressed. "You really didn't know about them?" I looked at Colm. "Tell me you've heard of them."

"I knew your folk see the Light in fireflies," he said. "I never knew why they were called blue ghosts."

"Not at all?" I asked.

"Remember that your monarchs haven't exactly welcomed foreigners into their country for the last hundred years," Mona said.

But even her testiness couldn't faze me. "What about the synchronous fireflies?" I asked Colm. "They coordinate their flashes." I flicked my fingers in the air. "They all blink at the same time. Have you heard of them?"

"No."

"*Oh.*" I clapped my hand to my forehead. "Great

Light, you can't imagine the sight . . . I wish I knew where they were likely to swarm this year. The best place to see them is the waterfall flowing from the palace at Lampyrinae. We call it the Firefall, because all the different kinds of fireflies—the blue ghosts, the synchronous ones, the yellow and green ones—they all float along the banks like embers rising from the water."

Arlen stretched and scratched his head with the Bird. "Well, don't feel like you have to take us there to see them. I don't fancy being nabbed by the king just to go bug-hunting."

I clenched my hands on my knees. I wanted to shake him by the shoulders, rattle his teeth for brushing off my folk's most hallowed creatures. Instead I stabbed my knife point back into my rabbit, tugging at the skin a bit too forcefully. It didn't help that I hadn't had the privilege of celebrating the firefly revelry for five years now. The last time I had seen the blue ghosts was just before a blindfold was wound over my eyes by apologetic Royal Guardsmen. That was the last glimpse I had, the magic of the ghosts winked out just like every other blessed thing the old king had taken away from me.

CHAPTER 4

We packed up the following morning, striking our camp and scattering the ashes from our fire. Laden with the gifts from the Hill-folk and the forest's edge, we turned toward the pathless slopes rising before us. I balanced my compass in my palm, found my bearing, and with a word to the three siblings, stepped forward under the eaves of the wood.

It was a balm, being back in the trees after so long. The loamy smell rose up around me, rich, dark, instantly familiar. Birdsong flooded the canopy, voices as plain to me as my own tongue. Little sights I had nearly forgotten about surprised me with every step—the iridescent sheen of a damselfly, the crisp white petals of bloodroot, the miniscule prints of mice pressed into the creek bed. Even the ground felt familiar under my feet, my soft soles finally planted back in layers of leaf litter. I drew in a deep breath of fragrant air. I was home—finally, *finally*, I was back where I belonged.

But it didn't take long for my grating reality to slink back amid my bliss. *I'm trespassing*, I told myself firmly. *I'm a vagrant with no right to be here.* I ground my teeth and hoisted my pack, my stride lengthening as my frustration grew. I ducked under a rhododendron bough, musing over the many things I would enjoy shouting at Vandalen's grave. I wondered if his old councilors were still pursuing his quest to turn the scouts into forest assassins or whether they were focused on destabilizing King Valien first. Frowning, I wove among the twisting rhododendrons, hating that I had been turned into an enemy of my own country.

"Dammit, Mae, slow down!"

I pulled up short at Arlen's shout and looked over my shoulder. The three Lake-folk were a good ten yards back, Mona in front, followed by Colm. She was frowning at a long scratch running under her forearm, while Arlen was struggling to free his pack from a tangle of greenbrier. Colm, the tallest of the three, was wiping a smear of grime off his forehead where he had decked it on a rhododendron bough.

"What's wrong?" I asked.

"You're moving too fast, Mae," Mona said irritably. "You ran us right through a briar patch."

"Why didn't you go around it?" I asked, looking down at the tangle of greenbrier.

"We didn't know what it was until we walked through it!"

I watched them struggle for a moment, garnering several more scratches as they sought to free themselves. Finally they puffed up the creek bed to join me.

"How long did I say it would take to get over the mountains?" I asked before I could stop myself.

"Don't you antagonize us," Mona said frostily. "You're our *guide*. You're supposed to *guide us*, not run off and leave us." She rubbed her arm. "Just slow down. Tell us if we need to watch out for something."

I shrugged and turned back up the creek. "All right. I'll try."

Was it normal, I would wonder an hour later, for reasonably hardy, well-traveled people to be so clod-headed as they moved through the Silverwood? Here were folk who could hold their breaths in frigid water for nearly five minutes, and yet they took to the mountains as well as fish to the rocky shore. The forest absolutely baffled them. They didn't know poison ivy from pokeweed or a hornet from a hawkmoth. They didn't think to check the spaces between trees for spiderwebs, and—*earth and sky*—they didn't know the first thing about moving quietly.

"Great flaming sun!"

Arlen was the worst of the lot, and I turned, whispering fiercely as he thrashed like a mouse caught in a talon, "Will you keep it down?"

"Do you *breed* spiders for size here?" He convulsed, running his hands through his hair and over his shoulders. "Thing was the size of my thumb!"

"Be glad for them," I shot back. "Unless you'd rather

be eaten alive by mosquitoes. Just check the branches in front of you."

"I'm too busy watching my blazing feet!"

"Well, at least keep your voice down if you're going to shriek again. King Valien can probably hear you from his throne at Lampyrinae." I started back up the banks of the creek.

"When will we stop for lunch?" Mona asked. "It's nearing midday."

"I was hoping to make it further, where this fork joins Drink-Your-Tea Creek."

I could hear the eye-roll in Arlen's voice. "Again with the bizarre names."

I stopped walking. "Shut up."

"Don't you tell me to shut—"

"No," I interrupted, turning back around. "Shut up and *listen*."

The siblings stilled their movements, letting the sounds of the forest rise up around us. Filtering from the treetops, plain as day, came the insistent command, the two-note pendulum swing finished with a warble. *Drink-your-tea! Drink-your-tea!*

"The towhee," I said quietly. "He's one of the first birds we learn as children.

> *"Phoebe gives a little sneeze,*
> *Chickadee says his name,*
> *Towhee orders drink-your-tea!*
> *Mockingbird says the same."*

I looked up at the trees, seeing the flit of black head, red shoulders, and white breast. A beautiful bird. "All our names mean something, Arlen. Shroud Mountain is always covered in mist. Skullcap Bald is a dome of bare rock that sticks up above the tree line. Kingsfall Ridge is where the king fell, one hundred years ago, and broke his leg. Everything tells a story."

We listened a moment longer to the song being passed through the trees, and then I turned without another word and continued, leading the other three up the slope. We walked for a minute in silence.

"Rivers to the sea," said Arlen irascibly. "I can't stop hearing them now."

I smiled vindictively.

We camped that evening next to a rocky cascade hung with moss and maidenhair ferns. A few yellow fireflies winked around the water's edge, searching placidly for their mates. We were several miles from where I had hoped to stop for the night, but the three siblings were so sweaty, scratched, and footsore that I was forced to give up the distance as lost.

"Are you sure we can't light a fire?" Mona asked mournfully, watching a school of minnows pluck skimmers from the water's surface. "We're so far from your folk's settlements."

I shook my head. "Honestly, we'd be safer starting one just outside Lampyrinae, because the smoke could be passed off as someone else's. The king's scouts are especially watchful of the mountains near the foot-hills, and they're quick to investigate any signs of in-truders. Smoke will bring them running."

"I will never understand," Arlen said, chewing on a piece of jerky, "why your folk are so blazing distrustful."

"Did you never take history lessons?"

"Sure I did," he said. "And I still don't understand. It all seems to stem from the changing of your monarchy three hundred years ago."

"Two hundred," Colm corrected him.

Arlen waved a vague hand. "The point is, your orig-inal monarchy was lost. The line of kings and queens that presided throughout the Luminous Years ended, and lesser folk took over the crown. Bad decisions have been made ever since."

"It wasn't because of the passing of the crown," I said. "It was because the silver mines dried up, and the moment trade through the mountains dissolved, all the surrounding nations started assaulting the country."

"Assaulting?" Mona repeated. "There were no as-saults."

"What do you call the Hill-folk felling whole swaths of trees at the forest borders, even after the king for-bade it? What do you call *your* folk, Your Highness, trying to build a road through the southern mountains without our consent? That would be like us building bridges through your pearl beds."

"Your king was increasing tariffs on all trade through the forest," she countered. "With it costing more and more to send our wealth to the delta, we needed better access to the southern ports."

"Yeah, and look where that got you. Alcoro came sniffing around. It's no wonder they invaded Cyprien to get closer to the lake, with you tripping over yourselves to ferry your pearls down the waterways."

"It still stems from your monarchy," Arlen said. "Even after your new silver mine was discovered, you refused to collaborate with the lake."

"We had just gotten through warring with each other!" I shot back. "Your folk were just as unwilling to collaborate with us!"

"But it's been a hundred years since the Silent War!" he protested. "Long enough that your folk should have gotten less paranoid—but your borders have remained closed ever since!"

"Peldalen," Colm interjected quietly.

I pointed at him triumphantly while still looking at Arlen. *"Right,"* I said. "King Peldalen. He was killed in a skirmish with a band of timbering Hill-folk barely forty-five years ago! Your own folk diverted rivers on the Palisades—the Palisades belong to *us*—just a few years later. Is it any wonder the queen felt the need to keep the borders closed? Our monarchy has only ever tried to protect its citizens and its resources!"

"You're awfully forgiving to a crown that ordered you banished," Mona said.

"I've told you before—that was Vandalen. He took his mother's caution to the extreme. Everything else you're talking about happened years before he took the throne. I have nothing against the kings and queens of the past except that they ultimately led to Vandalen. He's the one who twisted everything away from the protection of the forest. "

"Perhaps things will change," Colm said. "Perhaps his son will redeem the throne."

Arlen spread his arms wide. "What's changed? What's different? Here we are, on a journey that, if successful, could benefit the Silverwood as well as Lumen, and we still have to crawl through the mountains like vagrants. King Valien should be welcoming us with honors and trying to re-forge our old alliance if he really has his citizens' best intentions in mind."

"Would you trust him?" I asked. "After centuries of skirmishes and standoffs, would you trust him on just his word?"

"No," admitted Mona. "His father would have swooped in and driven Alcoro out of Lumen only to claim my throne as his own—if he hadn't been killed in the attempt, that is."

"Perhaps Valien sees his father's error," Colm suggested.

"Just a few months after his father was killed?" Mona said. "More likely he's in mourning."

I snorted. Mona looked at me.

"Sorry," I said.

"It's much too soon in Valien's reign for him to have developed any contrasting convictions of his own," she continued. "And as Mae said in Tiktika, he'll be under pressure from his court. Vandalen's old advisors will want to make sure their influence is still secure, and if they supported an invasion of Lumen under the old king, there's no reason to expect them to change their tune under the new one. Any offer Valien made to me would make me question whether it was still part of his father's power play."

I stretched. "So who's distrustful now?"

"I don't deny it. A queen can't hand out her trust without careful scrutiny."

"Except to half-drowned vagabonds who know how to use a compass."

She picked a few specks of dirt off her sleeve. "You're a scout, Mae, and a disgraced one at that, not a politician or a monarch. You have no influence in the Silverwood. Any motivation you have is purely personal. For wealth—and, I suspect, the opportunity to feel useful once again. You couldn't betray me without also betraying yourself."

I stared at her for a moment, rankled. Several different retorts boiled up inside me, but instead I rolled over and gathered up my bedroll. For the second time during our journey, I stomped away, heading to the other side of the clearing to avoid blurting something I would later regret. Furious and flustered, I settled down amid a patch of ferns. A firefly blinked idly by as I cast my cloak over myself. I wanted to shout back at her, topple her haughty sense of entitlement, but I couldn't, not with any conviction.

Because when it came right down to it, she was right.

We hit more of a stride the following day, though not without a steady litany of complaints from Arlen about how his cloak was wringing wet from the dewfall and he hadn't slept a wink for the cacophony of peepers all night long. I tried to ignore him, resigned to the fact that he would always find something to be unhappy about.

I tried hard.

We followed the path of Drink-Your-Tea Creek, the towhees serenading us during our climb, before leaving the banks behind us to take a more westerly route. The forest gradually changed from dark, snarled rhododendron thickets to towering stands of hemlock and tulip poplar. The ground was carpeted with the poplars' fringed green and orange flowers, and every now and then we passed an old moss-covered stump, remnants of the days of the timbering industry.

Our conversation was light and terse, delicately avoiding anything that had to do with the years of turmoil between our two nations. Mona's inquiries and commands were succinct and dignified, and I refrained from embellishing further on the narrative of the land we were hiking through. In fact, it wasn't until another day had passed that anything contentious came up.

I was twelve feet up in a tree, gripping the trunk between my knees while I tied a hitch into our rope. We were sheltering that night in a pine grove, fragrant and springy underfoot, but lacking in stout branches to hang our food off the ground. I had strung up a line between two trunks, suspending our packs out of harm's way. When the rope was secure, I shinnied back toward the ground. As I descended, my hand dragged over a glob of pitch oozing out from the trunk. I paused. The light was just beginning to fade, making it difficult to see, so I leaned forward, peering at the pitch. I looked up, squinting at the crowns of the pines surrounding me.

"What are you doing?"

I glanced down. Arlen was at the foot of the tree, looking up at me.

"Nothing. Checking the pines. Habit." I continued down to the ground. "Did you need something?"

"What are you checking for?"

I rubbed my sticky hand. "Sickness. Die-off. But they're producing pitch, and all their needles are green. That's good. That means they can fight off beetles."

"What does that matter?"

"What do you mean, what does that matter? If a tree gets infested with beetles, they'll spread to other trees. Sick trees have to be cut down before they get infested. Why are you looking at me like that?"

"You can't possibly check every tree in the wood?"

I raised my eyebrows. "Well, we don't go tree to tree or anything. Each Woodwalker heads a scouting party assigned to a certain range. Weak pines are just one of the things they look for."

"Seriously?"

"What did you think we did?" I asked hotly, stalking past him.

"I've never been entirely sure, to be honest." He pattered after me. "Birdwatching?"

I huffed and settled down a few feet from Mona, who was stitching up a rip in her cloak. "We're stewards of the forest. We keep an eye on all kinds of things. That's why we're called scouts. *What?*" He was staring at me with a look of amused disbelief.

"I mean, it's a forest." He waved around him as he sat down against a pine trunk. "Doesn't it sort of take care of itself?"

"If it was *just a forest*, yes, it would take care of itself." I unlaced my boot. "But there are a couple thousand people living up and down the mountain range, and we cause a lot of damage. Landslides, spoiled streams, overhunting—and that's not counting the impacts of the silver mine. If we put stress on a stand of timber, the trees will die, the mountainside will wash out, and folk will get killed. If we muck up a stream, the insects and plants will disappear, and then bam, we'll have no fish. The Wood Guard—and the Woodwalkers—were created to keep track of those things."

"And what about murdering wandering foreigners on sight?" Mona asked lightly. "Where does that factor in to your duties?"

I looked up at her sharply. "Why? Who was killed?"

"You tell me," she said, making a perfect, miniscule stitch in her cloak. "All I know is I received an extremely derisive letter a few years before the invasion warning me that King Vandalen's scouts were under orders to fire on foreigners in the Silverwood. Maybe that order came after you were banished."

On Mona's other side, Colm watched me curiously. I looked back down at my boot. "I suppose the idea was to stop the timbering and hunting along our borders. At least, that's what the council said their reason was. In reality, Vandalen wanted us to focus our efforts away from the mine, to ease our restrictions on it."

"So you *were* still a scout when this happened?"

I fingered the worn leather of my boot. "When the order came, yes, I was still a Woodwalker."

"Wait, are we going to be shot?" Arlen sat forward from the tree trunk. "I figured if we were found, we'd just be taken in and questioned, not killed on sight. Does King Valien still have his scouts shoot trespassers?"

I pulled my boot back on my foot. "I don't know what his orders are."

"Back in Winder, Topher said the Hill-folk weren't being fired on anymore," Colm said.

"Valien's only been on the throne a few months, and it's been wintertime," Mona said, cutting her thread with her teeth. "Fewer chances for folk to be abroad in the wood. I seriously doubt anything has changed."

Arlen shook his head and settled back against the pine tree. "Bad blood. Bad monarchy. You have to admit, Mae, the crown passed to the wrong family all those years ago. Maybe, if we're lucky, the line will destroy itself. Maybe Valien will be killed early on and a new family will take the throne."

Something flared up inside me, something I couldn't quite vocalize to these three royals, so sure in their right to rule their own country. "Don't place any bets on it. Valien is cunning, and he takes risks. I know. I lived in the palace at Lampyrinae, remember? He's a better swordsman than his father and grandfather were, and he's more desperate. He knows he has everything to lose, or gain." I took a breath, reining myself back in. "If he decides to pursue the crown of Lumen, you can be sure he'll do so with more tact than his father did."

"Well," Mona said matter-of-factly, smoothing out the seam in her cloak. "He won't get anywhere near it without a fight, and woe be to him if he tries and fails and I get my hands on him. I do not take kindly to people who double-cross me."

I rolled over and pressed my face into the fragrant pine carpet, pulling my cloak around my shoulders. "You don't take kindly to anyone."

I jerked from sleep that night to a sound that was instantly familiar to me: a shuffling, shambling, grunting noise at the periphery of our campsite. I groaned inwardly. If Mona woke to find a bear inspecting our hanging packs, her shriek would wake the entire forest. I lifted my head an inch off my bedroll. The night was clear, and the waxing moon threw enough light through the trees to make out the dark, slope-shouldered shape in the shadows. I held still, watching the big head snuffle the ground.

There's nothing here, I thought. *Our food's in the trees. We haven't used soap in days. Nothing here, bear.*

It took a few muffled steps on the carpet of pine needles and raised its head toward our dangling packs. With a heave, it lifted itself onto its hind legs, stretching its nose into the air. But the line I had tied was too high. It snuffled loudly and then flumped back down to the ground with a thud.

Nothing here, I thought again. *Go away before the queen wakes up and loses her mind.*

It sniffed the air again. Slowly, with many cautious pauses, it took several steps our way.

We were lying two-by-two with our heads facing together. The bear was closest to Arlen, who was lying on his stomach with his head pillowed in his arms. Mona was on his other side. The bear bent its nose to the ground a few feet from Arlen's hip. It huffed the air.

Colm was between me and the bear, lying on his back with one arm behind his head. Gingerly, I straightened my leg and prodded him with my toe. He twitched but didn't wake.

"Colm," I whispered. The bear lifted its head and snorted. I nudged him again. *"Colm."*

With a grunt, he broke from sleep.

"Don't startle," I said softly. "Don't shout. There's a bear next to Arlen."

He blinked several times but didn't speak. I could

see his head incline slightly as he searched for the animal, now standing tensely by Arlen's hip.

"I'm going to try to talk it down," I said. "I need you to stand up with me, slowly."

He nodded once. The bear grunted. Mona stirred.

"Hello, bear," I said in an ordinary voice. "Hello."

The bear startled backward. Slowly, I sat up.

"Sit up, Colm," I said in the same level voice. "Hello, bear. We're big. We're big and uninteresting." Colm pushed himself up on his elbows. "There's nothing here for you. Colm, stretch your cloak out. Look, bear, see how big we are?"

The bear took several swaying steps backward. It snorted again. In the moonlight, I saw Mona open her eyes.

"Don't scream," I said sharply.

She didn't scream. She drew in a sharp, audible gasp and scrambled upright. The bear snorted again.

Unfortunately, Arlen wasn't even *that* composed as he shifted and lifted his head.

"Flaming sun!" He bolted to his hands and knees.

The bear charged.

That's when Mona screamed. She flung herself off her bedroll and scrambled in the other direction.

"Don't run, Mona! No, Arlen, put it down!"

But he had already fitted a dart to the Bird, which had been lying in the crook of his elbow. He flung it as he scrabbled backward over his bedroll.

The bear skidded just short of him, and hurriedly

he groped for another dart. I couldn't tell where the first had hit. The bear slapped the ground with both paws.

"Put it down, Arlen!"

He flung his atlatl again, but his aim was off in his haste and the dark. The dart burrowed inconsequentially into the bear's foreleg. It charged again. Arlen reeled backward, scrambling for purchase amid the tangle of bedrolls and cloaks.

I was on my feet, stretching my cloak over my shoulders like absurd bat wings.

"Go on, bear!" I shouted. "Go on!"

But the bear wasn't interested in me. It bore down on Arlen, who grappled for the knife at his belt. In a swift move, he loosened it and plunged it into the bear's shoulder.

The bear bellowed and cuffed Arlen with a heavy paw, bowling him over. His darts spilled from his hand; the Bird sailed off into the brush. He rolled onto his side, clutching his arm.

Colm scrambled around the far side of the clearing. Mona, who had frozen in the middle of our campsite, took off running for the underbrush. The bear slapped the ground again and barreled after her. She screamed to wake the dead.

"Stop, Mona! Stop running!"

In the darkness, I didn't see everything that happened next. The bear staggered sideways, halting its instinctive pursuit. It turned in a half-circle, staggered again, and then buckled forward, landing on the pine carpet with a heavy thud. It snorted wetly, once, twice, and then it stilled.

Five paces away stood Colm, the Bird lofted in his hand. Two new darts had found their marks, one deep in the bear's neck, the other between its eyes.

A thick silence settled among us. Mona peered around the bole of a tree on the far side of the campsite, clutching her chest. Arlen lay on his side, his hand on his arm. Colm slowly lowered the atlatl. And I stood with my cloak bunched in my hands, my fists pressed to either side of my head.

I looked past the dark hulk of the bear to Colm, feeling an unexpected sense of betrayal. "It didn't have to die! You didn't have to kill it!"

"It was chasing Mona," he said.

"Because she *ran*." I whirled to her. "It's because you ran!" I spun on Arlen. "You stung it with a dart!"

"It was charging," he said angrily, rolling upright.

"It was *bluffing*!"

He pulled his hand away from his bleeding arm and waved it at me. "It gouged me!"

"*After you stabbed it!* Great Light, it behaved exactly as expected! You provoked it, and it cuffed you." I pointed at Mona. "You ran, and it chased you. That's what bears *do*!"

"You'll forgive me if I don't apologize," she said coldly, stepping out from behind the tree.

I marched to Arlen, gripped him under his uninjured arm, and hauled him to his feet.

"You hit me and I hit you back," he said fiercely.

I plunged my hand into the pocket of his trousers and drew out a handful of fruit leathers.

"I *told* you," I said through clenched teeth. "Everything goes in the trees at night."

"I forgot they were there," he said. "I was bringing them to you to hang in the bag when we started talking about sick pines."

I spun on my heel and stalked to the bear's side. I tugged at the dart in its neck. It slid halfway out before getting stuck.

"It's barbed," Arlen said. "The darts are barbed. You have to cut them loose."

I flung the fruit leathers at his face and then bunched my cloak over my eyes, wanting to scream. Earth and sky, this was as basic as any knowledge we learned as scouts. Most of us came into the Royal Guard already knowing how to act if we crossed paths with a bear. I supposed these three hadn't learned that at the lake, but they could have listened to *me*. I took several sharp breaths, trying fiercely to channel my anger into something useful. Slowly, I slid the cloak from my eyes. I glared through the darkness at Colm.

"I'm sorry," he said quietly. "But it hurt Arlen, and I thought it was going to hurt Mona."

I blew out the last breath I had been holding. I wasn't done being angry with him, but something about his direct, solemn statement made me bite back the rest of my rage. I waved my hand in resigned agitation.

"It's done. But we can't leave the darts in it. None of

my folk would kill a bear just to let it rot in the woods, and when the king's scouts follow the carrion birds, we don't want them finding atlatl darts."

"I'll get them out," Colm said.

"Good. Arlen, sit down over there while I get the medical kit."

As I headed through the darkness for the tree bearing our packs, I heard Mona say quietly, "That was a good shot, Colm."

I sucked in a sharp breath, forcing myself to continue to the tree instead of turning around and letting my anger spill out again. I clambered up the trunk, the needles slapping my face in the darkness. When I reached the line, I paused for a moment, resting my forehead against the rough, sticky bark. I breathed in the clean scent of pine.

Three days. Three days under the eaves of the Silverwood, and already I was wondering how—how in the great wide world—we could possibly complete this journey without killing one another.

Arlen's wounds were small but deep, and it took me some time to wash the grit out of them. When I had finally cleaned and dressed his arm as best as I could in the dark, I had everyone pack up camp. This met with little resistance—nobody wanted to hike extra miles in the middle of the night, but Mona was not about to sleep side by side with a bear, no matter how dead it was. Or maybe *because* of how dead it was—I was too irked to care. We trudged away from the fragrant pine grove and further up the mountainside. It took us almost an hour to reach another suitably flat stretch of ground. Of course, unlike our pine bower, it was studded with rocks and must have been located near a skunk den. We slept poorly.

It did not improve our dynamic.

In the following days creeping up the slopes, an unexpected loneliness settled around me like a heavy cloak. Mona and Arlen did not hide their disdain for the mountains. Sights and sounds I welcomed like old friends made them uneasy, like the rusty screams of two ghost owls that jarred us from sleep one night. A few days later, I came back into camp from filling our waterskins in a stream to find Arlen beating the underbrush with a stick. He overrode my shocked admonitions, saying there was a wildcat hiding nearby, stalking us. His face lit up in victory as the throaty mewling began again. I could have strangled him. What he took for a predator was, in fact, a fawn, cowering in the brush, calling for its mother. Enraged, I made them break camp again and move to another spot to allow the doe to return to her frightened infant.

When they weren't openly displeased, the best I could hope for was indifference. My heart warmed one evening when I found we had camped in a ring of foxfire, the rich, rotting wood glowing softly in the night. But Mona and Arlen were unimpressed, nudging the fungi with their boots, grumbling that it would have been better to find mushrooms we could eat rather than ones that glowed in the dark. Once again, our conversation ended with me storming off to take my own private solace in the soft light shining through the forest.

Colm, however, I couldn't read. If he shared his sibling's discontent, I couldn't tell. He did make an effort to keep the peace, often slipping a gentle word into heated conversations to ease the building tension. He helped with small tasks without being asked. He didn't complain. He gazed at the foxfire. But his joy was as buttoned up as his disdain. Whether this was a continued apology for killing the bear, I couldn't tell. I almost wished he would offer some contempt, if only so I might know where he stood. But he remained unshakable as stone. I was surprised to find this disappointed me.

In the years since my banishment, I had managed to tamp down the constant ache for a familiar face, a familiar voice, one that shared my culture and convictions and reverence for the forest. It was easy in the busy river towns and port cities to become just another stranger, another guest to serve, another foreigner passing through with nothing to contribute. But here, in my home, I felt more alone than I ever had roaming the eastern hills. Sometimes, before I opened my eyes in the morning, my hazy half-finished dreams would plant me back in my childhood bedroom, or in my bunk in the barracks, the windows open to the morning birdsong. My old daily routine would lift its head out of my sleepy fog: uniform, then breakfast, then out onto the ridge. But in another few heartbeats, this once-familiar veil fell away, and I found myself instead lying on my bedroll on the forest floor, wrapped in a rough cloak and leather shoes made far from home, the trees all staring down at me curled up at their feet, a question whispering through their leaves.

What are you doing here?

Colm caught on to me one evening. I'm not sure what gave me away, whether he saw the frequent glances I was stealing at Beegum Bald, visible from our campsite for the night, or if he simply guessed something was whittling away at me. Either way, he broached the subject.

"Where are we now, Mae?"

I jerked my glance back down from the bald to him. "Where on our journey?"

"No, where in the mountains?"

"We're in a saddle, sort of, between two peaks. Back there is Shroud Mountain." I pointed into the gloom. "Up there is Beegum Bald."

"Is that where you're from?"

"Oh." Was it that obvious? "Yes. I mean, I lived at Lampyrinae for seven years." I looked up at Beegum again. "But yes, that's where my family is from."

"Are they still there?"

I gazed at the bald, black against the darkening sky. If I squinted, I could pretend to see the flicker of lanterns twinkling on the slopes, lighting the carved wooden lintels of the cabins scattered in its hollows. I thought of my sister Sera, draped in gauze as she smoked her bees. I thought of my brothers. Meicah, the settlement's blacksmith. Jole, the drummer, taking up my parents' craft. And Persë, sweet Persë, who could play a tune lovelier than birdsong on any instrument he touched.

"I hope so," I said.

"Have you seen them since you were banished?"

Well, we were moving fast. I cleared my throat. "No. During the first year, I used to come to the border of the forest and light big, smoky fires. Most of the king's scouts were still my friends at that point, and when they came to investigate the smoke, I'd give them letters to bring to my family. But Vandalen ordered them to stop when he found out." I squinted at the distant bald. "My sister was pregnant when I was banished. I had been planning on going home for her labor."

"Did they get to say goodbye to you?"

I shook my head. "I doubt they even got news of my banishment until after I was released at the forest border."

"I'm sorry."

I looked at him, his face disappearing in the twilight. One of my own folk, dark-headed and dark-skinned, would have melted into the gloom already, but the gold of his hair was still visible in the dim light.

"Thank you," I said. I didn't know if it was loud enough for him to hear.

I hoped it was.

CHAPTER 5

The land soon became sharper, broken by steep ravines that yawned in the forest floor. These rifts were brushy and slick, and the bottoms were carpeted with rhododendron thickets. Our progress slowed to a crawl as we were forced to toil down these slopes only to start right back up them.

"Annoying, these," Arlen said as we rested at the bottom of one before beginning the climb up the other side. He, like the rest of us, was covered in grime from scraping through the rhododendrons. "Isn't there a way around them?"

"Most of them have bridges spanning them," I said, checking the bearing on my compass. "But we'd be running huge risk, trying to use them without being caught. This is much safer. No one traverses them like we're doing; it's too tedious."

"I'll say it is."

We came to the final ravine too late that afternoon, with not enough light left in the day to see us up the far side. Reluctantly, we made camp near the edge in a tumble of boulders as big as houses, carpeted with inch-deep moss. It was a pleasant campsite, and more of a rest than we had had since beginning our ascent. We lay on the cushions of moss, passing around bits of cheese and fruit leathers, watching the afternoon sky turn pink and gold.

"It's the Sea-folk who see the Light in the sunset, right?" Arlen asked, his hands folded behind his head.

"Sunrise," I said. "The shore faces east."

"Oh, right. Sunrise."

I turned my head to him. "You lived up and down the coast for three years. Did you forget?"

He shrugged. "I guess I never took much notice."

"You were never up that early," said Mona.

He stretched. "No, I suppose not." A yellow firefly blinked past us, unwilling to wait until darkness to search for a mate. "We haven't seen any blue fireflies yet, Mae."

"No, we haven't. Other than around Lampyrinae, it's difficult to tell where they're going to swarm each year."

"You said the blue ghosts are where your folk see the Light," Mona said. "But don't they only come out during the summer? What do you do the rest of the year?"

"We see it in the foxfire, too," I said. "That usually peaks in autumn. So we have something to look forward to from late spring to the first snows. And over the winter, we bide our time with the Festival of Emergence."

"Festival of . . . ?"

"Their origin story," said Colm, his fingers folded on his chest and his gaze on the sky. "Like our Overwater Feast."

"Ah," Arlen said with a grin. "Yes. *Mossgrubbers.*"

"Don't be rude, Arlen," Mona said primly.

"Oh, don't act like you've never said it yourself." He turned his head to me. "The story is that you dug yourselves up out of the dirt, right?"

"Succinctly, yes," I said, glaring at him. "Funny how we can contrive a week-long festival of light and dance from such banal beginnings."

He yawned. "You tell it, then. We've got nothing else to do."

Oh, he was needling me. "No, I don't think I will, if you're just going to snark at it."

Colm dropped his gaze from the sky to me. "I wouldn't mind hearing it as you tell it. I've only ever read it from other folk's accounts."

I looked down, pinching the thick moss in my fingers. Colm would listen. He wouldn't scoff. I decided just to tell him and pretend Arlen and Mona weren't even there.

THE WOOD-FOLK'S EMERGENCE

"Life started deep within the earth. All things were buried in the soil, silent and still. The first of our folk lay among the other plants and animals, simply existing in the emptiness. We were a quiet folk, and frightened, frightened of the crushing earth and absolute darkness. But we were frail and unskilled, and did not know that there was anything beyond the dark and silence. For ages we lay trapped in listlessness and gloom.

"But other beings were cleverer than we. They felt the call of the Light somewhere far above us, and they sought to find their way out of the darkness. One by one, each creature and growing thing used the skills and strengths that lay dormant within them, and one by one, they left us behind.

"The first to respond to the pull of the Light was the moss. It pushed its way up through the soil, the first living thing to rise from the depths. It was so amazed by the warmth of the sun and the shine of the moon that it simply sat on the mountaintops, covering the bare earth. After the moss came the other plants: shrubs and vines and finally trees, which revered the Light so much that they stretched up, up, up, trying to reach it.

"The animals began to follow, wriggling or crawling or digging their way to the surface. But we could not rise toward the Light. We did not know how. Now we were not only buried in the dark, we were left alone, abandoned by every other living thing. We mourned our fate, hidden in the press of the earth.

"But the other living things did not forget us. The first beings to come to our aid were the earthworms, who eased the soil around us, helping us move our limbs. The moles came next, teaching us how to use our hands to dig through the soil. The roots of the plants led us upward, until finally we pushed through the surface of the earth, emerging into the Light on the carpets of moss.

"We were stunned, still frightened, bare and exposed. The burning Light up above seemed so bright, so severe. We clung to the earth, pressing our faces into the moss, wondering if we should go back to the familiar depths. As our first day faded, the night enveloped us, and we were amazed to see that the Light did not wholly diminish. Under the deeps of the trees, the forest floor glowed with foxfire. The fireflies drifted through the underbrush, yellow and green and blue. These gentle things gave us courage. They gave us surety. They gave us the desire to remain above the ground, and when the morning dawned, we lifted our weak eyes to the sun once again, and our fear lessened.

"Our kindred did not abandon us. The growing plants showed us, slowly, patiently, how to sit; the trees showed us how to stand, how to stretch our arms to the Light. The cicadas taught us how to use our voices, unlovely and unpracticed as they were. The birds helped us to sweeten our speech, to create words and phrases and meaning. The mantids showed us how to take our first wobbling steps. The deer showed us how to run.

"We learned to forage from the bears and to hunt from the mountain cats. The spiders taught us to spin threads to cover ourselves, and the ants showed us how to build. The herbs and shrubs helped us to heal ourselves. And when we had mastered all the skills we needed to survive, the bees showed us how to dance, how to express our joy and our gratitude.

"And so we danced, rejoicing in our new lives, indebted to the dwellers of the mountains who had shared their gifts so that we might live in the Light. We revere those first humble sources, the fireflies and foxfire, for inspiring us to stay above the ground. We remember that we are not masters of the mountains, but caretakers and pupils. And we are reminded that we did not make ourselves."

"And so we celebrate with a week of dancing that ends in a night of pageantry," I said once I had finished. "It starts with all the lights doused. Two children, a boy and a girl, are chosen each winter to represent the first frightened Wood-folk. We all light lanterns to represent the fireflies, and we spread out glowing coals for the foxfire. As the story progresses, dancers in bright regalia sweep in, showing the pair how to master each skill as it's presented in the tale. By the end, everyone is dancing, and we don't stop until morning."

"You say your folk had to be taught how to move your arms and legs by *earthworms*?" Arlen chuckled. "Not giving yourselves much credit, are you?"

My cheeks burned, but Colm replied before I could. "I don't think that's the point. The point is that they don't take *any* credit. They claim nothing as their own—no skill or art was mastered without the help and inspiration of their homeland."

"I think it's quite charming," Mona said. My bubble of gratitude that had welled up at Colm's words suddenly deflated.

"Charming?" I repeated.

"Thinking up each animal and plant, and what skills they might contribute. It's a delightful story."

I spluttered like a frog with fluff on its tongue. "It's not *delightful*. It's a lesson in humility and respect. We *still* learn from the mountains. It's not something we just leave in the past. It's something we're doing *all the time.*"

She waved an airy hand. "Of course. I'm not criticizing it. Our origin story is equally fantastic. We claim we started out in the mud of the lakebed until we thought to cling to the bubbles rising to the surface. It's told to emphasize pragmatism and knowing your environment."

I stared at her, not sure what exactly bothered me about the way she spoke of her folk's mythology. She glanced at me in my silence, reading the look on my face.

"Oh, come now, Mae. You don't really believe—*truly* believe—that you started off buried in the dirt? How were the first people born? How did they breathe? What did they eat? How did an ant teach them to build, or a plant teach them medicine?"

"I suppose we don't believe it *literally*," I said. "Of course it's been simplified and poeticized over time. But yes, truly, we believe that every being in the mountains has something we can learn from . . ."

"Yes, yes," she said impatiently. "You're just proving my point. You believe in the *metaphor*. It's the same as our song of how we collected our first pearl." She prodded Colm's shoulder with her toe. "Sing the song, Colm. Go on."

He shifted uncomfortably. "I don't think that . . ."

"Go on."

His brow furrowed at the purple sky, he began.

THE FIRST PEARL

"Far under the lake lie the starry-bright pearls
The loveliest under the sun.
But they are laid deep in the dark and the cold.
Our folk could not reach even one.
The animals laughed at our tentative steps
As we skirted the water with care.
'If only your lot were as skillful as we,
You could bring up these riches so fair.'
'If only you could,' said the small water-bug,
'Glide over the water like me,
You'd skim to the spot where the pearls sit below
And win one for all folk to see.'
'If only you could,' said the sleek otter pup,
'Dive under the water like me,
You'd swim to the depths and dig up a shell,
And win one for all folk to see.'
'If only you could,' said the shiny red perch,
'Survive in the water like me,
You'd breathe in the lake and recover a pearl,
And win one for all folk to see.'
'If only you could,' said the white-speckled loon,
'Crack open the mussel like me,
You'd open the shell and take out its prize
And win one for all folk to see.'
Now the king and the queen were a wise, clever sort.
They studied the animals' ways.
They thought and they built and they toiled long nights

> *Away from the animals' gaze.*
> *To glide like the water-bug, they built a boat,*
> *And pushed it out over the beds.*
> *To dive like the pup, the folk practiced for hours*
> *In water up over their heads.*
> *To swim like the perch, they held deeply their breath—*
> *It cost them great labor and strife.*
> *To open the shell, like the white-speckled loon,*
> *They took out a razor-sharp knife.*
> *The king and the queen seized their very first shell*
> *And severed it open to find,*
> *The size of an egg and the shine of the moon,*
> *A pearl of rare beauty and kind.*
> *The animals sat in bewildered amaze:*
> *The Lake-folk, so clever and sly,*
> *Had mastered their tricks and were bringing up pearls*
> *Every color out under the sky.*
> *'Let it be known,' said the king and the queen,*
> *'To creatures of every kind:*
> *The folk of the Lake, while both strong and adept—*
> *Are most cunning of all with our minds.' "*

"A bit condensed, Colm," Mona said before I could comment on the richness of his singing voice. "You skipped the beaver and the crawfish. But no matter. The point remains. That song is sung to children in the cradle. We're raised with it. But no one actually *believes* the animals all laughed at the first Lake-folk.

We just like pointing to the skills of different animals and saying we've mastered them ourselves. We believe in the metaphor, not the reality."

"It is more of a nursery song," Colm pointed out.

"But there are similar songs that aren't," she said. "'The Overwater Ballad' lasts a full hour—the first verse is carved into stone at the Lakemouth docks. But most folk still see it as a fanciful legend, not historical fact."

"So you don't believe your mythology, and you don't believe in the Light," I said. "What do you believe in, Mona? Just yourself?"

"I believe in the tangible," she said darkly. "I believe in the values and strength of my folk, and of my role in my country."

"You know who else believes that?" I asked her. It was unkind, what I was about to say, but I couldn't resist the parallel. "King Celeno of Alcoro. He believes in his role, too."

"I'd be angry if I didn't know you were just trying to goad me," she said. "Celeno does not believe in anything concrete. He believes in a set of half-remembered ravings spit out hundreds of years ago. He believes in empty words and groundless claims. He believes in nothing. Not only that, his belief in nothing is propped up by everyone around him, from the queen right down to the lowest peasant. They *all* want to believe in the smattering of glyphs carved into the rock in Callais. If they can't believe in them, well then, what can they believe in?" She waved to the sky above us. "It's the same principle with the Light; we see an inspiring sunset and say it's something divine, something alive, when in fact it's just our silly selves wanting it to be more than pretty lights in the sky."

"Have you never stopped to consider what the Light actually *does*?" I said, irritated at her jaded convictions. "You're quick to point out that it's a dead, far-off thing, but think of what the world would be without it. The sun draws plants out of the ground. The moon moves the ocean tides. The stars help guide travelers. I wouldn't call that simply *pretty lights in the sky*."

"Only because we as humans have developed ways to use them for our own purposes," she said. "We've created lives that revolve around the lights of our world, because it makes sense to do so. That doesn't mean the lights themselves are sentient, guiding us down some unseen path. We honor them because they're useful to us."

"And what about my folk?" I asked her. "Fireflies and foxfire? Pretty to look at, but I'd hardly call them useful. What's made us cleave to them? If everything is about pragmatism, why do we as humans seek out beauty? Beauty is useless."

I thought surely I had won, that just this once I had had the last word. But she rolled onto her side, turning her back to me and the kindling stars.

"I never implied you were a rational people," she said.

Another dysfunctional night.

We had our first truly close call a few days later. We were making our way toward the last of the ravines; once we traversed this rift, it would be one long climb to the main ridge, the backbone of the mountains. We had been having good luck with both weather and terrain, with only a few light showers and reasonably open forest. We had just scrambled over a bulge of rock ribbing the mountainside, pocketed with patches of moss and fringed with dense azalea thickets. I was correcting my bearing; the siblings were behind me, holding some discussion. I found my landmark and was slipping my compass back into its pouch when the slightest noise filtered up the rock face.

"Hush, all of you," I said sharply.

Mona and her brothers quieted. It was a sign of how much progress we had made that they followed my instruction, willing to assess my concern before jumping in with questions. In another moment, my fears were confirmed. I beckoned frantically to the three of them, pulling them into the closest tangle of azaleas.

"Pull your cloaks over you," I whispered, stuffing them into the bushes. "Hold still. Don't make a sound." I wriggled in next to them, crouching so I could peer through the spindly branches.

Half a minute later, three figures appeared a stone's throw below us, crossing the bare rock face with silent, precise steps. They were wearing the uniform of the Wood Guard—moss green tunics over brown breeches, cinched at the waist with tooled leather belts. On their feet were soft-soled leather boots sporting a thick layer of fringe around the calves. Strapped to their backs were light packs; at their hips were quivers full of turkey-feather arrows. Each of them carried a flatbow, unstrung.

I recognized the foremost scout as an old barrack-mate, a few years my elder. The other two I didn't know. My gaze darted down the slope, lighting on every minute sign of our presence: a dislodged rock here, a squashed piece of moss there. As they passed over our path, the rear scout did a double-take at the ground, and my heart froze in my chest. But he said nothing to the others, and they continued on without stopping, crossing the rock face swiftly and silently, disappearing into the woods on the far side.

In the back of my mind, I chastised them for not paying more attention to their surroundings. Any sign of activity in such a remote place was well worth investigating. But this feeling was overcome by extreme relief. We were lucky, outrageously lucky, that we had crossed paths on solid rock and not the tell-all damp earth. Lucky, too, that they had been speaking quietly together before emerging from the woods, and lucky that the wind was blowing up the rock instead of down, so as to carry their words to us but not ours to them.

So, so lucky.

I held my breath long after they had melted back into the forest. In another few heartbeats, I was sure they were gone. We held still a moment longer, and then I let my breath out in a long, slow hiss.

"Scouts?" Mona asked in the barest whisper.

"Yes, but they weren't actively tracking anything, and there wasn't a Woodwalker among them. They're moving south, so my guess is they're heading back to Lampyrinae from some task in the northern wood. It's odd . . . this area isn't usually heavily traveled. Most folk would use one of the paths near the ridge."

"Did you recognize them?"

"One of them. We used to house together. But that doesn't mean anything. If I were on my own, perhaps I could persuade them to let me pass. But here I am leading three strangers through the country they're tasked to protect—they won't take kindly to that." I took another breath, trying to slow my heartbeat, and checked once more down the rock face. "All right, quietly, now. Let's keep the talking to a minimum. We'll be heading closer and closer to the ridge road, and your accents stick out like a raven among wrens."

As we came to the edge of the last ravine, however, I saw exactly why the three off-duty scouts had been picking their way across the pathless mountainside. I pushed through a scratchy stand of pines to find myself teetering on the edge of an unexpected precipice. The loose soil slid under my boot; I took several steps backward, latching on to one of the pines. My jaw dropped.

What had once been a steep, forested slope was

now a raw, open gash stretching away on either side of us. Even as I gazed down at the damage, loose mud slid without any provocation. The rhododendron thickets at the bottom were buried in a mire of rubble. Dozens upon dozens of dead pines littered the slope like piles of kindling.

Anger washed through me; I gripped the tree with a shaking hand, noting the rows and rows of pitch tubes left by invading beetles. I looked up at the red, brittle crown. This tree was going to die soon, too. This whole shelf would continue to slide until it was nothing but an impassable lake of mud.

Arlen whistled as he and the other two joined me. "Well, this makes things difficult."

Mona nudged a trickle of dirt over the edge. "Can we go around it? Cross somewhere north or south of here?"

They didn't care. Nobody cared. Nobody cared that this landslide could have been easily prevented. Nobody cared about the stream at the bottom that would never flow clean again. Nobody cared about the creatures that had been caught under a collapsing wall of liquid earth. Nobody cared that this was the very basis of a Woodwalker's job.

My job.

With a cry of frustration, I snapped off the brittle branch I had been holding and hurled it into the oozing scar. It fell with an unsatisfying *splat* into the thick mud.

Out of the corner of my eye, I saw Mona raise her

eyebrows, but I didn't care. I turned and elbowed past all of them, heading back the way we had come. "Come on," I said. "Get away from the edge before the whole damn thing collapses."

We trudged until we were back among healthy trees. I stopped and pulled out my compass, glaring at the face as I let the needle settle. Colm, who had been at the back of our group, drew up beside me.

"I'm sorry about the trees," he said.

The compass shook in my hand. "I used to range this ridge, early on in my training. We knew it was vulnerable. Even when Vandalen moved our focus down to the foothills, we used to send scouts this way to keep an eye on the trees." I snapped my compass shut and took a breath. "Obviously they stopped."

Mona and Arlen caught up with us; I could tell Mona was still judging me for my outburst.

"So what do we do?" she asked coolly.

I took another breath, trying to regain my composure. "Well, there's no point swinging north. The scouts we saw earlier were traveling down from the north, so we know there's no crossing that way."

"And the south?"

"The south could work . . ."

"But?"

"But there's a bridge," I said, furrowing my brow in thought. "That's where those scouts must have been headed. Before we could reach the end of this slide, we'd hit the bridge. It's not often used, but if folk are having to divert around this mess, it'll be seeing heavier traffic." I bit my lip, uneasy with the thought of leading the Alastaires anywhere close to a scout path.

"Could we cross the bridge quickly, and then disappear back into the woods?" asked Colm.

I blew out a breath. "I think we're going to have to. Listen, though. There won't be any time to stop, understand? We get to the bridge, we get across, and then we get out of there. No speaking, no doing anything stupid. It's an older bridge, so we'll have to go one at a time."

"I think we can manage it," Mona said.

"I hope so," I said, turning to the south. "Because otherwise this would be outrageously reckless."

I led them along the ravine, far enough away from the edge to avoid dislodging any more earth. They were good about not speaking, at least, though they still seemed to find a way to snap every stick and kick every stone we came across. I thought through the land before us; the path on the far side of the ravine would bend away into the south almost as soon as we crossed over the bridge. We could head directly into the woods, continuing our western route, and hope that our trail leading away from the path would go unnoticed.

Hope, and pray.

I was glad to find as we approached the bridge that there were no signs of any recent use other than the three wayward scouts we had just seen. Even so, I made the Alastaires hide deep in the shadows while I crouched against a fir, eyeing both sides of the ravine. I was sure that at any moment, an official scouting party would materialize out of the forest. But several minutes passed without any appearance, and so I finally beckoned to the siblings, my heart fluttering in anticipation.

"All right," I whispered to them. "We have to be quick, understand? One at a time. Straight across and into the woods. Let's go."

I broke from the fringe of trees along the edge of the ravine and darted across the open ground. Without pausing at the edge, I leaped up onto the cable, splaying my boots out so it ran under the arches of my feet. Gripping the two waist-high ropes, I ran out over the ravine. The breeze blew down the rift, making the cable under my feet swing, but I had experienced worse on previous traverses. I made it to the middle of the bridge with no shout from either side, no arrow whistling through the air. Another few strides and I was nearly across. I peered into the trees. No stirring, no whisper of my folk. I reached the end of the bridge and jumped off onto the lip of the ravine. I turned back around.

I nearly screamed in frustration. Mona was not stepping up to the bridge, following in my footsteps as soon as I touched down. She was standing idly at the far side, her mouth open in astonishment.

"Come on!" I whispered desperately, hoping my voice would carry over the rift. I did not want to have to shout.

"You said *bridge*," she exclaimed—quietly, but not as quiet as I'd have liked.

"What are you . . ."

"This," she said indignantly, "is not a bridge."

"Oh, great Light!"

"This is a rope, Mae!"

"It's a walkwire!" I gestured to the cable spanning the length of the ravine. "You hold on to the ropes on either side!"

"There is no possible way."

"Earth and sky, Mona! Stop being stupid! This is how we cross ravines on *all* the scout paths! Come on, now, before someone shows up!"

"We can head south. We can try to find a way down the ravine."

"*No,*" I said fiercely. "Further south takes us into the settlements. We're here, we're going to cross. You can't politicize your way out of this, Mona."

If I hadn't been so agitated, I might have relished seeing her so undone, but this was the worst possible time for her to fall apart. I had seen this kind of meltdown once or twice with new scouts—often the ones with the biggest swagger were the ones to freeze up on their first lofty traverse. Desperately, I looked past her to Colm, motioning frantically with my hands. He understood: *get her on the bridge.*

I didn't hear what he said to her, but I could see her taking long breaths through her clenched teeth. At long last she managed to put one foot on the cable.

"This is impossible," she said.

"I just did it, didn't I?"

"Then it's lunacy," she snapped.

"Other foot, now, Mona, come on. That's it."

She gripped the ropes and moved a fraction of an inch out over the ravine.

"What if the cable breaks?"

"It will if you don't hurry up," I said.

This was the wrong thing to say. She clenched the ropes until her knuckles were white, her eyes squeezed shut. I checked the woods over my shoulder.

"Mona," I said, my mind whirling. "Tell me about your family."

"*What?*"

It was a trick we sometimes used with the scouts who fell apart on a traverse. Get them talking, keep their mind occupied, and the feet often followed. "Tell me about Blackshell. What color is your banner?"

"I know what you're doing!"

"*Talk to me*, Mona! What color is your banner? I don't remember."

"It's blue. Blue and white." She took a tiny step. "Two crossed bulrushes, surrounded by twelve pearls." Another step.

"Why twelve?"

"For the twelve islands, of course." Another step.

"Which island do you live on?"

"We don't . . . Blackshell's on the shore! You know that! I know what you're doing!" She froze again.

"What about your parents, Mona? What were their names?"

"You know their names!"

"You think I can remember every little nuance of Lumeni history?"

"Myrna," she said, wiggling her foot a little further. "Queen Myrna and King Cael."

"Who was the better diver?"

"Father. He was the lead advisor for sustaining the pearl beds before he married my mother."

"Good," I said as she inched along the cable. She was a quarter of the way across. I checked over my shoulder again. "What's the biggest pearl you've ever found?"

"Great Light, I don't know . . ."

"What's your favorite color pearl?"

"Gray."

"Gray?"

"Like the surface of the lake in winter."

"Lovely. Favorite lake bird?"

"I don't know . . ."

"Favorite fish?"

"This is absurd!" She stopped again, clutching the ropes.

I needed to find the right topic. "I've never seen your crown, Mona. Tell me about your crown. I suppose it has pearls?"

"Twelve of them, like the banner." Good, she was moving again. "All white, set in silver. It crests like a wave."

Whatever that meant. "And you have jewelry that goes with it?"

She was halfway across. Unfortunately, at that moment, the breeze picked up, and the cable swayed under her feet. She yelped and bent at the knees, trying to grip the ropes with her arms.

I wracked my brain, trying to think of relevant conversation. "You said your folk sing across the water. When do you do that?"

"At the solstices, and other events . . . the Overwater Feast. Weddings, funerals." She squeezed her eyes shut.

"Stand up, Mona. One foot at a time."

She straightened just enough to inch forward, her eyes still closed. "One person starts," she said without prompting. "They stand in a boat in the middle of the lake, and they light a lantern. All the boats around them take up the song when they hear it, lighting lanterns as they go." She was in a stride now, creeping forward as she spoke. Her eyes were still shut. "It spreads along the shores until all the islands are alight and music is ringing across the water." The wind gusted again, and she took a sharp breath.

"Have you ever been the one to start the singing?" I asked. "The one in the middle of the lake?"

"Once. At my mother's funeral."

Oh, dear. Not a good topic. I jumped to change the subject, but to my surprise, she pressed on.

"She told me not to, before she died. It was this mantra of hers—don't do something if you don't think you can do it well. 'No one can *be* perfect, but a queen must *act* perfectly.' " I raised my eyebrows, but she still wasn't looking. "She didn't want my first act as queen to be making a fool of myself. She thought I would be too grieved to start the singing."

"Weren't you?" I asked in surprise, forgetting for the moment that I was supposed to be coaching her across the bridge.

"Of course I was. But I knew I could live up to her mantra. I knew, in that moment, the greatest way I could honor her was by *acting perfectly* in the face of everything." She inched along, her face screwed up in concentration. "And so I did. I pushed everything else down, and I held myself like she always taught me, and I sang—and I sang *well*. I sang *perfectly*." The breeze wobbled the cable again, but now she was moving too steadily to notice. "My parents were old when I was born, you know. Years of trying to produce an heir, and finally I came along. And then Colm, a year later, and then—surprise! Arlen. Three children born so suddenly to an aging king and queen. From my very first breath, it was common knowledge that I would take the throne as a child. And so my mother had to prepare me. She gave me all the tools I needed to run my country—how to act, how to govern, when to trust others, and when to trust myself. She didn't want someone running the country behind my back because I was too naïve to do things myself."

I was listening in silence now, astounded at the words spilling from her mouth. The wind whistled against the cable, and I wasn't sure whether or not Colm and Arlen could hear her from the far side of the bridge.

"She used to make me give speeches to the council," she continued. Her eyes were still shut. "She used to make me draft ordinances. Once, one citizen quarreled with another and set his dock on fire, and she made me make the final judgment on the man's punishment, and she made me read it aloud to him. All this before I was eleven. She made me demand respect for myself, because she knew once she died there would be no one else to do it for me."

"Mona," I said. "You made it."

She gave a small start and opened her eyes. She stood at the very end of the bridge, her feet hanging over solid ground. Gingerly, she stepped down off the cable and loosened her grip from the ropes. She stared for a moment at the dirt between her feet, and then lifted her eyes accusingly to me.

"That was a dirty trick," she said.

"Got you across, didn't it?" Behind her, Arlen had already climbed up onto the bridge. He gripped the ropes with white knuckles like his sister and shuffled forward with miniscule steps. I looked back to Mona. "So. I understand a bit more now—not much of a childhood, was there? No time to imagine mermaids or dragons if you're busy writing legislation. Perhaps that's why you're so skeptical of the Light. Sounds too much like a fairy tale."

"Enough," she said coldly. "I overspoke."

Arlen wobbled on the bridge, pulling the ropes in toward his waist. "Out, Arlen," I called to him. "Push out." I put my arms out to illustrate. "Push onto the ropes, don't bring them to you." I turned back to her again, cocking my head. "Can't imagine you had many friends, did you? Only allies."

"I said *enough*." The icy barrier that had dropped away was back up. "Don't press me, Mae." She pointed out to the ravine. Arlen was almost to us. "You have a job to do here, and it's not done yet. Focus on that, not on making snide comments."

But I had been doing my job, and whether she liked it or not, hearing her monologue had made the job a bit easier. Now I knew, just a little, who I was dealing with.

I took Arlen by the arm and guided him off the cable. He wiped the sweat off his brow with a shaky hand. On the far side of the ravine, Colm stepped up onto the cable. He took short steps like his siblings had, but his grip on the ropes was less dire.

"All right, Colm?" I called.

"All right."

He crossed with barely a wobble. As soon as he joined us, I led the three of them into the brush, showing them where to step to avoid leaving a swath of destruction in our wake. We moved carefully through the woods, seeking to put as much distance as possible between us and the bridge. When we had finally gotten far enough away, I brought us to a halt.

"Not so bad, was it?" I asked.

Mona was glaring at the forest around us, as if angry with her very environment. "Let's get going."

I turned back up the slope, wondering how she was going to make me pay for laying bare a little bit of the substance below her crown.

CHAPTER 6

The following morning, a thick fog rolled into our campsite. It shrouded the trees and trickle of a creek, pressing down on us like a blanket. I woke up slowly in the uncomfortably heavy air. Oh, how we used to gripe in the Wood Guard about the damp—how it rusted our blades and spoiled our food. But now I greeted the sensation like an old friend, relishing the way it condensed on my skin and corkscrewed my hair. The way it hid us. As I drew in a deep, humid breath, however, my quiet reflection was broken by an un-queenly groan.

"Oh, rivers to the sea, this is *disgusting!*"

I opened my eyes to see Mona sitting up, peeling her drenched cloak away from her skin. The hair that had frizzed out of her braid was plastered to her damp face. I threaded my hands behind my head as she clambered to her feet, slicking her hair back. Arlen stretched out with a grimace, rubbing the stickiness from his eyes. He opened his mouth and stuck his tongue out as if trying to air it out.

"You can't tell me the lake isn't foggy in the mornings," I said with amusement, watching Mona stalk to the creek.

"Not like this," she said, her mouth twisted with displeasure. "We have mist—light, cool, refreshing. This is like soup. *Ugh*." She untied her braid and threaded it loose, the fine strands crimped into waves. She crouched over the water and splashed her face.

Colm sat up as well, running his fingers through his own hair. It stuck up, molded into shape from the humidity.

"The first thing I'm going to do when we take back the lake," Mona declared vehemently, pouring handfuls of water over her hair, "is dive into the channel between Blackshell and the Moon Beds and swim until I'm purged clean."

"I'm going to find Sorcha," Arlen said with a sigh, lying spread-eagle on his bedroll. "I'm going to sweep her off her feet and vow to her that we'll never be separated again."

"She despises you, you twit," Mona snapped.

"Well," I said, quirking one eyebrow, "somebody's crown is a bit too tight this morning."

"I'm sick of these wretched mountains," she said. "I'm sick of waking up soaking wet and covered with dirt, and I'm sick of having bugs crawl over me while I sleep. It's no wonder your king has his eyes on Lumen.

I'd be looking for an escape for my folk, too, if this is what I faced every morning."

I rolled over onto my elbow, my eyebrows snapped down. "You sure don't talk like someone who wants to rebuild an alliance between our two countries."

"I hardly have high hopes for an alliance," she said with a sniff. "I want security for Lumen, and for your folk to leave us alone. Believe me, I'm looking forward *immensely* to having nothing to do with the Silverwood once we're finally on the other side."

"And what makes you think the king will just leave you alone?" I asked. "Are you planning on annoying him into submission?"

She fanned her shirt. "I have several plans in mind, none of which are worth explaining to you."

I glared at her with deep dislike. "I could leave you, you know. Right here, right now, without a second thought. Don't you think that would influence your power play?"

"Fine," she said. "Go on, abandon us. Go back to mending nets for the Sea-folk or shoveling dung from the Hill-folk's stables. Maybe you can scrape together enough copper to buy boots that aren't falling apart, though you may have to avoid feeding yourself in the meantime."

"You'd have a snowflake's chance in a forge of getting to the lake from here, you pretentious tick. I give you three hours before you're snapped up by the Wood Guard."

"Less. I know we can't get out of the mountains

without you; we won't even try." She got to her feet with staggering superiority. "I'll pile up all this wet wood and light a big, smoky fire, and when they march me to your king, I'll tell him exactly where we left you, so he can send his runners out to scoop you up as well. What did you say your sentence would be upon recapture? Execution, wasn't it?"

I sat on the wet ground, astounded at her arrogance and seething with rage, while she made a great show of braiding her hair once more into its crown. Arlen was still splayed out on the ground, staring straight ahead, his eyebrows raised up to his hairline. Colm scratched wearily at his beard. A few birds chittered through the fog, filling the vacuous space between us.

"Well," I said contemptuously. "I suppose we'll just press on, shall we?"

She stepped primly out of the creek. "Yes, let's. Only I'm eating something first, before we go anywhere."

It was a dismal start to the morning. We ate handfuls of fruit leathers in frosty silence, all of us avoiding each other's eyes. The sun shot down through the trees in golden spikes, but instead of burning off the fog, it only heated it up, keeping us just as damp and sweaty as we were when we woke. When we had finished our meager breakfast, Mona filled her waterskin in the creek and Arlen tottered off to find a rock to pee on, but Colm coiled our rope and packed up our food bags. It was the first time on our journey I hadn't had to do this task myself. He didn't say a word, stowing the supplies in his pack and cinching it down. Whether it was a wordless apology for his sister's harsh remarks or simply an effort to get us moving as fast as possible, I allowed him a silent gratitude. Perhaps if I could find a private moment away from his brother and sister, I'd apologize, too, for prodding Mona a bit too far. But not in front of her.

When everyone was ready, we struck out up the steep slope. The forest became denser, the shade deeper, and we puffed with exertion as we scraped our way through the trees. The fog slowly dissipated, though it left behind its humidity. Mona was directly behind me, and on several occasions I let branches whip back into place, hearing her aggravated tut as they caught her in the face. Childish, and petty, perhaps, but it brought me a vindictive pleasure.

We had not been climbing long when we broke through the deep shade into a surprise clearing. A large tree had recently fallen and had taken several smaller ones with it, its massive root ball thrust up out of the earth. A thick carpet of greenery was taking advantage of this windfall light, each plant vying for the sweet rays of sun that shone down through the canopy. I stopped to consult my compass and peered into the thick forest ahead to find a suitable landmark. I was just about to press on when Mona's shriek split the air and a heart-stopping crash resounded through the forest. I whirled around.

All three siblings were on the ground. Mona was scrambling backward like a crab. Arlen was on his back, and Colm was facedown, half-buried in the thick undergrowth. A buzzing noise filled the air, like a twig caught in the spokes of a spinning wheel.

"What?" I barked, striding toward them, my heart in my throat. I couldn't see any trigger, any sign of alarm, though Mona had her feet tucked up underneath her as though a toothed fish might come along and nibble them off. "What's wrong? Are you hurt?"

"Careful!" she cried, flinging out her hand.

I stopped in my tracks and looked down where she was pointing. Curled up in an unmistakable coil of aggression, its head drawn back in a diamond wedge, was a long black snake as thick as my arm. Its tail buzzed, hidden in the leaves.

I looked at the snake and then at the three of them splayed across the forest floor. Mona had evidently startled backward into her brothers, who had fallen prey to the steep, slippery grade and tumbled into the underbrush. None of them were looking particularly regal at the moment; Colm was trying to lift his head from the leaves under the weight of Arlen's leg across his shoulders.

I took a deep breath and burst out laughing.

"Stop it!" Mona commanded breathlessly, her hair frizzing once more out of its braided crown. "How dare you . . ."

I couldn't help it. I tried to stop, I did, but the sight was so delightfully pedestrian—and the sharp words from earlier still so fresh in my head—that I leaned against the root ball of the tree, clutching my stomach in laughter. I couldn't tell who was angrier, Mona or the snake.

"Stop it!" she ordered again.

"Useless," I managed between gasps. "Useless, the whole lot of you."

"It's rattling!" she protested, pointing again to the affronted snake. "It's a rattler! I nearly stepped on it! It's poisonous!"

"*Venomous*," I said. "And no, it's not." I picked up a branch. With the tip, I flicked away the leaves covering its tail, smooth and ordinary. "See what he's doing? He's quivering his tail in the leaves, making them buzz. He wants you to think he's a rattler. He's even pulling his head back to make it a wedge, like a venomous snake's." I gave the clever creature a gentle prod, its body tensed in alarm. "But he's just a rat snake, no more venomous than you, Your Highness. You startled him."

Her mouth worked in chagrin, her eyes as icy as they had ever been, flicking back and forth between the snake and my face. I nudged the snake again, coaxing it to move along. After one prod too many, he thrust his head into the leaves and hurried off, rustling the underbrush as he moved. I tossed the stick aside and turned to help the siblings to their feet.

Which is when I screeched to a halt at Mona's side and then skipped backward as if teetering on a precipice. "Oh!"

"What?" she asked acidly, trying to pick herself up off the slope.

I flapped my hands at the three of them. "Oh, great Light. Stay still! Don't shift around!"

"Very funny," Mona said. "I've had enough of your—"

"Stop moving, you idiot!"

"*What?*" Mona demanded, furious now.

"Poison ivy. Earth and sky, you're swimming in it. Colm! Pick your head up!"

"I've been trying," he said, brushing a leaf off his lips.

"Ah." I skittered around the periphery of the sunny clearing, viewing the scene with dismay. Mona only had one arm in the patch, and Arlen had avoided too much contact thanks to his pack and cloak, but Colm had landed facedown in the stuff, his forearms and neck bare from the exertion of our climb.

"All right," I said, trying to assess the damage. "All right, try . . . try not to touch anything. Just get up, carefully, and get over here."

They did as I directed, Arlen moving like a bear on its hind legs, his arms bowed out by his sides. I blew out a breath of frustration.

"Sand," I said. "We need to get you some sand, and jewelweed. Especially you, Colm. If we're lucky, you won't have much of a reaction, but the oil will spread like wildfire, and you absolutely do not want to rub it in your eyes. Come on. Don't touch anything."

"Where are we going?" demanded Mona as I doubled back the way we had come.

"I told you, we have to find sand. We need to get

back to the creek. You need to scrub your skin with wet sand, to get the oil off. And I need to find you jewelweed."

"The creek was half an hour ago," she said.

"Look, believe it or not, I'm actually trying to rectify the situation, not force-march you up and down the ridge. Just, for once, suppress your need to control every detail. Trust me. You don't want this stuff to spread." I started down the slope. And then, because I couldn't help myself, I shot back over my shoulder, "And it wouldn't have happened if you hadn't lost your frizzy head over a harmless rat snake."

She shouted. I don't remember what. Names, how-dare-yous, curses on my head and my family's. We stomped back down the mountainside with a veritable thundercloud over our heads. When she finally wound down, a furious silence settled among us, swirling and smoking. We descended in half the time it took us to climb, but this made nobody happy, as we all knew we only had to hike back up again. We clattered into the water, and I bent down and worked up a wet handful of pebbly grit.

"Scrub," I said. "Wherever you think it touched you. Colm, try to get your face, if you can. Don't use water; you'll spread the oil around. Arlen, scrub off your cloak and pack, too." I dropped my pack by the water's edge. "I'm going to look for jewelweed. Don't leave this spot."

Before I could hear any more royal protests, I headed down the trickle of a creek, scraping through the tangled rhododendron thickets on either side. We were too high up for jewelweed to be abundant, but if it grew anywhere, it would be near the water's edge. If our altitude wasn't bad enough, it wasn't blooming season for the freckled orange flowers, making the plant even harder to spot. I skittered down the creek bed, scanning its shoulders for the telltale serrated leaves.

It took me nearly ten minutes to find a patch. I sliced off a handful of thick stalks and tucked them into my belt before turning around with an aggravated sigh and jogging back the way I had come. The air had grown hot and heavy, unseasonably warm for this early in May. Probably heralding a thunderstorm, I thought bitterly. Just in time to crest the ridge. I could only imagine the mutiny I would face if I turned our party around to seek even lower ground. Any explication on the dangers of lightning would fall on hostile ears.

Scratched and sweaty, I climbed into view of where I had left them to see Arlen standing astride a mossy rock. When he saw me appear, he started waving his arms. And shouting.

I slogged forward, scattering stones. "What?" I called when I got close enough. "What's wrong?"

"It's Colm," he said, beckoning frantically.

I scrambled over the rise to find Mona crouched over her brother, who was lying on his back with his feet in the water. She looked up as I approached, the frostiness in her eyes banished by distress.

"He just collapsed," she said, her voice higher than

usual. "Two or three minutes ago. He didn't say a word."

I dropped to my knees and pressed two fingers to his neck. An angry rash was creeping up his skin. His pulse was rapid, ticking, but faint.

"Colm," I said, my voice level but overly loud. "Colm." I shook his shoulder. He didn't stir.

"What's happening?" Mona asked frantically. "The poison ivy?"

"He's having some kind of reaction." I remembered the leaf on his lips, and my stomach turned over. "He got it in his mouth."

"What does that mean? What will that do?"

"I'm not sure. Some people are more sensitive than others, but I've never had to deal with someone who swallowed the oil . . ." I held the back of my palm close to his mouth, my own heartbeat hammering in my chest. His breath came in shallow puffs against my skin. I waved to his legs, still in the stream. "Arlen, prop his feet up on something. Get them elevated." I unbuttoned the collar of his tunic, swiped aside a chain around his neck, and pressed my ear to his chest. His lungs rattled with each short breath.

"What do we do?" Mona asked, clutching Colm's hand. "What does he need?"

I hit my fist to my forehead. "We used to carry joint-pine in our scout kits, but it's exotic, it grows away west in Alcoro. I never thought to purchase any from the markets."

Thunder snapped like a whip-crack over our heads.

Mona gave a small start, clutching Colm's shoulder. "What do we do?" she asked again. "Mae? What do we do?"

"First thing we do is calm down," I said, holding up my hand. "Panicking won't do anything. Let me think a moment."

As I flicked through the options available to us, something trickled back to me, an old mantra we were taught from the beginning in training. I remembered Reuel, the grizzled old Woodwalker I served as a scout, repeating the phrase during every exercise.

"Always determine what's *important*, and what's *urgent*. Prioritize."

I chewed my lip. Thunder rumbled again.

"We need herbs," Mona said, unable to maintain her silence.

"I know," I said. *Prioritize.*

"We need to be able to brew them."

"I *know*." I took a breath. "There's a risk we could take. But it will take effort, and a tremendous amount of good luck."

"What is it?"

"The old silver mine at Lowback Gap. It's abandoned now, and not that far from here, less than an hour if we hurry. We could shelter in the entryway, get a fire going." I closed my eyes. "But it's so, so close to the main road."

Mona looked up at the darkening sky. "But if it's raining . . . people will be inside their homes. The king's scouts might not be about. Right?"

Wrong—but they didn't need to know that. "Maybe. We can at least hope the rain will muddle our smoke."

"But we don't have the right herbs," she said again. "What do we brew?"

I blew out a deep breath, looking back down at Colm's flushed skin. "I have another idea, even more reckless than the first. But I think we should focus on getting to the mine. Nothing else will matter if we get stuck out here in a thunderstorm." A few fat drops spattered down among the stones.

"Can't you build a shelter or something?" Arlen asked.

"Of course I can. But it's not going to keep all the rain out, and he's going to have a time fighting off the chills in his state."

This, the chills, I knew they could grasp. It would be a constant specter for their folk, living half their lives in the cold lake in all kinds of weather. The cold and wet would not find them easy prey, but I knew they would at least understand the danger. I took another breath.

"We need somewhere enclosed that we can get a fire going. The closest, safest place for us right here, right now, is the mine."

Colm drew in a rattling breath and coughed. Instinctively, I felt his pulse again.

"How do we get there?" Arlen asked pointedly.

I looked up the slope, steep and loose. The rain would make it muddy and slick.

"We're going to have to carry him," I said.

I thought they might protest, start their scrutiny all over, but Arlen only nodded. "Can you carry my pack?"

"You can't do it yourself. Not up this slope. We'll have to hold him between us . . ."

"No sense in that. We'll move at a snail's pace."

"He's big, Arlen," I said. "Bigger than you. Have you done this before?"

"I've portaged a canoe," he said, stripping off his pack. "How different can it be?"

If I had to guess—very different.

We made short work of lashing his pack to mine and Colm's pack to Mona's. In that brief period of time, the rain went from a few stinging drops to a downpour, a late spring deluge. Cold drops thumped off our shoulders and bent heads. I split the stalks of jewelweed I had gathered and rubbed them over Colm's skin, hoping it might at least slow the spread of the ugly rash. I bent forward to listen to his chest again. As I did, I disturbed the chain around his neck, and it slid out from under his shirt. Looped around it was a ring, small and delicate, capped with a row of pink pearls.

We all three hesitated a moment, and then Mona reached forward and pushed it back under his shirt.

"His wife's?" I asked.

"Yes."

The rain became loud, deafening, pouring through the tangled branches and splattering in the rocky creek, and that was the end of the conversation. Thunder rumbled up and down the mountainside. Arlen finished cinching our packs and crouched down next to Colm. He hauled his brother upright and threaded his shoulder between his legs. Still on his knees, he steadied his footing in the creek with Colm slumped over his back.

"Arlen," I said again. "Are you sure about this? We can try to make some kind of litter . . ."

In one heavy movement, he straightened his legs, his knee cracking as he stood. "Positive. You'd better get those packs on; I'm not planning on standing around like this." With that he began staggering up the slope. I slung my awkward pack over my shoulders and hurried to get in front of him.

It was grueling work, slogging up the now unmercifully steep mountainside. The rain persisted, a steady hiss, until we were waterlogged and shivering, and the loose ground often slipped out from under our feet. Doggedly we climbed, though every now and then Mona put her hand out to steady Arlen as he swayed under his brother's weight. Occasionally I made him stop so I could check Colm's pulse and breathing. As I did this, I noticed with dismay the churned trail we were leaving in our wake, ruffling up the wet leaf litter and sinking our footprints into the mud in our haste. But there was nothing I could do. Time was racing against us. Colm's breath remained shallow, his pulse rapid and weak—we needed to get him to shelter before his airways closed up completely. I could only hope the rain might wash away the evidence of our passage before the king's scouts came across our trail.

After half an hour, the hardwoods gave way to spruce and fir. The temperature dropped, slicing easily through our wet garments. I didn't slow my pace, feeling like a mouse being watched by a cat, aware that a pounce could be just a heartbeat away. The rain muffled all other sounds, a blessing and a curse. Sharp-eared Woodwalkers would have trouble picking up the racket we were making, but even the freshest scouts would be able to move silently across the wet earth; we would have no warning of an approaching party until they had surrounded us, bows drawn.

As we neared the ridge, the rain began to sting—it was turning to sleet. Our pace became frantic, the frozen pellets numbing our faces and hands. Mona didn't even react when she staggered face-first into the mountainside. She just scrambled back to her feet, wiping mud off her freckles, her fine hair now adorned with leaf litter and twigs. A few minutes later, I placed my foot on the sodden earth and it slid, grating against the pebbly soil. This was too much for my worn-out boots, loosening the seam along the right insole. A flood of water and grit washed over my bare foot. Fortunately, Arlen did not fall; he placed his feet with the utmost care while Colm dangled head-down off his shoulder. Thunder raged around us, lightning split the sky, and vaguely I prayed that any scouting parties nearby would be doing the sensible thing and seeking lower ground, away from the toothy trees on the ridges, the lightning beacons. I shook my head, trying to clear it of my instinctive apprehension; lightning was one foe nobody pretended to stand against. Eleven people downed by one strike on Brambletop Bald the first year I was a scout . . . I pushed down my concern. Shelter. That was all I could focus on. *Prioritize.* One crisis at a time.

The wind picked up and whistled through our clothes, stealing away what heat we built up as we climbed. It was with great relief that we crested a familiar rise to find the grassy hollow of Lowback Gap spreading away before us. A dark, unassuming door yawned in the hillside with a weather-beaten wooden grate propped against the opening. Our sanctuary.

We hurried forward, our feet squelching in the waterlogged grass. I pulled down the grate. Half of it had been shielded from the rain by the lintel, and I shoved it into the mine entrance to use for firewood. The tunnel sloped down into the darkness, the air cool and damp. I gripped Arlen's elbow and guided him inside, helping to slide Colm off his shoulders. Without a word, he put his back against the mossy wall and slid to the ground, his legs splayed out frog-like in front of him.

"Hey," I said to him, settling Colm against the opposite wall. "Good work."

He groaned.

I turned to Colm, reaching forward to press my fingers to his neck, but my hand froze in midair. The flush had drained from his cheeks, leaving his skin as white as birch bark. His blistering rash burned red against the pallor. My hand flew from his neck to his forehead. I sucked in a sharp breath.

"What is it?" asked Mona, kneeling down beside me.

"He's burning up. He's come down with fever." I held my hand in front of his mouth again—his breath was the faintest whisper. "Oh, earth and sky, Colm . . ."

"From the poison ivy? Does it cause fever?"

"I've never heard of it before, but spending an hour in the sleet surely didn't help him." I waved to her and Arlen. "Gather up some of these dry twigs and moss. We've got to get a fire going."

While the two of them got on their hands and knees, I scuffed out a hollow just inside the doorway and piled up the moss they gathered, tenting the twigs around it. I pulled off shards of timber from the grate, building up the cone of kindling. My hands numb from cold, I fumbled with the tinderbox and struck a shower of sparks into the moss. At first nothing happened, and I worried everything was too damp. I struck the steel against the flint again and—earth and sky—they caught. Little worms of orange light spread through the tinder, and I lay flat on my stomach, my face inches away as I puffed air into the moss. The lights squirmed, they danced, they flared—a tongue of flame sputtered to life, darting up into the seasoned wood. Golden light flickered through the entryway.

Arlen sat back on his heels, his shoulders drooping with weariness. "What a beautiful sight."

I continued breaking apart the grate. "Get the pot out of my pack." I piled the dry fragments well away from the door and stacked the damp pieces into a wall across the threshold.

"What are you doing?" Mona asked, passing me my blackened cooking pot.

"Firewall," I said. "Reflect the heat, dry the wood." I filled the pot from my waterskin and positioned it over the flames. Into the pot went a bundle of black willow bark from my medical kit. I left the water to simmer and crawled back to Colm's side. Mona joined me, twisting her hands in anxiety.

"Is he going to be all right? Fever . . . fever can be brought down."

"It can, though he's already fighting off this reaction." I pressed my ear to his chest again. His breath rattled in his lungs. "I worry more about his airways. I don't have anything to open them up except for peppermint."

She leaned over me, her face creased with worry. Hoping to give her something to do, something to keep her occupied, I gestured to our packs. "See if there's anything dry to cover him with. Arlen, get the rope out of my pack and string it up a few feet down the tunnel. We can hang up some of our wet things and trap our heat."

While they worked on this, I set a cup of peppermint to steep in the flames. The water in the cooking pot began to sputter, and I lifted it off the fire, pouring the tisane into Colm's mug. I handed it to Mona. "Try to get him to take some of that."

She trickled the tisane into his slack mouth, holding his chin upright. He gagged and coughed, his chest shuddering as he fought to draw breath. I reached out and pinched his nose shut, beckoning her to try again. She did, her face screwed up tight. He took short swallows, spluttering between each one. Arlen, having finished stringing up our dripping cloaks, slid back down to the ground, resting his head against the wall.

"Sleep, Arlen," I said to him. "You've earned it. Rest while you can."

Without any more persuasion, he keeled over onto his side and curled up into a ball with his back to us. Mona continued holding the mug to Colm's mouth until he had emptied the cup. She still had her nose scrunched up, focusing intently on her brother, and I realized after a moment she was trying not to cry.

"This wasn't your fault, you know," I said with some surprise. "All this."

She looked away, busying herself with pouring more tisane into the mug. I pulled a damp kerchief from my pack and wet it in the rain. As I pressed it to Colm's forehead, his eyelids fluttered. He slit them open, his eyes overbright.

"Hi, Colm," I said. "How are you feeling?"

He stirred feebly. "Ama," he said, his voice raw.

Mona ceased her busying with the mug. I leaned forward. "What?"

"Ama." His fingers edged along the ground, searching. They found the fabric of my cloak and closed over it in a fist. He sighed.

I patted his hand awkwardly. "Sorry, Colm. I'm not your mother."

"No."

I turned to Mona. She was sitting very still, clasping the mug. "Ama," she said, watching Colm as he sank back into sleep. "His wife."

I looked back at him, his chest rising and falling with shallow breaths. The chain around his neck was just visible under his collar.

"Did she die that day?" I asked.

"Yes. They had been married less than a year." She glanced down at the mug in her hands. "You said I couldn't have had friends as a child. You were wrong. I had one. Ama, the daughter of one of my councilors. She was one of the very best divers in Lumen, able to get to the deepest beds few others could reach." Mona lifted her gaze to Colm. "And she died saving us, giving us our escape from the Alcorans."

The rain was a steady hiss outside the door, sputtering occasionally in the fire. Mona shifted so her back was against the wall and slumped wearily against it. She dragged her own cup from her pack and splashed some of the tisane into it.

"She had a delightful sense of humor." She clutched the cup. "She used to tease me—the only person, really, to treat me like a teenage girl rather than a queen. Colm always liked her, ever since we were small, and after a while, she decided she liked him back. They were obnoxiously happy together." She held her face close to the steam curling from her tea but didn't drink. "Their wedding was grand—lanterns on the water, boats and flowers and food . . . she wore an incredible gown. Arlen sang. Colm wept."

She took a few sips, and I didn't say anything for fear she might stop. "I don't know how much you know about the day Alcoro invaded. I know you were exiled at the time. But I've always wondered if your folk could hear the sounds of the invasion from up on high. I wondered if they could see the smoke and flames up in Lampyrinae. We were utterly unprepared for the assault; we had traded with the Alcoran monarchs for decades with no aggression. They weren't the most generous of allies, but then, that's not the kind of people they are. Their strength lies in their strategy, and their cunning, and their military prowess. And of course, their drive to see their wretched prophecy realized. If I had thought about it, I might have anticipated their desperation. King Celeno, the Seventh King of Alcoro, had ascended to power only a few years earlier, and it fell to him to make the prophecy come true. We presented the most logical target.

"That day started like any other day; their ships sailed up the southern waterways from their stolen ports in Cyprien, but there were more of them, and they didn't anchor at Lakemouth like they were supposed to. Instead they clove a path straight for our palace at Blackshell, spreading out to cut off the waterways between the islands and the shore. It was the morning; folk were diving all across the channels. We were scattered before it even began.

"And then, of course, the ballistae started, the fire and smoke. Even if we had been prepared for the attack, our meager army could never stand against theirs. Some tried to fight back, but it did little except increase the death toll among our folk. The Alcorans sent their skiffs to the islands and began ransacking the homes there. I can still remember hearing the screaming from all the way across the water."

She paused, sipping from her mug again. Colm's hand had relaxed its grip on my cloak, but I didn't move it away. "They marched up the shore to Blackshell. There was no time for any kind of front; no way to rally our swordsmen or archers. Arlen had the old ceremonial atlatl he had grabbed from the wall, and that was it. We ran—the three of us and Ama—through the palace, while the Alcorans swarmed it. Arlen and Colm engaged a few times, but at that point they were only trying to get me down to the southern docks. If we could swim, we thought, we could get out of harm's way, and form some kind of plan, a counterattack. We weren't sure we could make it, though. The grounds were crawling with Alcorans by that point. As we bickered amongst ourselves, Ama handed Colm her ring. We didn't even pause to ask her why. As we neared the doors to the grounds, she reached out and plucked the crown off my head. 'For safekeeping,' she said. I didn't think to question her. Nothing made sense at that point.

"From there, it was a flat-out run to the docks. No stopping, no turning back, no time to hesitate. We broke from the palace with the Alcorans pursuing us and dove into the water. We swam like we had never swum before, staying down for as long as we possibly could. But when we finally surfaced amid the destruction, we realized there were only three of us."

"She didn't jump in with you," I said quietly.

"No," Mona said. "She didn't. In fact, she didn't even follow us from the palace. We could hear the shouting from Blackshell. There's a great terrace there, you know, for gatherings and speeches and such. And there was a tremendous commotion.

"They had captured the queen.

"They were dragging our banner down from the palace and hoisting up their own. And kneeling in the courtyard was Ama, wearing my crown."

I rested my chin on my knees, hoping she might say that they never saw the execution. But her eyes were far away now, seeing the scene all over again. In the firelight, Arlen shifted slightly.

"They did it upright," she said. "Instead of putting her head on a block. You know, so folk could see. They didn't even have the decency to blindfold her, or tie back her hair. Their swordsman was good, at least. One clean, sideways swipe. And then, incredible noise . . . sounds of victory and defeat, all mingled together. Screaming and weeping coupled with trumpets blasting a fanfare.

"I thought we might lose Colm right then. He was trying to swim back, and he was shouting, swallowing all this water. We had him under the arms, trying to drag him toward the mouth of the river that flows away from the lake. Truth be told, I was barely hanging on myself. I couldn't believe what she had done, what I had let her do. But now I knew we had to escape. 'Don't waste it,' I kept yelling to Colm. 'Don't waste what she did.' She had died to keep them from hunting us down, to make them think my throne was theirs. We could do nothing less than take the opportunity she had bought for us.

"The waterways south are difficult to navigate; there's a reason we wanted to build a road through the southern Silverwood all those decades ago. It took every bit of our skill to swim them without drowning or being caught by the Alcoran ships patrolling the ports. It was a miracle we made it to Matariki at all. We hauled ourselves out onto the shore a few miles north of the city, and that was when it overcame Colm. He was paralyzed with grief, blaming himself—we couldn't get him to do anything. He felt she had tricked him, and so he was angry, too, but it was mostly at himself, for leaving her, for not checking to be sure she was with him. But honestly, who would have thought she'd be anywhere but at his side?"

She went quiet for a moment, staring into space and sipping her tisane. I looked down at Colm. Automatically, I covered his forehead with my palm. Still hot.

"As awful as it sounds," she began again, slowly, "I think it helped me. I couldn't focus on myself, on my own grief. I could only focus on my brothers. We had nothing but what we'd grabbed in our flight, nothing to barter or sell except the few things that we could never part with." She patted her chest. "My pendant, an heirloom and symbol of my throne. Ama's ring.

And Arlen's atlatl. He won a sword sometime later, in a game at a tavern, but he sold it when we were trying to find a way through the Silverwood." She shook her head, looking at his curled-up form. "You can imagine, after all that, how angry I was at him for giving us away in Sunmarten. After everything Ama did for us, he could have thrown it all away in that stupid brawl."

"Is that what his scar is from?" I asked, gesturing to my own cheek, where Arlen's smile-shaped line sat.

The corners of her mouth twitched. "Oh, no. That's older. He got that on one of his first deep-water dives. He misjudged his entry and scraped his whole face along the Brown Beds. He was lucky he didn't break his neck." She shook her head, closing her eyes. "Such an idiot. So incredibly dense."

"As are most brothers," I admitted.

She rested her cup in her lap. "I know I snipe at him too much. He doesn't mean to cause so much trouble. He's like me; he doesn't take well to change, and having everything he was used to taken away so violently . . . it's no wonder he's always fighting for his name. He was barely fifteen when it happened, just when he was figuring out his role in the monarchy." She brushed a wisp of hair out of her face. "And honestly, he's gotten us out of several scrapes. Carrying his sick brother halfway up a mountain, for one. Fighting, too. I've never taken to combat, and most of the fight went out of Colm after we lost Ama. We'd have had several close calls if Arlen hadn't been quick to act. Cocksure fool."

"I'm awake, you know," he said without turning over.

"I know," she replied.

Thunder rumbled outside, and the rain increased its volume. I got to my feet to pull the peppermint away from flames, dipping my kerchief into the tincture. As it soaked, Mona turned her empty cup in her fingers, silent. After a moment, she cleared her throat.

"You can imagine, with all that's happened, why I might be kicking myself for endangering not just our mission, but Colm's life as well."

"It's not your fault, though," I said once again. "All that with the snake, and the poison ivy . . . it was all just a messy accident."

"I chastised you earlier this morning. I provoked you. If you hadn't been angry at me, you might have led us around the patch, or warned us of it."

"I barely thought about it," I insisted. "I'm so familiar with every plant and animal that I react unconsciously. There was a bare sunny spot; I knew there might be poison ivy or nettles growing there—or maybe a snake sunning itself—and so I went around it. I didn't think to tell you to do the same. It's as much my fault as yours."

She stared fixedly at her battered tin cup. "I have not been . . . entirely fair to you, Mae. A queen who antagonizes those who are helping her can hardly be considered wise, or noble." She looked up at me. "I used to abide by that principle, and to the virtue of being kind to those from different cultures. I'm not entirely sure what's happened to that leader in our exile, but I'd like to try to get her back."

A few seconds of silence passed between us, filled only by the rain. I prodded the fire, sending a cloud of sparks dancing into the air. "Nothing will change a person like grief and hardship."

"Rivers to the *sea*." Arlen rolled onto his stomach and crossed his arms over his head. "How can a person be expected to sleep with all these nancing heart-to-hearts? Give it a rest; I just carried a grown man up a mountain!"

Mona and I looked toward opposite ends of the mine shaft, hiding our smiles, while Arlen buried his face in his arms, muttering.

CHAPTER 7

As the afternoon waned, cloaked in sheets of gray rain, it looked as though Colm might pull through. The peppermint poultice I spread on his chest eased his breathing slightly. After another mug of black willow tisane, the smoldering in his head lessened and his color improved, but his skin was still dry to touch. During a lull in the rain, I threw on my damp cloak and hunted around in the gap until I found mullein, hoping it might induce sweating and break his fever. This didn't help, however, and by twilight, his temperature was climbing and his chest was closing up once again.

I thought desperately of all the exotic herbs tucked into neat, labeled pouches that each scouting party carried, joint-pine chief among them. I steeped rosemary and let him breathe the steam, knowing it would do little, knowing it wouldn't open up his airways—but

I had to do *something*. I switched to brewing spicebush and later sweet birch, hoping it might touch his fever, but like the willow, it didn't slow the heat in his head. When spasms started wracking his chest with each breath, I finally faced the looming prospect that had been dogging me since we left the creek.

"There's a cache," I said wearily, wetting the kerchief once more and handing it to Mona, who pressed it to Colm's burning forehead. "The Wood Guard have them scattered throughout the mountains. Spare weapons, tools, supplies . . . and kits. Each cache contains one fully equipped medical kit. Joint-pine, camphor laurel, ointments, oils . . . things that could help him. The closest one is a little ways south of here; I could probably make it there and back in an hour and a half."

"Will there be scouts around?" Mona asked.

"I wish I could say. The caches are checked and resupplied every two months; otherwise, they're only used if the need arises. I'd like to think there's no reason for scouts to be concentrated close by."

She looked back at Colm, shivering in his sleep. "And if you get caught?"

"I won't."

"If you do?"

I sighed. "Keep brewing tea. If Colm wakes, don't hang around. Strike out west. Once you hit the Palisades, you'll be able to see the lake. Watch for loose rock as you descend. Be careful of wind shears near the edges. Avoid traversing too far to the north." I ran my fingers through my hair. "And about a hundred other cautions. But it doesn't matter. I'll be back before midnight."

She and Arlen looked as though I had just signed their execution sentence. I ignored my own misgivings and tucked my pack against the wall. I gestured to the dwindling firewood. "If the rain stops, douse the fire. And keep quiet."

Mona followed me to the threshold of the mine as I drew my cloak around my shoulders and stepped out into the curtain of rain.

"Mae . . ."

I looked back at her, but she couldn't seem to verbalize her thoughts. "It's all right," I said, hoping I sounded reassuring. "Just keep Colm comfortable. I'll be back before you know it."

I turned my back on her troubled face and jogged away into the growing night.

I was glad to find I couldn't smell any traces of the campfire near the edges of the gap. As I reached the stand of firs on the far side, I glanced back toward the mine entrance. No flicker of firelight. As long as the rain remained steady, it would cloak the signs of our presence. I allowed myself to trust in this small comfort before heading into the forest.

It was liberating to be able to travel like I used to, without the pace and noise of the Alastaires niggling away at my patience. I ran, ducking fragrant evergreen boughs full of rain, swerving through trunks over the needled carpet. The snarl of thunder and lightning had blown away into the west, leaving the forest bathed in the steady hiss of rainfall. The chill from our climb had been chased away by the fire, and I ran with a warmth brought on by the urgency now jangling through my head.

I knew this ridge. I knew her folds and her pockets, her sharp promontories and graceful swells. During the day, the boughs would ring with the ethereal downward-spiral calls of veeries. The air would be rich with the scent of fir, kissed with a constant coolness not present in the lower slopes. Lowback Gap created a convenient bowl in the range, an intersection between the miners' settlements to the south, Lampyrinae to the north, and the towns nestled on either side of the ridge. Much of the country's population was concentrated here. As a result, this had always been an important stretch of mountains for the Wood Guard, tasked with keeping the road connecting New Mine and Lampyrinae clear, the forest healthy, and the citizens safe.

This was bad, I reminded myself, trying to ignore my instinctive pride toward this stretch of land. The scouts who patrolled this ridge were among the best, assigned to protect this vital artery of the mountains. They could spot an errant footstep in the dark and hear the careless brush of a cloak in a breeze. I knew, because I had been one of them. I kept my senses on alert, weaving silently among the trees, steering well clear of the handful that occasionally harbored firewatchers in their branches.

The night grew deeper; the storm did not lessen. A few intrepid barred owls called dolefully through the rain. *Who-cooks-for-you? Who-cooks-for-you-aaallll?* On I ran, the loose seam of my boot flapping with each wet footfall. Just as a blustery wind picked up, scattering the rain sideways, I neared the cache. I slowed my pace, stealing among the boles of the trees and peering through the gloom. Surely, I thought, there would be no scouts about, not now. They would be tucked into the trees, wrapped in their cloaks as they kept their lookouts, or else sheltering for the night. I crept forward until I reached the trunk of a lopsided juniper standing next to a patch of empty ground. The wind had swept the heavier clouds away into the west, and the hiss of rain was lightening. I paused, feeling again like a mouse, this time preparing to snatch a morsel of cheese out from under the cat's nose. My heart thumped in my chest as I crouched, tense, alert.

I would be lying if I said I didn't feel a twinge of guilt. This was thievery, and from my own kin, no less. I envisioned a desperate Woodwalker rushing an injured scout to this cache only to find the kit plundered, but I made myself push down that thought. I was only here for the joint-pine. If there was enough, I might even leave some behind. And any injured Guardsman would have options I didn't—the ability to call for help, to seek assistance at the closest settlement, to hurry back to the healers at Lampyrinae. This was my *only* option. I waited a moment longer, straining for any sign of another's presence, and then I darted forward into the clearing and plunged my hand into the sodden leaf litter.

I dug away the layer of needles and twigs, uncovering the rough plank lid of the cache. I heaved it to one side and peered into the box sunken into the ground, rubbed with pitch to keep the moisture out. Packed inside was a lumpy oilcloth sack. I fumbled with the knot and opened the sack, rifling in the dark through the contents. A set of knives, a coil of rope, a box of arrowheads, a tinderbox, a few pitched pine torches . . . my hand closed on the roll of thick canvas. I pulled it out, hovering over it to shield it from the rain, and unrolled it on the ground. My fingers fluttered over the kit—little vials of oil, stoppered containers of ointments, packets of dried herbs, each tied with a series of knots to distinguish their contents in the dark. My heart in my throat, I felt along the cords until I found the right one. Flat braid, five knots . . . jointpine. I breathed a sigh of relief and plucked the packet out from its fellows. I felt the contents; it was a small amount, enough for two, perhaps three doses. I would need it all. I thrust the packet deep into my pocket. On impulse, I removed the vial of camphor laurel as well, hoping it may be more effective than the peppermint in soothing Colm's chest. My thieving done, I rolled up the canvas and set it back in the sack. The rain had lessened now into a drizzle, pattering down through the trees. After cinching the oilcloth sack closed and arranging it back in the box, I dragged the lid into place and piled the leaf litter back on top of it.

I was finishing this task, trying to disguise the signs of recent use, when the slightest sound made me jump. I crouched on all fours, hunched over the hidden cache as I strained my ears through the patter of rain. In another heartbeat, I scrambled, panic-stricken, for the lopsided juniper and launched myself into the scraggly branches, climbing arm over arm through the boughs. The sharp, stubby needles drove into my hands, but I paid no heed to them, stopping only when I was a full ten feet off the ground. I shrank into the shaggy bark and held my breath, my blood raging in my ears.

A voice filtered through the drizzle. "Left, left, Teo, there."

A lumpy shape emerged awkwardly through the trees across the little clearing. Two scouts, holding up a third between them. A fourth followed with an extra pack. I silently thanked whatever luck still clung to me for the racket they made as they moved clumsily through the forest, and for the lessening of the mask of rain at just the right time. I pulled my collar up over my mouth to stifle my breath.

I recognized the Woodwalker as Deina, a scout several years my elder, but one who had risen up the ranks more slowly than others. Consequently, she worked hard for each advance she made; I could remember her sitting away from the rest of us in the evenings, poring over botanical illustrations and topographic maps. Most of our calls to join in the camaraderie around the fireplace were met with her hands over her ears as she muttered facts to herself. I was glad for her—sometime in my exile, her hard work had paid off. She had finally become a Woodwalker.

"There we go." She and the other scout eased the third to the ground as he held his foot in the air. She gestured to the other. "The kit, Teodór."

"Someone's been here," he said, flicking through the loose litter I had piled back over the lid.

"Must have been Howel's party. This is his range." She snapped her fingers. "The linen, Teo, come now."

Howel Tanager was in charge of my old range? Great Light, no wonder I hadn't been waylaid. Howel was skilled enough but obsessed with rank and formality, jumping at every mundane opportunity to earn a new lapel pin. No wonder Vandalen thought him a fitting replacement, if he was fed up with me disregarding his orders. Or had Valien appointed Howel? What a dunce. A clever dunce, if he was hoping this range would remain poorly watched.

Teodór swept the mess off the lid and opened the box, digging for the kit. There was a flare. The fourth scout had lit a torch. In the flickering light, I could see the injured scout examining his injury; his trouser leg was rolled up, and a length of linen was bound around his ankle. Blood seeped through the dressing.

Teodór handed Deina a roll of linen and a vial of antiseptic. She unwound the dressing on the injured leg, revealing a shiny abrasion, as one might get from slipping in scree on the top of a bald. As she daubed antiseptic on it, the wounded scout sucked in his breath.

"Easy, Deina, easy!"

"Don't squirm. I'm trying to get the grit out. I *told* you to watch that ledge, Otto. You were moving too fast." She rolled his ankle in her hands. "Does that hurt?"

He yelped. "*Yes.*"

"I was afraid of that. So it's not just a tweak. Jenë," she said to the fourth. "Make him a splint."

I fought to hold down a cry of surprise. I had been so preoccupied with Deina and her injured scout that I failed to see that the fourth guardsman was my cousin Jenë. She had only just started her training when I was exiled, a young, fresh-faced trainee who believed in the integrity of the Guard. I watched her now as she busied herself with her task, filled with a dozen different emotions. Pride, trepidation, joy, heartache . . . how long had it been since I had seen anyone I could call family?

Otto was gritting his teeth as Deina tended to his ankle. "*You* were the one who decided we should go over the Tooth, rather than taking the low path. One of us was bound to skid at the pace you were leading us."

"We've got to bring this news to the king, you know that. Alcoro wouldn't move a fleet like that up the waterways if they didn't have a reason for it. And now you've gone and hobbled your foot." Despite her sharp words, she was gentle as she wrapped his calf in clean linen.

"Joint-pine is missing from this kit," Teodór said, fingering the empty spot. "And camphor laurel."

"Someone must have gotten stung. We'll have

to make a report that this cache needs resupplying. But first we need to get Otto somewhere that he can shelter."

"What about the ledge near the Mudbug spring?" asked Teodór.

Jenë lifted her head, her dark curly hair wound into a knot at the back of her head like mine. "No good. It's colonized by swallows now, and they attack anyone who comes near."

"Old Bear Cave?"

"Collapsed," Deina said. "No. I tell you what we'll do. Do you think you can make it to the Lowback Mine, Otto?"

I stuffed my fist in my mouth to avoid groaning in dismay. All thoughts of my good luck vanished.

"I suppose. If we go slowly."

"It'll be easier on the road. We'll make for the mine and get you settled. Teodór will stay with you. Jenë and I will head back to Lampyrinae to bring our news to the king, and we'll send a rider out to collect you in the morning."

"Fair enough." Otto gritted his teeth again as Jenë bound his leg in a splint. I watched her careful hands, my pride in her skill eaten up by the dire situation now presented to me.

"Close up the cache, Teo. Let's get going. I want to reach Lampyrinae by first light."

They placed everything back in order and piled the leaf litter back over the box. Jenë shouldered Otto's pack once again, and Deina and Teodór hauled him to his good foot, putting their shoulders under his arms. With a great deal of noise, they limped across the clearing, passed directly underneath me, and shuffled away into the forest, making for the ridge road.

I let a whole two minutes pass before I felt safe enough to relax my iron grip on the juniper tree. I reeled with trepidation. They were heading for the mine. What could I do? Even if Colm's fever had broken and I could get the siblings away from the gap, Deina and her scouts would see the clear signs of our presence. It would be a simple task to track us down, made easier by the crawling pace we would have to adopt for Colm.

What if I could overtake them on the road? I nearly laughed out loud. Yes, I thought, what if? What could I do, what would I be willing to do, to keep them from reaching the mine? I was not yet so wretched that I would attack my own folk, my own *cousin*, and one tired ex-Woodwalker against three able-bodied scouts was hardly a promising match. I could perhaps distract them, lead them away down the mountain, and hope, pray, that they might bypass the mine for another shelter . . .

Oh, great earth and sky—it could not possibly work.

I gripped the packet and vial buried in my pocket. Colm needed this medicine, and he needed it quickly. Would I have time to bring it to him before turning around and engaging Deina's party? I tried to gauge how fast they might move on the open road. Slower than I would, with Otto's injury. But by how much?

Important, and urgent. Important. Urgent. Which was which? Woodwalker Reuel growled in my head. *Prioritize.*

My head ringing with uncertainty, I slid down the juniper tree, the loose seam of my boot fraying against the bark. Without pausing to second guess my actions, I sprinted off into the woods, angling away from the line Deina and her scouts had taken.

I made a wide arc away from the road and ran back through the forest, digging juniper nibs out of my palms. Piercing the layers of concern now weighing upon me was the snippet of news Deina had let slip— the Alcorans were moving a fleet up the waterways. Were they acting on the news that Mona was alive and returning to reclaim her throne? How long would it take them to reach the lake? I estimated the time-frame. Deina and her scouts had seen the fleet from southern lookouts, which overlooked the Cypri waterways. At a usual scout pace, it would have taken them three, perhaps four days to come this far. Otto had injured himself on Coon's Tooth, probably this past evening, and they had limped to this cache for additional medical supplies.

Then the Alcorans were close, I thought with growing anxiety. We had perhaps six days before they reached the lake. Maybe more, if the storm had affected them as well.

I tore back through the forest, forcing myself to remember that a scout party—besides Deina's—still patrolled this ridge, even if it was Howel Tanager's.

Without the downpour to mask the sounds of my hurry, I slowed just enough to control my movements, praying that I would continue to avoid detection.

A fog was rising along the ridge when I finally reached the open swath of Lowback Gap. I ran through the grass, the ragged seam of my boot flapping with each step. The flicker of the Alastaires' fire prickled through the fog.

Arlen's face appeared white-skinned in the gloom, eyes wide. "Oh," he said in relief. "You're back. She's back!"

"Hush," I hissed, pushing past him over the threshold. "Listen. Stop, don't talk. Listen. There's a scouting party making for the mine."

Mona drew in a sharp breath, but I overrode her and crouched down next to Colm. "How is he?"

"I think his temperature is better. But he hasn't woken up, and his breathing is so ragged . . ."

I pulled out the packet and vial from my pocket. "Joint-pine. Brew it all, and then douse your fire. It doesn't have to be strong. Put the extra in one of the waterskins." I handed her the vial. "Camphor laurel. Spread it on his chest and throat."

"Where are you going?" she asked. "What are you going to do?"

"I'm going to try to lead them away. They've got an injured scout, so it won't be easy to get them to leave the road, but if I make enough of a disturbance . . ."

"And us? Should we stay here? Should we try to move?"

I wracked my brain. "Stay. Just stay. You'd leave a trail anyway, and there are still other scouts about. Keep working on Colm." As I stood, a thought struck me, and I held out my hand to Arlen.

"Give me your atlatl."

I could see a protest rising in his throat; he hesitated for a full three seconds, but the urgency of our situation won him over. Gingerly, he passed it to me, followed by a handful of darts.

"Have you ever used one before?" he asked, and silently I applauded him for keeping the disdain out of his voice.

I hefted it in my hand, the pearls winking in the firelight. "No." I clapped him on the shoulder. "But how hard can it be?"

He twisted his mouth, desperately wanting to retort, but Mona cut in. "You're not thinking of firing on them . . ."

"No. I don't know. I don't know what I'm thinking." I turned for the entrance. "I can't give you any promises. I'm sorry. I'll be back as soon as I can."

I couldn't read the expression on her face. It wasn't fear. Resignation? "Good luck."

"Don't hurt it," Arlen called after me.

I ran back out into the fog, veering right to follow the disused path to the main road. It took me very little time to reach the packed-dirt track, and I was again reminded what a risk we were taking sheltering in the mine in the first place. I had no plan, no flash of inspiration. My mind reeled as I ran, jarred by each footfall.

After fifteen minutes, I slowed my pace, straining to hear the sounds of Deina and her scouts struggling up the track. They were moving slowly; Otto must have broken his ankle rather than sprained it. The road here was rocky and rutted with wagon tracks, flanked by a steep drop-off to the west. The fog made the way more treacherous than usual. I slunk to the side of the road and crept from tree to tree, listening to their murmuring drift through the fog. After a few moments, I realized they weren't actually moving; they must have stopped to let Otto rest on the road.

"Leave me, I'm telling you, leave me," Otto was arguing. "We've slept in worse cots than this."

"I'm getting you to the mine," Deina said. "I don't care how I do it."

"Just let me stay here. You need to get to the king, and at this pace we won't reach the gap until after midnight. Just go."

I prayed for Deina to accept this offer, to leave him with Teodór and continue up the road, bypassing the mine. But I could hear the determination in her voice.

"No, Otto. You're bleeding and covered in lavender oil. You smell like a well-seasoned breakfast for a bear. I'm not leaving you lying out on the road."

Otto groaned, he huffed, he argued, but Deina did not back down, and in another minute, they were gathering themselves to continue their struggle up the road. Luck was against me tonight. I would have to do something.

I still had no idea what, though.

Silently, I retreated a short distance into the woods and waited for them to pass me by. I pulled the hood of my cloak up over my head. And then, gathering my courage, still acting on impulse, I plunged forward through the underbrush. I rattled tree branches, kicked up wet leaf litter, and snapped sticks underfoot until I skidded back onto the road. I glanced up the track, where the Woodwalker and her scouts had frozen at my sudden appearance, their faces wide with surprise. Jenë stared, unable to see my face through the fog. A brief moment of stunned silence ticked by. And then Deina slouched Otto off her shoulder and slung her flatbow upright.

"Stay where you are, stranger. Lower your hood. State your name and your business."

I took a breath and streaked away in the opposite direction, leading them away from the mine, forcing myself to run flatfooted to continue making a ruckus. Deina gave a shout, and in between my heavy foot-falls, I heard her ordering Teodór to get Otto to safety. No. I couldn't have that. I fit one of the darts into Arlen's atlatl and turned, stumbling. I flung the thrower as I had seen Arlen do and watched as the dart jumped forward to strike the dirt only a few paces in front of me. My hands shaking, I loaded another dart and tried a second throw, aiming for a straighter flight. This dart sailed with alarming force and buried itself, quivering, in the rocks at Deina's feet. It did the trick. I turned and focused once again on the road, hearing her changing her orders to the others.

The chase along the road didn't last long. It couldn't have, not with the thickening fog and precarious drop-off along the path. As I looked over my shoulder to check the scouts' progress behind me—they moved silently, of course, ghost-like—I felt a sickening drop in my stomach as my foot cut through thin air. I fell forward into blind space and threw my arms over my face to shield my landing. I bounced against the rocky slope, loosening stones and debris. I struck a log; it slithered in the scree, freeing more rubble, sending it tumbling into the night. As I was caught up in the clattering momentum, I caught a last breath in my throat and shouted over my shoulder, "Come and get me!"

It was a desperate, grueling night. The western slopes were loose and sheer and shrouded in fog, and I fought to stay far enough ahead of Deina without appearing overly adept at navigating the landscape. I led them far into the north, praying they would then continue to Lampyrinae with the alarming news that there were intruders up on the ridge. When I thought we were finally far enough away from Lowback Gap, I abandoned my sloppy path through the scree and stole back up the ridge, taking the utmost care to keep my passage invisible. I reached the road and turned back to the south, running wearily through the fog.

When I finally limped back through the dewy gap, lit with watery gray light, I felt as though I had been dragged behind a wagon. I was scratched and aching, with bruises blooming on my knees and calves. The seam of my right boot was connected in only two places, and it flapped like a tired dog's tongue with each step. In my hand I clutched the Bird, all the darts spent. The air was heavy and clean, with no trace of smoke, and silence rang throughout the gap. As I approached the dark mine door, the thought occurred that the Alastaires had been found and taken away despite everything. I hurried the last few steps to the door, stopping abruptly on the threshold.

My sudden appearance startled Mona, who slopped tisane down Colm's front. "Mae! Rivers to the sea, where have you been? What happened?"

I sighed in relief and slouched against the doorframe. Arlen stirred and lifted his head from his cloak, blinking owlishly. But the most welcome sight was Colm, now clutching the cup in his own hands. His hair was damp with sweat, and his cheeks were flushed with color.

"Hi, Colm," I said.

"Hi," he replied, his voice hoarse.

"My atlatl," Arlen said, scrambling forward and plucking it from my fist. He held it this way and that in the weak light, searching for any harm.

"The darts are gone," I said wearily, moving forward into the mine.

"You knocked one of the pearls out! Great Light, I told you not to hurt it!"

I ignored him and joined Mona next to Colm, pressing my palm to his forehead. The heat in his head had lessened to a dull warmth. The tang of sweat was mingled with the bite of camphor laurel. "How's your chest?"

"Better."

"He started breathing easier as soon as we gave him the tisane," Mona said. "His fever broke close to midnight, and he woke up not long afterward."

"Dizzy?" I asked him. "Sore?"

"A bit," he said. "Not much. Thank you, Mae. Mona told me what happened."

"*I* want to know what happened last night," Arlen persisted, fingering the empty setting of his now one-eyed Bird. "How did you use all the darts?"

"I spilled them," I said heavily, slumping down onto my pack. My body buzzed with exhaustion.

"You *spilled* them? You didn't even throw them?"

"Arlen, be reasonable," Mona said, the usual sharpness in her voice banished by weariness. "She spent all night risking her own safety for us."

A vague amusement registered through my fatigue as I thought back to the harsh words she and I had exchanged less than twenty-four hours previously. Earth and sky, that argument seemed years ago.

"I threw two darts," I said. "Just to get their attention. They left their injured scout and followed me, but I slipped off the path . . . I started a rockslide."

"A *rockslide?*"

I rubbed my bruised legs. "I did a lot of shouting with a Hill-folk's accent, trying to make it seem like I had companions. I certainly made enough noise for a large group, but I don't know if they believed it or assumed that I was just a madwoman having a fit. At any rate, they followed me down the slopes, close to where the head of the Palisades begin. I led them far enough north that it would make more sense to continue on to Lampyrinae, rather than double back along the road. They'll want to bring the news of a raucous band of intruders to the king with the rest of their report."

"What report?"

"Oh." I slung my arm over my face, my weariness growing at the thought. "Didn't I say? They were a scouting party from the southern fringes of the mountains. They were bringing news to King Valien that a fleet of Alcoran ships is moving up the waterways toward Lumen Lake."

Mona clutched at the fabric of her trousers with white knuckles. "No."

"Yes. I thought it through in my head. We have less than a week to get to the lake in time."

"And how close are we?" she asked, her voice tight with tension. "How many days from here?"

I glanced at Colm. "If we can move at the same pace as before? Three days. Three days over the ridge and down the Palisades."

Mona looked at Colm as well. His eyes were cast down, his brow furrowed. "So when do we leave?"

"Tonight," I said, closing my eyes. "We're too close to the road to move safely during the daylight. But once word gets to the king about the disturbance last night, they're going to start doubling the watch along the ridge. We need to be out of the gap by tonight. With luck, we can start our descent down the Palisades before morning." I settled my head back into the mossy wall and drew my cloak around my shoulders. "And after that, I sure hope you have your grand plan squared away, because I don't have the faintest idea what to do on the other side."

CHAPTER 8

I could have slept for a week, but I forced myself back out into the gap around midday, heading to the spring near the mine to refill our waterskins. I washed out the cuts I had sustained in the grinding tumble of rock the previous night and daubed salve on my bruises. I rinsed out Colm's shirt; it was stiff with sweat from the drop in his fever. I stole back to the mine entrance and spread it out to dry on the branches of a laurel growing up against the hillside.

As the day waned, I threw caution to the wind and crept through the forest to the road, trying to determine the best route to lead the siblings over the ridge and down to the Palisades. There were few accessible routes down the steep slopes to the escarpment, and I couldn't risk another rockslide like the one I had started last night. I picked my way along the road, staying deep within the shadows of the trees, and searched for the gentlest grade. I needed to hurry the Alastaires through this area as quickly as possible, but if any of them were hurt during the descent, there would be few havens to shelter us.

Just as I turned around to make my way back, I picked up a curious shuffling sound coming from the road up ahead. I couldn't think what creature would be making that kind of noise—a dull snap followed by the crunch of pebbles underfoot. I snuck through the trees until I could see the figure through the trunks. I let out a sigh of relief, followed by a heavy wave of guilt. It was Otto, laboring up the road. He had a stout stick in each hand and was planting them in the ground before hopping forward on his one good foot. His injured ankle was hovering just an inch off the ground.

My mind raced. Why hadn't anyone from the palace come to fetch him with a cart or a horse? Surely Deina and her scouts were back by now? I moved forward a little more. He had his pack, that was good, but his skin was pale and running with sweat, and his face tightened in pain with each step. And then, with a swoop of unease, I noticed his wooden canteen, hanging upside down from his belt, unstopped. Empty. My stomach surged. This ridge was dry for another ten miles; the closest spring was back at the Lowback Mine. He wouldn't reach water for hours yet.

I crouched against the bole of a fir, trying to tame the urge to hurry forward and help him. No, I told myself. No, I couldn't worry about Otto. I was treading a knife's edge as it was. I stood up slowly, preparing to turn back for the mine. As I watched, his good foot slipped on a loose stone and he paused, leaning heavily on his walking sticks, his chest shuddering in and out. His hand fluttered toward his empty canteen before closing back on his stick.

I took one step away from the road, stopped, took one step back to him, and stopped again, chewing my lip. I glanced up at the sky; the light was melting into the golden glow of afternoon. Not much time. I hesitated a moment longer, and then turned and ran away from the road, leaving Otto gathering his strength. But I didn't make directly for the mine. Instead I hurried parallel to the track, hoping there was enough tree cover to hide me from the road. When I was far enough ahead of Otto, I slipped back through the trees. I slid my full waterskin over my shoulder and placed it on a prominent rock in the road. Hopefully it would see him through to the next spring. Up the path, I heard the *snap crunch* of his walking sticks, and without waiting any longer, I turned and fled through the trees once again, leaving the road behind me.

I made it back to the mine as the sun was edging down toward the treetops. In the light that was left to me, I sat in the grass just outside the mine door and stitched up the seam in my boot. The needle I carried was too slender for the leather, and I kept snapping my thread as I tugged at the stitches, my hands jumpy with unease. It was so risky, this lull in our progress. Every slight noise made me still my work, straining to determine its source. Colm rested against the doorway, his shirt unbuttoned in the late sunlight. He had just used the last of the camphor laurel and was taking deep, slow breaths. Behind him, Mona and Arlen slept in the cool darkness of the mine.

"This is when we'd look up to see the Light."

I glanced up from my work. Colm was gazing at the sky, streaked with the first fingers of orange. "Just before the sun sinks behind the western peaks, it shines straight across the lake and hits the waterfalls on the Palisades."

I stabbed my needle back into the leather. "For some reason, I always thought your folk saw the Light in your pearls."

"That's partly true. We see it in reflections. The moon glinting off the lake, the sun rippling on the lakebed. And, yes, the colors and shine of our pearls."

His voice had a longing that I recognized. "It's hard to be stuck somewhere where the Light is different, isn't it?"

He fingered his shirtfront idly, and I knew he was unconsciously plucking at Ama's ring. "I didn't think it would be. The Light is the Light, after all. It shouldn't matter where folk see it, how they revere it." He frowned slightly. "But it does. For months after we arrived at the coast, I found myself turning into the east at sunset, expecting to see the waterfalls lighting up. Not seeing that event, every night, it left me . . . I don't know, I can't describe it. Not sad, just . . ."

"Drifting," I offered. "I understand. The fireflies used to anchor me to the Light, too. Even after years of traveling, I could never find the same reverence for the turn of the moon, like the Hill-folk, or the first rays of sunrise, like the Sea-folk. The closest I came was in Alcoro."

"Was it?" he asked. "The stars?"

"Yes, the stars," I said, looking up at the sky, its clouds now streaked with pink. "The land there is so dry and so open that the skies go on forever and ever. A whole dome of stars." I gestured around us. "It was remarkable. But still. Not quite the same."

He leaned his head back against the moss. "I know Mona wants to stop feeling tied to the Light, because of what it drove Alcoro to do." He glanced into the mine, where she was sleeping under her cloak. "She doesn't want to admit she may share something with King Celeno, even something as lovely as revering the Light."

"A little stiff-necked, your sister," I said, looping another whipstitch. "Though I suppose that's always been her reputation."

"You have to understand, though, she's eased up since the invasion. She used to be much . . ."

"Worse?"

"Different," he said. "Extremely particular. She's had to weather a great deal, and it's made her more adaptable, I think. I know it doesn't seem that way . . ."

"No, I understand." I forced my needle through the leather again. "She's been through more than most. I'm guessing she didn't get much chance to grieve your folk's losses on her own. Especially Ama."

I was absorbed in my whipstitches, so it took me a moment to understand why he was staring at me. I paused my work and lifted my gaze to his. He had straightened, sitting forward from the doorframe. A span of silence stretched between us.

"You *were* talking about it yesterday," he said. "Great Light, I thought I was just having fever dreams."

The silence was pierced by a few crickets starting their evening song. My hands were frozen above the seam of my boot.

"She told you about that day."

"Yes," I said softly. "You said, 'Ama.' "

He stared at me, his chest rising and falling as his breath quickened. I didn't know what emotion was building inside him. Was it anger? Embarrassment?

"I'm sorry," I said quickly. "I wasn't trying to pry."

"I could see it, every word of it." His voice was sharp. "Happening right in front of me again."

"I'm sorry."

The tension buzzed between us a moment longer, and then he slumped back against the doorframe. "It's okay." He ran his fingers through his hair and then did something I didn't expect—he laughed. It was the first time I'd heard him do so, but it was a bitter sound, mirthless. "I'm not mad, Mae. It was the most vivid image I've had of her since she was killed."

I swallowed, entirely unsure of how to respond. He pulled Ama's ring out from his shirt and held it on the end of his little finger. It barely fit down past his first knuckle. "You would have liked her, I think. She was passionate about what she did, like you. A miraculous diver." His mouth twisted as he gazed at the row of pink pearls. "I told Mona in Tiktika that I would follow her anywhere, and it's true. But I'm not happy to be going back to Lumen Lake. Not at all. She and Arlen both have something to return to. She has her throne. Arlen has Sorcha, or at least he thinks he does. I have nothing. Only Ama's absence."

I tried to clear the block in my throat, my mind still a blank. "Maybe . . ."

He turned his head to me, and I was startled by the hardness in his eyes. "Maybe what, Mae? Maybe I'll find someone else? Start all over again? It'll all just fade into the past while I walk past the spot where she was murdered, day after day? That's a fool's notion. You try to live with that kind of loss, see what it does to you."

I sat stunned under the blow of his harshness, finally looking back down at my boot. My last four whipstitches had only caught one edge of the leather. Determinedly, I aimed my needle once again and worked it through the seam, my face hot. The light was fading in earnest now, and my stitches were wide and uneven, as haphazard as my heartbeat. I managed four more loops before my needle jammed in the thick material.

"I'm sorry."

I didn't look up.

"Mae. I'm sorry. I . . . that was uncalled for. You have lived with that loss. That was selfish of me."

I wriggled the needle, trying to force it through the

seam. "No, you're right. My family is still alive. My sister and brothers, my aunts and uncles, my cousins, my friends . . . the man I was going to marry. They're all still alive."

"But they were taken away from you. I know. I'm sorry. Perhaps that's worse, knowing they're continuing on without you, that you can't be a part of their lives."

"It's not worse," I said. "And it's not better. You can't quantify grief." My fingers slipped on the needle and it bent, driving into the pad of my thumb. I cursed vaguely and sucked at the spot, tying a reluctant knot in my thread and shoving my ruined needle back into its pouch.

"You were engaged?"

"Only just. He proposed the same week I was banished."

I could feel him watching me. I pulled my poorly repaired boot back on my foot. "I'm sorry," he said again.

"Stop saying that." I tied my laces and took a deep breath, trying to banish the tension in my chest. I looked back up at him. His hair glowed in the last light. "It never goes away, does it?"

The hardness had dropped from his face, and he looked tired, and sad. "No," he said. "It doesn't." He watched me a moment longer. And then—"Why were you exiled, Mae?"

I plucked up a blade of grass. "I thought I told you."

"No, you haven't. Not really. You said you spoke out against Vandalen."

"Yes."

"You never told us what you actually said to him."

I pinched another few blades of grass, thinking back to that day, and the days that came after.

He waved his hand quickly. "I suppose now I'm the one prying. Never mind, you don't have to tell me . . ."

"It almost doesn't matter what I shouted at Vandalen," I said, looking up at him. "I could have said anything, and the outcome would have been the same. Though I think you've already worked out that it had to do with the order to shoot trespassers."

He turned Ama's ring in his fingers. "I recall getting the letter around the same time you say you were banished. I remember, because I had just purchased this." He held the little ring between his finger and thumb.

"I see. Well, it wasn't just that order. Things had been going wrong before that." I stretched out my boots on the grass. "I suppose you know about the family that took over the crown when our original monarchy died out all those years ago?"

"They were silver magnates, weren't they?"

"Yes. Oversaw the mines. Naturally, the monarchy that stemmed from them always had a vested interest in the mines. But mining is a destructive industry—it's one of the biggest reasons the Woodwalkers were created in the first place. And after a while, the mission of the Woodwalkers began clashing with the interests of the monarchy."

"I suppose they began trying to do away with the office?"

"Well, we were useful, you know—they weren't *entirely* stupid. They knew we played an important role in protecting the mountains. But they began trying to downplay our influence, alter our objectives to ease the restrictions on the mines. Vandalen just happened to be worse than most. Over time, he shifted our focus from protecting our resources to glorified border patrols. None of the scouts were happy about it, but I was . . . more vocal than most. And I had lots of friends in the Guard."

"A dangerous combination."

"For him, yes. And I used to bypass his orders— I'd take the minimum number of scouts I needed to accomplish whatever inane task he had given us, and then I'd send the rest of them to do the real work— checking the runoff from the mines, felling and burning infested trees, all that. But he had a few loyal eyes in the Guard, and word eventually got back to him. He gave me warnings, assigned me extra work, threatened to demote me. But the more his orders changed, the more antsy the Woodwalkers got. Apparently we made him nervous. So something had to be done— someone had to be made into an example."

"And that turned out to be you?"

I toyed with the grass some more. "Well, it wasn't just a wrong-place, wrong-time scenario. He was clever about it. He called me up in front of the council, alone, without the support of the other Woodwalkers. He gave me the order to shoot on sight in the forest and told me to disseminate it to the rest of the Wood

Guard. He knew I'd lose it. It was absurd—we're not armed infantry. That's the Armed Guard's job, and even then they're more focused on training for battle, not murdering travelers. That's when I did the shouting." I pursed my mouth, remembering how he had let me rail against him, giving me a nudge of provocation here and there to keep me going. "I made it perfectly easy on him. He didn't have to prove anything to his council. No need for a trial. I was in a prison cell an hour later, and before dawn the next morning, I was being marched away from Lampyrinae."

"How did the other Woodwalkers find out? Do you know?"

"Oh," I said, unable to keep the bitterness from my voice. "They were there."

"Where?"

I crushed a blade of grass between my fingers. "In the courtyard, where I was formally sentenced and led away. They didn't know why I had my outburst, just heard that I had lost it in front of the king. All the Guard was there—Wood Guard, Armed Guard, Palace Guard. Even the trainees. Vandalen . . . made a point of making it a show."

I hated remembering those moments—the sea of faces standing at attention before me, forced out of bed two hours before wake-up call. "He had me get all polished up in my most formal uniform, and then he trotted me out in front of everyone. He called up the other Woodwalkers and had them strip off everything that denoted my rank. They took my silver shoulder cord and lapel pins; they took off my tooled belt and double-fringed boots." I remembered Jenë standing near the back with the other trainees, watching with wide eyes. "He made them snip off the insignia on my tunic. They even ripped the embroidered hem off my cloak. He made them break my bow, the moron—it could have at least gone back to the armory, but no, he was making a statement."

I burrowed my fingers into the soft dirt, glaring at nothing. "He read out my sentence for everyone to hear, officially removing my rank and pronouncing me a foreigner to the Silverwood. He laid out the orders for any party that might intercept me in the forest in the future. And then he had the Woodwalkers bind my hands and blindfold me—as if I couldn't walk the whole mountain range with my eyes shut." I remembered looking determinedly over the heads of my friends at the last few fireflies drifting around the edges of the courtyard as the blindfold was passed in front of my eyes.

I brushed grass off the toes of my boots. "Over the last five years, I've sort of clung to the idea that his show had the opposite effect of what he intended—that instead of scaring his Guardsmen straight, it would deepen their disregard for him."

Colm turned Ama's ring on its chain. "That's why you were so upset about the landslide."

I looked out over the darkening gap. "Nothing's changed. No one has the courage to keep doing our real job. Instead they're prowling along the old road, scaring away Winderan kids collecting mushrooms.

Meanwhile we lose stands of timber to beetles and kill waterways with runoff." I heaved a sigh. At that, he gave the barest chuckle. "What?"

" '*My strength is in my integrity.*' " He tucked the little ring back inside his shirt. "No one can say you aren't still a Woodwalker, Mae."

It was the casualness of his comment that hit me, I suppose. For years I had been fighting tooth and nail to hold on to my old sense of purpose, consumed by the directionless, meaningless void my life had become. Hearing him give me my old title with no fanfare or doubt made unexpected warmth swell in my chest. I looked down, my collar suddenly hot.

A yellow firefly blinked lazily between us, indifferent to our conversation. It jerked me back to the present. Dusk. Time for us to go. I brushed the grass off my trousers.

"We should wake your brother and sister." I got to my feet. "How do you feel? Do you want me to carry your pack for a while?"

"I'm fine. No pain. You've done more than enough. I'm grateful to you, Mae." He held up his hand, palm-up, in the manner of my kin. "Thank you."

The impact of this gesture was not lost on me, and I smiled as I went to wake Mona. "It would have been a lot more trouble hauling your unconscious body down the Palisades, Colm. I'm just glad you're still breathing."

I caught the edge of his grin before reaching down to shake his sister.

We shared a quick meal of fruit leathers and the last of our smoked meat before slinging our packs over our backs. I directed Mona and her brothers to start up the rise leading out of the gap while I hung behind, attempting to disguise the signs of our presence. I scuffed up the grass we had trodden down during our stay and scattered the ashes from our fire. Dusting off my hands, I followed in the wake of the siblings. Mona was cresting the rise, trailed by her brothers, but when she reached the top, she froze, her silhouette black against the deepening sky.

"Oh," I heard her gasp.

I tensed, my heartbeat quickening with my footsteps. "What? Mona, what's wrong?"

She didn't turn back toward me, but raised a hand, beckoning us up the slope. "Come here, now."

We scrambled to her side and drew up short, staring down the gentle hill into the hollow below. I swayed in sudden shock, my hand jumping to grip my chest.

Below us, silent as nightfall and as bright as the moon, the blue ghost fireflies were swarming. Rivers, cascades, eddies of starlight, never blinking, only glowing as they drifted calf-high off the ground. They flowed among the trunks of the trees, drifting like mist over the underbrush. There were so many stretching away into the twilight that the whole forest glowed, the trunks bathed in blue light. In the branches above, their yellow cousins flickered and flashed, adding their own twinkle to the display unfolding below them. I found myself pressing my palms to my cheeks, my throat constricting in sudden emotion. How long, how long had it been since I had last seen this sacred sight?

Too long.

Mona's arms hung limp by her sides. "Oh," she breathed again, as if in sudden comprehension.

I felt a soft touch at my elbow. Colm. "Your Light," he said.

I swallowed, unable to speak. Somewhere in the trees, a towhee joined the cricket song. *Drink-your-tea!* The final gray light slipped from the cloudy sky, leaving nothing but the dazzling sight twining through the hollow. A few loners drifted our way, and away from their fellows, I could see the faint blue glow each one cast on the ground below. So unconcerned, so plain, these dark little beetles, seeking quietly for their mates. The crickets sang, the towhee called, and the rivers of starlight continued, drifting among the trees.

I was full, I was brimming, I was heartsick . . . so much so that my sluggish brain didn't latch on to that glaring towhee, shouting its call all alone, at far too late in the day, at much too high an elevation, nor did it apply this logic to the handful of pewees that called back to it. No, I stood like a statue until my subconscious finally nudged me into alert, but by then it was much too late. It barely took one breath for the figure to detach from the trees, standing sideways in the cloud of fireflies, an arrow nocked on the bowstring.

"Don't move," commanded a muffled voice, and in that instant I was shattered glass, staring at the pieces of my foolishness spread across the ground. "You are surrounded by the Wood Guard of King Valien Bluesmoke of Lampyrinae." The speaker's face was hooded and covered by a dark cloth; the only visible part of her was her eyes, flickering in the blue light. In her bow hand she held three more arrows, one for each of us. She moved forward slowly, her arrow trained on us. "You will not speak or reach for any weapons. You will present your hands to be bound. You will be taken to the king's court at Lampyrinae, where you will . . .

"Ellamae?"

She straightened in sudden astonishment, her bow drooping in her arms. She blinked several times, the pinpoints of blue light winking.

It was my cousin Jenë. My heart crashed to my feet.

"Great earth and sky . . ." She pulled back her hood and jerked down the cloth covering her nose and mouth, and even in the dim light I could see distress in her face. She strode forward and grasped my arms. "What in the world, Ellamae . . . what in the world are you *doing* here?"

I gripped her back. "Jenë, please, let us pass. We're only trying to get through the mountains. You can't take us in."

"I . . . Ellamae, I already . . . didn't you hear me signaling? I've got Howel's scouts convening on us *right now*." Her eyes flicked between my three companions. "What are you *doing*? Who are *they*?"

"They're no one, Jenë. Just travelers. We mean no harm to anyone. We're just trying to get through."

"It wasn't . . . great Light, it wasn't *you* last night, was it? On the path, down to the Palisades?" Her grip grew tighter on my arms. Her eyes jumped to the Alastaires again.

"Jenë," I said, almost shaking her arms. "Let us pass."

"I rode out to get Otto on the road," she said, her voice high. "He said someone left a Winderan waterskin out on the path. He thought perhaps the intruders from last night were still up on the ridge and suggested I check the closest spring . . ."

A Winderan waterskin. Damn everything.

"And the closest spring is here, of course." Even as she panicked, I could hear the near-silent sounds of scouts hurrying through the trees, brushing against bark and ruffling leaves in their haste. "And it . . . and it was *you*?"

"Jenë, listen . . ."

She swiveled her head around as a chirp rang out from the trees. While she was turned, I reached out to Mona and jerked the pearl pendant over her head. Hurriedly I balled it in my fist and stuffed it down into my boot.

Jenë turned back to us, her eyes creased in anguish. She took several steps back and bent her flatbow again. "I . . . I can't . . . I'm sorry, Ellamae."

I turned to Colm. "Quick," I whispered urgently. "Give Mona your ring, before they bind our hands."

He fumbled with the chain, slipping the pink-pearled ring into his hand and passing it to his sister.

She pushed it down onto her left ring finger just as figures began emerging from the deeps of the forest. Bows creaked on all sides.

"Present your hands to be bound," ordered one of the figures, his face hooded like the others'. Running over his shoulder was a woven silver cord, and his boots had a double band of fringe around the calves. His lapels glittered with an absurd number of pins. "Surrender any weapons you carry."

"Which shall we do first, Howel?" I asked him. "Get your sequence straight."

"It's Ellamae Hawkmoth, sir," said Jenë quietly.

I saw several arrows waver. One scout to my left actually straightened his bow and pulled down his mask, like Jenë had.

"Stay on your guard!" Howel snapped, and the scout jerked his arrow back up. My hopes sank even lower—Howel had always been one to err on the side of the king rather than his more furtive comrades. He looked between me and the three siblings. I could sense the stiffness in Mona's silhouette.

"Correct me if I'm mistaken, but you're supposed to be serving out a lifelong banishment, are you not?" Howel asked.

"You're correct."

"Then what are you doing here, now, in the company of foreigners, so far up the mountainsides?"

"We're passing through only, Howel, as innocent travelers. If you weren't aware, Tradeway Road is still impassable, so anyone trying to get from one side of the mountains to the other has to beat a path through the middle."

"And why," he asked, passing his gaze over the Alastaires again, "would you want to get from one side to the other?"

"I commend you on your rise to Woodwalker," I said carefully, "but I'm afraid I'm still not at liberty to tell you."

His face twitched under his mask. "Then I suppose you'll just have to tell the king and his council."

"Surely the king can't be bothered with a few harmless travelers?"

He gestured to his scouts. "Bind their hands."

"Sir," said Jenë with a hint of desperation, "you do know what the council ruled all those years ago?"

"That's hardly our concern. If we let them pass— which, I may remind you, would be considered a form of treason—in all likelihood they'll be apprehended again, and word may get out that they first encountered our party, who did nothing. I don't need to tell you what will happen to your rank and reputation in such an event." He snapped his fingers agitatedly at his hesitant scouts. *"Bind their hands, Guardsmen, or I will report all of you to the king!"*

Several of them sprang forward and busied themselves with our wrists. Arlen let a curse slip when one of them pried his atlatl from his hands.

"Shall we blindfold them, sir?" asked another scout reluctantly.

Howel hesitated. "No," he said. "These foreigners

are going to have a hard enough time in the dark as it is. No need to drag out the journey."

And with that, I knew that was all the leniency I was going to get from my former comrades.

At least we weren't dead.

Yet.

We walked through the night. In a vague, detached way, I was glad we had rested during the day, or else the Alastaires never could have kept up with Howel's pace. Our way was buffeted by the fireflies, but now their glow seemed to only illuminate my many failures. I fought down the desperation churning in my stomach, my mind flickering from one bitter thought to the next like a bird afraid to perch. How had I forgotten that Otto would immediately recognize the waterskin as a Winderan product? Why had I not thought he would connect it to the intruding Hill-folk from the night before? How had I missed the calls of the Wood Guard ringing through the forest? What on earth was I going to tell the king? Would his council recognize Mona and her brothers? What would they do to them?

What would they do to *me*?

The ridge road was hard-packed and wide, but still uneven, and I heard the siblings stumble several times behind me. I thought anxiously of Colm, so recently recovered. The other scouts were carrying our packs, so at least he wasn't bearing any extra weight, but this brought me small comfort. On one particularly rocky stretch, I heard him stagger, spurring a coughing fit. I turned, walking backward with my wrists bound behind my back. "All right, Colm?"

"All right."

"Don't speak," commanded Howel.

We stumbled along through the deepest part of the night and into the dawn. As we moved further north, we passed intersections with other paths leading away down the mountains. I thought of the Wood-folk in these settlements, the earliest risers just now beginning to kindle fires and draw water, and I wondered if there was a soul in the Silverwood who might possibly risk their safety for mine. I thought of my family, away north on Beegum Bald. I could never get word to them in time. And my friends in the Guard? Would they be willing to risk their ranks and titles for an ex-comrade, now leading strangers through the land they were charged to protect?

At last, as shards of light shot through the morning mist, we broke through the trees to see Blue Ghost Mountain sloping away above us, the palace of Lampyrinae perched on its summit. My heart gave a wobbly leap, fatigued and anxious though I was. The winding towers were still as familiar to me as the day I was blindfolded and led away from the gates. Built into the living mountain itself, the turrets and arches rose above the trees, glinting in the early light. The great Firefall was still in the clinging shadows on the western slopes, plunging out of sight down the sheer drop to the Palisades, but the sound of its foaming rapids still reached us at the feet of the rise.

But the sight didn't grant me welcome for long. Howel urged us into the trees at the foot of the hill, and as the palace disappeared behind the canopy, my desperation came flooding back to me. This was not my home. This was not my refuge. This was not even a place of safety for me anymore. This was danger and despair and failure. I clenched my fists behind my back, hating that the place that should have brought me joy now filled me only with dread.

Folk were well into their morning routines amid the settlement ringing palace walls. The scent of wood smoke and baking cornbread wafted through the air, pierced by tendrils of acrid smoke from the black-smith's forge. I couldn't help but glance to my left and right as we made our way up the track, quietly observing what had stayed the same and what had changed in my absence. There was the chair caner and the broom-maker, the tanner and the farrier. There was the sorghum mill and the cider press. Above the morning's activity filtered the groaning of the waterwheel, powering the gristmill for the day's corn. There was a new bowyer, it seemed, and the silversmith had expanded her shop, but the old tavern was no different. A gaggle of children tumbled around on tommy walkers outside the front door. One girl sat with a limber jack in her lap, making him dance to the laughter of the others. They all stopped their games to stare at us as we passed, the loose wooden limbs of the jack dangling limply like a hanged man.

I tried not to take it as an ominous sign.

When we finally reached the carved wooden gates, I was surprised to see that the motif engraved into them hadn't changed. Traditionally, whenever the crown passed to a new king or queen, they would have the old gates taken down and order new ones to be carved with their desired symbol. But the doors that rose before me still bore Vandalen's eagle swooping down upon the mountains, its talons outstretched as if to snatch away the trees on the peaks. I didn't have time to ponder this, however, because a moment later the gates swung open with a groan to admit us into the space beyond.

We passed through the great courtyard, the site of the annual feasting and revelry for the citizens of the Silverwood, lorded over by a branching oak as ancient as the country itself. During summer feasts, musicians would sit in the arms of the tree, surrounded by the synchronous fireflies, driving the dancing taking place below. But now the courtyard echoed with silence, broken only by our hurried passage. Howel ushered us up the sweeping staircase to the front gates of the palace, nodding to the Palace Guards posted at the door. They did double-takes as I passed by them.

"Ellamae . . . ?"

But a moment later, we were inside the arching front hall, the morning sun illuminating the dust motes drifting through the air. I was awash in a spectrum of emotions. This palace. My home. My prison. My victory.

My downfall.

Howel didn't lead us straight ahead to the throne hall, but veered off down a side passage. So we were going to the council chamber. I fought down a wave of dread and cleared my throat, breaking our long silence.

"Are the councilors the same?" I asked. "None of them have, I don't know, died of bitterness in the last five years?"

Howel quickened his pace, as if to get away from my irreverent words.

"No," Jenë said quietly from the back of the line. "The council's the same, Ellamae."

"Hellebore and Blackthorn?"

"Still there."

Damn.

The palace windows were thrown open to the spring breeze, and the sun gleamed off the polished wood lining the hallways. Intricate wrought-iron lanterns hung from the rafters, interspersed here and there with chandeliers of mirrored silver. The country's banner, a silver tree on a green field, was draped throughout the palace. In the Luminous Years, the roots of the tree would have been embellished with blue pearls, representing the ghosts, but as goodwill dissolved between Lumen and the Silverwood, so did our supply of pearls. Now the only banner to bear these gems was the one in the throne hall. The rest were embroidered with knots of blue thread.

The door to the council chamber brought back memories that made my stomach roil. Howel lined us up in the corridor outside the chamber and left to bring word to the king, leaving Jenë and the three other scouts flanking us. For the first time since our arrest, I made eye contact with Mona and her brothers.

"I'm sorry," I said.

Mona glanced at the scouts, expecting one of them to silence us, but they were all looking determinedly in opposite directions. I felt a small spark of gratitude.

"Don't be," she said. "I'm the one who convinced you to come back."

I looked past her to Colm. He was staring solemnly at the opposite wall, where a carving of the Firefall stood, scattered with beads of silver to represent the swirling fireflies on its banks.

"So," she said quietly. " 'Ellamae Hawkmoth'?"

"A relic of when I used to belong here," I said wearily. "The name the king shouted out during my sentencing. Some things you prefer to leave behind."

"Hawkmoth is your family name?"

"Actually, Ellamae is more so. My sister is Seramae. My mother is Ilamae." I shifted my weight. Her pearl pendant had rubbed a hot spot into my foot where it sat in my boot. "Hawkmoth is my epithet. We all choose one when we turn thirteen, which usually means they're picked for stupid reasons. My brother Meicah's, for example, before he got married, was Woodcock, because he was an idiot. My sister's was Tuliptree, because she thought the flowers were pretty."

"And yours?"

"I don't suppose you've ever seen a hummingbird hawkmoth?"

"No."

"They're amazing little creatures. At first glance you're not sure if it's a moth, or a hummingbird, or a bee. It looks like all three at once. I thought they were very clever, being able to masquerade like that." I leaned back against the wooden wall. "Normally, you get a second chance at choosing your epithet, either when you get married or achieve some kind of status in your profession." I closed my eyes. "Neither one seems very likely for me at the moment."

Behind the door leading into the hall came a murmur of voices, and my heart, which had quieted, began to pound once again. Despite all our precautions, all our efforts, we would come face to face with this new king, after all. The door opened and Howel stuck his head out.

"Come."

But as we entered the room, I saw with surprise that the king was not among the five councilors seated at the high table. I stared at his chair, conspicuously empty in their midst. Where could he be, that they would bring us in without him? Was he out in the wood? Was he ill?

After overcoming my initial consternation, I turned my attention back to the familiar faces at the high table. Councilor Hellebore shuffled a few sheaves of parchment. He was a spidery-looking man, his dark skin made dingy by years of indoor work directing the economics of the silver mines. He peered at me with beetle-black eyes. He would well remember the trouble I gave him over his constant requests to ease mining restrictions. I met his gaze without blinking, and after a moment, he turned his attention to Howel.

"So, Woodwalker Tanager," said Hellebore. "Begin your report. Who are these intruders, and where did you find them?"

Howel paused. "With respect, Councilor, shouldn't we wait for the king?"

"The king is burdened with other tasks at the moment. We will give him a full account of our interrogation. Give me your report."

I ground my teeth. So this was the relationship between the council and the new king. They were undermining him outright. I tried to will Howel to stand his ground, to insist on proper protocol. But he was too bound to title and rank to reject an order from a councilor. He cleared his throat.

"At dusk this night past, my party was called to rally by Scout Jenë Junco at the Lowback silver mine. We convened on the gap to find these four intruders. Three, as you can see, are foreigners, with the look of the lake about them. The fourth is Woodwalker Ellamae Hawkmoth."

"*Former* Woodwalker," corrected Hellebore, looking at me with a creased brow. I refused to lower my gaze under his glare. "Was there any struggle?"

"No, sir. They've all been compliant."

"What weapons were they bearing?"

"An atlatl of Lumeni make, and pocket knives. We haven't had a chance to search their packs more thoroughly."

"See that you do it." Hellebore swept his gaze back to me. "What excuse do you have, Hawkmoth, for being found in the heart of the mountains with three strangers?"

I had rehearsed my desperate story in my head the entire night. I wished I could have discussed it with the Alastaires first.

"I'm well aware I'm violating my banishment," I said. "Up until now I've accepted my misguided sentence and haven't ventured into the mountains for five years. But I met these three Lake-folk in Paroa by chance, and they expressed their desire to make their way through the Silverwood to Lumen Lake. They were among the only folk who managed to escape the Alcoran attack." I took a breath, feeling Mona's sideways glance. "These two"—I gestured with my elbow to her and Colm—"were forced to leave their child behind. They haven't seen or heard of her in three years and are attempting to return to her. With them travels their cousin." I nodded to Arlen. "They asked me to lead them swiftly and safely through the Silverwood, and nothing more. They have no animosity to the king, nor any particular influence in Lumen. They only want to find their child."

I held very still, striving to keep my eyes on the council and not the siblings. Councilor Blackthorn leaned forward.

"Do they not face enslavement upon their return?" She eyed my companions.

"It's worth the risk," Mona said evenly. My heart hammered in my chest.

Councilor Kestrel cleared her throat. She was the only one of the five who had shown anything close to reservation upon my sentencing, having once been a scout herself. She had abandoned the Royal Guard when she couldn't rise to Woodwalker and took up politics instead. "Why didn't you appeal to the king, and seek his permission to travel through the Silverwood?"

"How could we have communicated with him?" Mona asked. I wished she and her brothers would lower their chins; they were giving off a distinctly regal air. "There are no paths into the mountains open to foreigners, and no system to send a message through. We tried for weeks to attempt the crossing ourselves, but we realized we could never get through without a guide. This woman was our first chance in three years to try our return."

"What on earth is your plan upon your arrival?" asked Hellebore. "You'll just be locked up with your daughter. What do you propose to do?"

"That is none of your concern," Mona said with authority. Earth and sky, she might as well have commanded them to kneel.

Hellebore's frown deepened. "Your presence in our country makes it my concern. We can't have the Alcorans believe we're helping to smuggle your folk through the mountains." He straightened. "You will all be imprisoned, and questioned separately . . ."

"Please," I said, overriding him. "Lock me up, if you must, but let these three continue on their journey. They won't betray you to Alcoro—there's nothing they could give away. You only need to escort them down the Palisades to the border . . ."

"You face a heavier sentence than mere imprisonment, Hawkmoth, and you're in no place to make requests," Hellebore said fiercely.

"And you have no place to interrogate captives without the presence of the king," I said, my anger finally rising. "What's your plan for the changing of the crown, Hellebore, or haven't you picked out a replacement monarch yet?"

He turned a marvelous shade of purple. "You," he said with venom, "would do well to keep silent, lest we order your execution before the day is out."

"What's in your boot?" asked Kestrel.

Everyone in the room looked at her, and then down at my foot. I glanced at my poorly repaired seam and cursed her scout's eyes, her namesake. Spilling out of the ragged edge was the fine silver chain of Mona's pendant.

I opened my mouth to reply, but before I could fabricate an answer, there was a sharp grind behind us as the heavy double doors were shoved open. The Alastaires and I half-turned.

On the threshold stood the king, his face as dark as thunder. He was dressed in a variation of the moss green Guard uniform, though the embroidery was finer and his tunic clasps were set with gems. His boots, inlaid with silver and hung with bands of fringe, were damp with earth. A circlet of silver ran across his brow, disappearing into his black hair. His eyes swept the four of us, jumping from one sibling to the next before alighting on me.

Great Light, he looked exactly like his father when he glared like that, though his eyes were sharper and more cunning than the previous king's. His gaze slid from us to the row of councilors, his jaw working.

"My king," Hellebore greeted coolly. "We heard you were out on the ridge this morning."

He stalked past us, his cloak billowing behind him. "I've been there for most of the night, Hellebore, though by happy coincidence I returned a short time ago to hear that intruders were being interrogated without me. I thought perhaps it was a matter worth my time." He turned back to me, jabbing his finger at my face. "You should not be here."

"I know," I said pointedly. With his right hand inches from my eyes, I could see the mess of scars spreading out from his palm. The only vague explanation the Guard had had for this injury was some kind of childhood accident.

"She has admitted to leading these three foreigners through the mountains," Blackthorn said. "They were found at the Lowback Mine last night on their journey to Lumen Lake."

"How is it that a past-prime scout and three cutfoot

divers made it halfway through the mountains without being caught?" the king asked. He honed in on Howel. "Well, Woodwalker?"

Howel was somewhat taken aback. "I . . . we're assigned to range the ridge, my king. It's Yrien and Clera who command the eastern slopes . . ."

"I still want to know what's in her boot," Kestrel said.

King Valien dropped his eyes to my foot. He snapped his fingers at Jenë. "Take off her boot, Guardsman."

Jenë hurried forward and crouched down at my feet. I reluctantly lifted my foot for her, wobbling with my elbows splayed out like an ungainly turkey. She pulled, but instead of my boot coming off, the whole seam simply fell apart. The sole flopped to the floor. Out dropped Mona's pendant.

"Sorry," she whispered to me, lifting the necklace to the king. He plucked it out of her grip and dangled it from his scarred fist. His face took on a wary, closed look.

"What is it?" Councilor Hellebore asked, peering forward. "A gem?"

"A pearl," the king said.

"A *large* pearl," said Kestrel.

I clenched my hands behind my back. How common knowledge was it that the monarch of Lumen Lake bore a large pearl pendant? The Alcorans in Rusher's Junction had known.

Hellebore looked back at me. "Hawkmoth has sug-

gested that these three Lake-folk are simply common-
ers, with no influence among them, but if they bear a
valuable pendant . . ."

"Nonsense," the king interrupted, balling up the
pearl and chain in a swift move. "All it suggests is
that our former kinsman has fallen on difficult times.
Taken to thieving, have we, Ellamae?" In a swift move,
he passed the chain around his own neck, settling the
pendant under his tunic.

I could almost feel the heat radiating from Mona
as her rage smoldered. I shrugged as well as I could
with my arms bound behind my back. "I have to get
on somehow."

"Clearly." His eyes roved from my ruined boot to
my ragged tunic.

"My king," said Hellebore with impatience. "I really
think we ought to . . ."

"You'll forgive me if I ignore your current request,
Councilor," said the king sharply. He reached into his
cloak and withdrew a slender shaft. He held it out to
Jenë, the tip inches away from her face. "Guardsman."

She shrank from him slightly, her eyes on the
object. "My king?"

"Tell me what this is."

"A dart, my king."

"Is this the same variety of dart that was thrown at
your scouting party two nights past?"

"Yes, my king."

"Are you learned in projectile weaponry, Guardsman?"

She didn't know how to respond. Up at the high table, Hellebore pursed his lips. "With respect, my king," he said in a voice that belied his address, "I don't think that this . . ."

"Do not presume to tell me my place, Hellebore," Valien commanded, pointing at the councilor with the dart. "Let me help you all. A dart of this make is too short for a bow, and too light to throw by hand. A dart of this make is generally used with a spear-thrower." He turned and without hesitation, held the dart up to Arlen. "Tell me, lakeman, which one of you is skilled with an atlatl?" He eyed the smile-shaped scar on Arlen's cheek.

"I am," he said curtly.

"I thought as much. Then it couldn't have been you. It was a poor shot, you see. And not you." He moved past Colm, waving the dart dismissively. "And not you." He swept past Mona, ignoring the contempt pouring off of her. He stopped in front of me again. "Ellamae, tell me, what were you doing on the ridge two nights ago, firing on my scouts and endangering those living along the Palisades?"

"I was trying to lead Deina's party away from the Lowback Mine," I said evenly. "Where we were sheltering from the rain."

"Yes, and to recover, I suspect, from some kind of illness, if the plundering of the ridge cache is any indication." He turned away from me, striding toward the high table. Hellebore was watching him like a hawk. "Not only do you violate your banishment, but you do so in the interest of bringing strangers into the heart of the Silverwood. You steal from my caches and injure my scouts."

"I never hurt anyone!" I said with surprise.

"No?" he asked, pausing on the steps. "I don't suppose you count the dislocated knee my Woodwalker sustained while pursuing you?"

So that was why Deina had been so late getting back to the palace. I felt a swoop of guilt.

"I admit I've acted against the Silverwood," I said. He stood on the steps before the high table, twirling the dart agitatedly in his fingers. "Lock me up. Do what you must. But let these three go free. They have no quarrel with you, and they must get to the lake."

A moment of silence passed through the room, a moment that apparently lasted too long for Hellebore's peace of mind. He shifted and cleared his throat. "My king." His voice was just a bit too loud, a bit too forceful. "My king, I must insist that you deny this request . . ."

In that instant, I saw the young king's exact predicament illustrated before us, caught like quarry between two opposing fronts. His councilors' eyes bored down on him, but he didn't wait to let another person speak. He turned sharply with a swipe of his earth-stained cloak.

"You *insist?* Hellebore, be silent. Despite what you may think, you do not, in fact, possess the authority to insist I do anything." He stalked around the high table to his place amid his council, but he didn't sit down. He pointed at me with the dart, his face dark as night. "Ellamae Hawkmoth, I hereby hold you to the sentence my father placed upon you five years ago and sentence you to death by hanging at first light tomorrow morning. As for the three of you, you will be held in prison until I decide how you might serve me most effectively." He jerked his hand at Howel. "Take them away, Woodwalker."

Mona's voice broke from her in a hiss. "You wretch! You poison your country like an apple rots a barrel! How dare you . . ."

"*Away*, Woodwalker!" he said loudly.

Howel and his scouts muscled us out the door and into the corridor. I dared a glance back over my shoulder before the doors swung closed; King Valien stood as stiff as stone, watching our exit with an intense, calculating stare.

My whole body buzzed with shock. Of course the reality of my sentence had been looming over me since we first entered the wood, but it had been distant, abstract. Even as we marched along the ridge after Howel, I knew what must eventually lie at the end of our journey. But hearing the king say it aloud, so absolutely, shook me from the inside out. First light! He hadn't even allowed me a whole day in prison. What on earth could I do in such a short period of time? I moved blindly along the path to the stairwell, following Howel into the deep, dank air of the dungeon.

When we reached the first block of cells, Jenë pushed forward through the other scouts to busy herself at my wrists. Howel and his scouts led Mona and her brothers further down the corridor.

"I'm sorry, Ellamae," she said when they were out of earshot. Her voice was tight with constricted emotion. "I wish I had known it was you. I wouldn't have signaled the others."

"You did your job, and you did it well. I'm proud of you. You're a good scout."

She loosened my bindings but didn't swing the door closed. I stood on the threshold of the cell, rubbing my wrists. She took a breath, glancing down the passageway.

"We won't let you be hanged. We won't let him."

I allowed a mirthless half-smile. "You and who else, Jenë? Who would risk the condemnation of the king for the sake of one disgraced Woodwalker?"

She blinked at me. "A lot of people, Ellamae. More than you might think. It wasn't popular with the Guard, what Vandalen did to you. You had the courage to voice what everyone else was thinking. You know Reuel Goldenseal resigned over it?"

Reuel, my grizzled old Woodwalker. I remembered his face close to mine as he had been forced to snip the insignia off my uniform. It had been tight, deeply furrowed. At the time, I thought he was disappointed in me. My breath caught in my throat. "He didn't."

"Yes, he did. The very day you were led away. Left Lampyrinae, walked away from it all. Almost forty years a Woodwalker, and he couldn't take it anymore." She glanced down the corridor again. "A lot of the others kept their positions but started stepping around their orders. Little things, you know, that nobody could *technically* punish them for."

"There's a stand of dead timber along Kingsfall Ridge," I said. "The ravine is wiped out."

"Well, yeah." She looked back to me. "Not everyone is as bold as you were."

"But what about now, under Valien?" I curled my fingers around one of the bars of the cell. "Obviously he's changed the order to shoot trespassers on sight. Hasn't he redacted some of his father's other orders?"

"Not yet." She picked morosely at her wrist guard. "We were all so relieved when he inherited the throne, after all Vandalen did to decimate the Wood Guard. You know Valien was well-liked as a prince. But suddenly, the crown and the court fell to him and . . . I don't know, Ellamae, he just vanished into the role. When he took the name Bluesmoke on his coronation, we all tried to find meaning in it; we hoped it meant he was as devoted to the mountains as the mist on the slopes, but as time went on . . ." She shook her head. "Now we say it's because he moves about in a cloud of smoke. No one can tell what his motives are."

"And the council?"

"Well, you saw how things went between them. You were right, you know, what you said to Hellebore. They're trying to usurp him, if they can manage it. I don't think they trust him to maintain his father's agenda, and there's never been a better time to begin a new line of monarchs."

"What about the Guard?" I asked. "Who do you side with?"

She flicked her eyes back down the corridor before inching closer to me and lowering her voice. "We have no idea. Some think Valien will be overthrown before the year is out. And then some of us . . . Ellamae, I think he's going after Lumen Lake again. He's doubled our watch over the lakeshore and has us report any irregularities in the Alcorans' pattern. But he's doing it independently of the council, like he doesn't want them to know."

"Would you follow him?" I asked. "If he moves the Guard against the lake, will you follow him?"

She opened and closed her mouth several times. "We'll have to," she said finally. "But I don't see how he thinks he'll be successful, or how it will help the Silverwood, unless he knows something we don't."

I leaned on the bars. "Maybe he does. He was a sneaky prince." I ran my fingers through my hair. "Though I suppose it doesn't matter for me at the moment."

She shook herself. "We won't let him go through with his father's sentence, Ellamae. No Silvern monarch has ordered the execution of a kinsman in over a hundred years. We won't stand for it."

Up the corridor, a faint jingle of keys sounded. Howel and his scouts were making their way back up the passage. I stepped into my cell and let Jenë close the door behind me.

As she fumbled to turn the lock, I grasped her arm.

"Before you go—our family. How are they? How are my brothers and sister? My parents?"

Her expression melted into sadness. She gripped me back. "They're fine. All fine. Seramae had another child, a daughter. Avamae. Your parents are well. They miss you, but they're well."

I exhaled. "Thanks."

She reached forward and pulled me by the shoulders against the bars, embracing me. I hugged her back, the cold metal biting into my chest and forehead. It was a sensation I remembered from my last stay in the king's prison, separated from the person I loved by a row of unforgiving iron.

She kissed my forehead and released me, dashing her thumb under her eyes. Howel reappeared with his scouts, hurrying past my cell. "Best not linger, Jenë."

"I know," she said, turning to follow him. "Hold on, Ellamae."

"Don't worry about me. Goodbye."

The Wood Guard filed silently up the corridor and disappeared up the staircase. The door on the landing swung closed with a metallic screech. The lock clicked into place. And then I was left with nothing but darkness, and silence, and my last word to Jenë echoing in my head.

CHAPTER 9

It's a cruel thing, time. Some days stretch into a thousand lifetimes, endless in their drudgery. Some flip over as quickly as the turn of a book page. And then some seem to do both at the same time, speeding you along faster than you can blink while still allowing you that slow, simmering dread deep in your stomach. I lay on the pallet in my prison cell, my hands folded on my chest, my eyes on the ceiling, living in that in-between time. The position, I eventually realized, I would probably be in when they nailed up my coffin.

After that I rolled onto my side.

I slept. What else could I do? I was bone-weary from the last few days, exhausted mentally and physically. I had already shaken the row of metal bars set into the stone, but they were solid, strong. Nothing that could be undone in the short handful of hours left to me. The three remaining walls were hewn out of the mountain itself, impenetrable to everything except the slow seep of water. I had pressed my face against the bars and called down the corridor, hoping one of the others might be within speaking distance. But the walls distorted my voice, and I couldn't make out the faint words that Mona called back to me.

And so I slept, desperately trying to shut out the passage of time. The cold crept in among the folds of my tunic, prodding me awake throughout the day. The guards had taken my cloak away with my other belongings, and I had thrown my useless boots in the corner. As the day waned, my limbs began to shiver and shake, cramped from being balled up so tightly against the chill.

Several times that day, the soft tread of feet marked the passing of the routine guard. I considered calling out to one, but I decided against it, recalling the good-natured rift between the Wood Guard and the Palace Guard. At this point, I doubted I could talk a Wood Guard into helping me, but a Palace Guard was even less likely. They would have no particular loyalty to me. Most of them hurried past my cell without looking in at me, and so I ignored them as well, until the metal slot at the foot of my door rattled. Wood scraped on stone as a tray bearing the evening meal was pushed into my cell.

I rolled over to see the prison guard straightening to continue down the corridor.

"Wait," I called to him. He hesitated, took a step

down the hall, and then turned back to me. He was young, unfamiliar to me. "What's going on upstairs?"

"I'm not sure."

"Are they building a scaffold?"

He paused. "Yes."

"Do you know my cousin Jenë? Jenë Junco?"

"I know who she is."

"Do you know what she's doing? Is she in the palace?"

He shook his head. "The king sent her out into the wood with a few others to call the rest of the Wood Guard back to Lampyrinae. She's out on the ridge, I imagine, or down on the slopes."

Earth and sky. I was sure she had been our chance for escape. My nerves, which had numbed somewhat, grew tense again. I pressed my head against the bars of my cell.

"Thank you," I said wearily.

He turned and took another few steps down the corridor. "Enjoy," he said over his shoulder.

It struck me as an odd thing to say, but he didn't turn around again. I dragged the tray to my side and lifted the heel of bread, my stomach growling, but I paused halfway to my mouth. On the tray where the bread had lain was a pat of sweet butter, a smear of thick jam, and, behold, a fried egg. Peeking into the accompanying mug, I found not water, but blackberry wine, of the kind we might drink at festivals. I craned my head against the bars to look back down the hallway, but the guard was gone. Did he himself prepare the meals for the prisoners? Or did someone else? I had a hard time believing the king had become so lavish in feeding his captives. With so little comfort left to me, I took it as the subtle message I hoped it was: that somewhere up above me, I had friends tiptoeing around their orders, still loyal to the cause we used to stand for before our way was made dark.

As the night grew deeper, marked only by the changing of the guardsman on patrol, I found I couldn't sleep anymore. I grew jumpy with anxiety and paced around my cell like a restless mountain cat. If I couldn't think of something, if I couldn't contrive some escape, I doubted any intervention on the part of my old friends could stop the council from following through on Vandalen's sentence. I tried the bars again, shaking them, searching them for places the water might have eaten away at the metal. I rattled the heavy lock on the door. I clambered up the bars, clinging like a tick, and poked my fingers in the spaces between the bars and the uneven ceiling. But there was no weakness, no give. I slid to the floor and rammed my shoulder in frustration several times against the door, but the only thing this achieved was to leave a long bruise blossoming on my arm.

Sometime past midnight, I was circling the small space, hoping some epiphany might strike my racing mind, when I heard the faintest sound up the corridor. Near-silent footfalls of soft-soled leather boots pattered swiftly toward my cell. But it wasn't time for the routine patrol. I stopped my pacing. A figure appeared like a specter at my door, swathed in a cloak, hidden behind the hood and mask of the Wood Guard uniform. He or she hesitated at my door just long enough to squeeze a shapeless bundle through the bars, and then they melted away like a wisp of mist.

I stood stock-still as the footsteps were swallowed up by the darkness, my eyes on the little bundle. And then I scrambled forward and tore it open. Two things: my silver compass. And a single key.

In half a minute, I stripped the laces from my ruined boots and tucked them with my compass down into my tunic. I thrust my arm through the bars of my cell, bending it awkwardly to reach the keyhole. There was a muffled click as the tumblers slid back, and the door drifted inward with a rusty creak. Without waiting a moment longer, I slipped out, locked the cell behind me, and stole barefoot down the corridor, my heart in my throat.

Mona was not asleep, her pale face wide with surprise in the lantern light. I opened her door and stepped back to allow her to join me in the corridor.

"How . . . ?"

"I don't know," I whispered back. "I don't know who it was, but someone's on our side. Come on, quiet as you can."

Colm was sitting up against his cell wall, but Arlen had to be shaken awake, flailing in surprise and letting out a squawk that we all shushed fiercely. I wondered if there would ever come a time when he would wake with more composure than a frightened toddler. But no one came running at the sound, and we all let out a collective breath. After locking his door behind him, I led them up through the corridor, the cold stone biting my feet.

We huddled at the base of the stairwell, listening for sounds of the guard.

"What do we do?" Mona whispered. "How do we get out? Is there a way that isn't watched?"

My mind whirled, muddled with anxiety. I tried to patch together my knowledge of the palace. I was only truly familiar with a handful of wings, and even some of them had been made vague by the passage of time.

"A few," I said. "Though it will be a job getting through the halls without being seen, and even harder getting across the courtyard to the front gate. And from there . . . we'll have to sneak down through the village . . ."

"One crisis at a time," said Colm.

I could have laughed aloud. "Yes. One at a time. All right. The closest exit onto the palace grounds is the terrace off the healing wing. Two floors up. Come on. Try to keep those boots quiet."

We crept up the stairs, pausing every now and then to listen. The way was silent, with no jingle of keys, no routine footsteps echoing down the stairwell. I was just blessing our benefactor for facilitating our escape in between the guard's patrol, when I realized I had forgotten the prison door on the landing. Surely it took a separate key from the cells themselves. But when we reached the door, we found it ajar. Of course. I pulled it open and led the others into the corridor beyond.

"Great Light!" Mona gasped. Slouched on the bench next to the door was the prison guard, his head lolling on his shoulder. His midnight meal sat half-eaten beside him.

"Poisoned?" she whispered, her fingers on her lips.

I waved my hand under his nose and then swilled his cup. "Asleep. Poppy, most likely. He'll have some pleasant dreams tonight."

"Great Light, Mae . . . someone has gone to an awful lot of trouble."

"I know." I started down the hall. "We'd better make the most of it."

We snuck through the halls, the crescent moon casting our dim shadows across the polished wooden floors. Each footfall from the Alastaires' boots sounded like a thunderclap to me, and several times I made them stop and shrink into a patch of shadows, sure someone could hear our progress. But no one appeared. No one called out. On we went.

I was familiar, at least, with this wing. Between my own inconsequential injuries and those sustained by my friends in the Guard over the years, I had spent a decent amount of time in the healing wing. After two more corridors and a short staircase, we arrived at a set of arched double doors, carved with a botanical motif.

"Okay," I whispered. "These doors lead to the antechamber. Past that is the healing hall; to the left is the door to the terrace. There are always people in the hall, so keep quiet." I thought of Otto sleeping in one of the beds, hopefully under some narcotic. I eased the heavy door open with the faintest creak and ushered the others inside. Across the room was another set of doors, slightly ajar. I led the way past these to the glass-paneled door off to the side; the flagstones of the terrace beyond shone pale in the moonlight. I placed my fingers on the handle, but it didn't budge.

"Locked?" I whispered aloud, pressing harder. "Locked! Why in the blue-eyed world would it be locked?" I wrung my hands at the handle, resisting the urge to kick the door. "Okay. All right, fine. The patio off the ballroom. Another floor up. Great Light, let's go."

"I can pick a lock," Arlen whispered.

Mona looked at him, surprised. "You can?"

"I need a knife or something, and a pin." He looked around. The antechamber was lined with shelves and baskets, bearing piles of linen, empty ointment jars, and bundles of herbs waiting to be sorted. I picked along one shelf until I found a case of knives used to prepare herbs. Near it was a box of straight pins. I handed these to Arlen, who knelt down at the door handle.

"I didn't know you could pick a lock," Mona said, watching him work with one eyebrow raised.

He looked a little sheepish, his eyes on his work. "That sword I told you I won in a tavern game?"

"Yes . . ."

"I didn't win it."

She managed to refrain from rebuking him, eyeing his progress with disapproval. He wiggled the tumblers with the pin, his tongue between his teeth. There were a few promising clicks.

"Damn," he said. "Slipped. Hang on . . ."

"Locked, is it?"

We whirled around. Arlen dropped the knife.

A figure stood in the doorway to the healing hall, gripping the frame. The moonlight lit up the white shift she wore.

I swallowed. "Deina."

"The narcotic Otto's on was making him sleepwalk," she said. "Made it halfway across the terrace before someone saw him hobbling away. So the healers locked the door."

Silence stretched between us. Her eyes flicked over the scene before her, her expression unreadable.

"They told me it was you," she said.

"I'm sorry about your knee," I said. "I didn't mean for anyone to get hurt."

"You ran the risk of doing a lot more damage than just a dislocated knee." She took a ginger step forward. "I should report you."

"Please, Deina. This is so much bigger than me.

We're not hurting anyone. We just want to get out of the palace, away from the Silverwood. I won't ever come back again."

"You'll never face justice for what you did."

"*Deina*," I said exasperatedly, nudging Arlen to get him to continue his work. "We're both Woodwalkers; we both believe in the same cause. I never abandoned our real mission."

"You did the moment you brought strangers among our own folk. You haven't been a Woodwalker in a long time, Ellamae."

She turned her head to the main doors and shouted in a voice to wake the dead. *"Palace Guard! Palace Guard to the healing wing! Prisoners on the run!"*

We collectively lunged away from the door, scrambling across the antechamber for the corridor. Deina limped after us, her shouts chasing us down the lofty hallway, magnified in the echoes bouncing off the walls. We ran flat out up the corridor and clattered around the far corner, passing a sleepy palace attendant hurrying to see what the noise was about. He turned in shock, watching us sprint past him, before adding his own cries to Deina's.

"Here, here, this way," I said breathlessly, flinging open a servants' door and pushing them inside. We thundered up the narrow flight of stairs, emerging— thankfully—near the ballroom. But as we turned down the corridor that would lead us to the patio, a mass of shadows played against the far wall, accompanied by the call of confused voices. We checked our flight and sprinted back in the opposite direction, rounding the corner just ahead of the knot of Guardsmen. We fled down the adjoining corridor, pursued by ringing voices. Somewhere, someone took up a horn call. I swore aloud.

"This way, this way." I stuffed the three ahead of me into a wide room used for musical performances for the king and his court. This room I'd only ever glanced in, but I knew where it must let out. We wove among the rows of chairs toward the far door. The room had only one window, a paneled glass circle set high in the wall, and the ambient light was barely enough to see by. We had almost reached the door when there was a terrific crash—Arlen had collided with an upright bass and sent it toppling into a stand of lap dulcimers. The resulting dissonance reverberated through the air like a peal of thunder.

"Run, run, to the right, Mona, the right!" We burst from the chamber into the far hallway, with voices echoing down every passage. Doors slammed, lantern light flared. I went from tracing a logical route to playing a desperate game of cat and mouse, dodging through whatever door seemed darkest and quietest. By now we were well out of my domain. I knew the public passages and a few well-known shortcuts, and I knew the Guard wing—the barracks, the mess hall, the target ranges, the sparring rings. But we weren't anywhere near there. My home was in the woods. I could move like mist through the woods. Here I moved like a bear in a potter's shop, disoriented, bewildered. The

Palace Guard knew where to cut us off and where my frantic route would lead us.

After three totally unfamiliar corridors and some kind of butler's pantry, we burst out into a hall I recognized as being near the council chamber. The corridor was lit by a great three-sided window at the far end, the pudge of a moon sitting exactly in the middle. We were close to the intersection with the next hallway when a voice rang out from around the corner.

"My king! We lost them near the map rooms, but we think they're heading this way . . ."

In the angled panes of the great window, I saw the reflection of King Valien striding up the hallway. The footfalls of guardsmen were running to meet him. In another few breaths, they would meet in the intersection directly in front of us. I shoved Colm against the wall in the shadow of a tall carved sculpture, flattening Mona and Arlen next to him. I crouched against the base of the sculpture, knowing that if the king and his guardsmen turned down this hallway, it would be over.

"Get to the armory!" The voice of the king was a snarl.

The footsteps clattered to a stop. Guardsmen began begging his pardon.

"I said, get to the armory! Great Light, do we want three armed Lake-folk running loose around the palace? Go secure the armory!"

"Yes, my king."

We held our breaths as the king stalked after them, his cloak billowing in his wake. His sword was drawn in his hand, white as a tooth in the moonlight.

He disappeared up the far hall after his guardsmen. We waited a minute longer, squashed together against the sculpture, until the sounds in the corridor died away. We let out a collective breath. I let my bare feet splay out into the hall, my knees shaky with relief.

"We're fortunate your king is an idiot," Mona said, her hand pressed to her heart.

"He's not my king," I murmured, my eyes closed against the press of our peril. I took another slow breath and then got to my feet. "All right. Let's take a moment." I covered my forehead with my palms. "They've covered the healing wing and the ballroom. I suspect they'll have blocked off the main gate. That leaves the wagoners' courtyard off the pantries and the feasting hall. The feasting hall is closer, but it's back toward the ballroom . . . I doubt the way is clear . . ."

"How high is the Firefall?" Colm asked.

I looked up at him, bemused. He was staring at the sculpture we had been sheltering behind. It was the tall, graceful carving of the waterfall, scattered with silver fireflies.

"How should I know? What does it matter?"

"How deep is the pool at the bottom?"

I opened my mouth to reply, and then his meaning hit me like a lightning bolt. "No, Colm, great earth and sky, no. Don't be stupid, I'm trying to think."

Mona's face widened with comprehension as she looked at the sculpture. She whirled on me. "How deep is the pool?"

I put up my hands. "I've got no idea, we don't go in it. It spills away down the mountainside; you'd get swept away . . ."

She ran her hand over the sculptor's depiction of the pool at the bottom, an artistic bowl of swirling wood. "Rocks?"

"I . . . yes . . . no . . . some, I don't know. Look, this is stupid, that's not a way out . . ."

"It is if you can swim," Mona said.

I looked between her and Colm, agape. "I *can't* swim."

"Where's the head? Off the western wings, isn't it?"

"Look, people have *died* in those cascades, they slip and get sucked in . . ."

"Where is the head?" She was silhouetted against the window, the moon crowning her hair.

"Near . . . near the library," I said weakly. "But, Mona . . ."

Somewhere up the hallway, a door slammed.

"I'll help you," said Colm. "I won't let you go."

"Your folk will have to follow on foot," Mona pressed. "Think of the distance we'll put between us and them. Tell me honestly—do you really think the three of us could outrun your kin in the dead of night?"

I stood before them, my stomach churning. Arlen jerked his head up the corridor. "Better make up your mind, quick."

"Great earth and sea and sky." I turned back down the passage, my heart wobbling with fright. We hurried through the corridors toward the library, a sprawling two-story hall with a massive staircase spiraling down to the floor below. As we ran, Colm drew up alongside me.

"Spoons," he said, cupping his hands. "Not forks." He splayed his fingers apart to demonstrate. "Stroke from your shoulder, not your elbow."

"Don't forget to kick your feet," said Arlen.

"Keep your chin tucked on the dive," added Mona.

"Pinch me when you need to come up for air," Colm said.

I thought of punching him instead.

We reached the library just as a knot of guardsmen rounded the far corner of the corridor. We scrambled through the doors, hearing them cry for the king. We sprinted across the balcony of shelves, swung onto the spiral staircase, and clattered down to the floor below. The guardsmen entered the library behind us, demanding we halt in the name of the king. We hit the polished floor and streaked across the great room while the staircase rattled with the footsteps of the guardsmen. I glanced over my shoulder and saw, at the head of the staircase, the king beginning his descent, his sword catching in the light.

We burst into the hall beyond, lit by the paned-glass doors leading out to the walkway over the falls. The thundering of the cascade echoed off the walls, growing louder as we approached the doors. The guards en-

tered the passage just as we pulled the doors open and
spilled out onto the walkway.

The cold stone stung my numb feet as we reached
the low wall at the head of the falls. The earth
dropped sickeningly away on the far side. The air was
filled with the roar of water, an angry, powerful force,
filling the night with foam and spray. I froze in place,
terrified.

Mona stepped up onto the wall. A thread of irony
prickled the haze of fright in my head—I thought back
to the walkwire over the ravine just a few days ago.
How afraid she had been, how at ease I was, simply because of the absence of water. How things had changed
now. Below her, like embers rising from a campfire,
swarmed hundreds of fireflies. Blinks of green, swoops
of yellow, drifts of cool, careless blue. I tried to slow
my breathing.

"I'll go first," said Mona. "Colm, you go next with
Mae. And then Arlen."

"Good luck," said Colm.

She bent at the knees, pointing her arms backward
and then in one decisive moment, she swung them
over her head, spurring her leap. Her body arched
gracefully in the night, and she disappeared into the
thundering spray.

I felt ready to vomit. Colm stepped up onto the
wall, pulling me up by my elbow. I swayed at the un-
hindered drop, the mists swirling like smoke in the
moonlight.

I looked up at him, trying to swallow down the fright in my throat. "Please help me not to die."

Behind us, the doors to the walkway burst open and the guardsmen swarmed out—Palace Guard, Wood Guard, and Armed Guard alike had been roused from the barracks. I looked back at the sea of familiar faces, parted from behind as the king urgently pushed his way to their forefront. He had a look of horror on his face. He flung out an arm as if to draw us back, but in that moment, Colm wrapped his arms around me, crushed me to his chest, and leaped from the ledge into the vast, empty air.

With my eyes squeezed shut and the unchanging roar of water filling my ears, I pretended for a brief moment that nothing at all was happening to me—I was simply suspended in a void, unmoving. I pressed my forehead against Colm's chest, twisting his tunic in my fists. He put one hand at the nape of my neck and pulled the other one away, stretching it above his head. I had just enough to time wonder if any new trees had fallen into the pool when we plunged into the churning water.

It was like being struck with a block of stone. The impact drove what meager breath I had managed to hold right out of my body. Water rushed into my nose and ears. The force of the current was astonishing, grinding us against the rocky bank like a carpenter might sand a piece of wood. We tumbled through the foam, my hands cramping around the fabric of Colm's tunic. We struck a log and I bounced away from him, biting down panic, but he reached out and closed his hand around my wrist, guiding my arm under his own. I regained my grip on the back of his collar.

By chance, the raging water tossed us up into the air. I was so shocked by this sudden change that I almost forgot to draw breath; I managed a ragged lungful before being plunged back under the surface. Colm was swimming now, moving in short, powerful bursts, directing us into the smoothest currents. We shot through the water, meeting several sickening drops as the cascade foamed away down the mountainside. I was getting ready to pinch his neck, my chest tightening on my meager supply of air, when the water seemed to slice down on top of us. A jumble of rocks grated along my back—we were down on the riverbed. And then, the most terrifying sensation.

We stopped.

Water poured down on top of us, pressing us into the riverbed, holding us in place. I panicked, let out my slip of air, thrashed against the press of Colm's body on top of mine. But he didn't lose his grip on me or his own composure. He gave a great push with his legs, forcing us out of the eddy. We shot to the surface and broke out into the stinging air.

I coughed and immediately sucked in a mouthful of water as we bobbed down the rapids. He put his hand under my chin and tilted my head back above the surface. I drew in great gulps of air as we swirled away downstream.

There was no distinguishing event in that harrowing flight—everything was a constant press of water and noise and darkness, broken only by the sudden drops in the rivercourse. I could feel the birth of a bruise in every collision with stone and wood. In the occasional break in turbulence, when we swirled into a basin, I could see Arlen and Mona, both alive, swimming with decisive, controlled strokes through the current. The fireflies along the banks swept by in streaks of light; the moon disappeared behind the ridge at our backs. After what seemed like a lifetime, the banks fell away on either side of us and the river widened into a shallow, rocky series of eddies. For the first time, Colm lifted his chest from the water and ground his feet against the pebbly bottom. He dragged us to a halt against the bole of a fallen sycamore, its bark worn smooth and slick by the current. Gently, he unclenched my hands, frozen into fists from the cold and dread, and draped me across the trunk.

"All right, Mae?" Arlen had one arm hooked around the trunk. He was grinning. "Kind of fun, isn't it?"

"I hope you choke," I gasped, clutching the tree before succumbing to my own curse.

Mona heaved herself out of the water and threw one leg over the trunk. Her hair had been pulled loose by the river and hung in a curtain down her back. "Well," she said, winding her shoulder. "That could have been a lot worse."

I wanted to give a scathing reply, but I couldn't deny that she was right. We had not been instantly killed in the dive, and we had not drowned in the perilous rapids churning down the mountain. We had put several miles between ourselves and the palace; the Wood Guard would have a hard time catching up with us even if they ran through the night. What's more, we had come to the very head of the Palisades. It would be much harder to track us over the expanse of solid rock now sweeping away on either side.

I edged along the sycamore for the shore, the current swirling around my waist. I could barely feel where I placed my feet on the rocky riverbed. Numb, battered, and stiff with cold, I crawled out of the river and collapsed against a protruding rock. Colm clambered out after me, sitting down an arm's length away.

"Colm," I said while Mona and Arlen made their way to the bank. "Thank you." I unfolded my palm where it lay on the ground.

"It's no more than what you did for me, Mae." He took off his boot and emptied the water out of it. "If everything somehow goes according to plan, if Alcoro is driven out and we survive it all, I'll teach you how to swim. It'll be a lot easier in the lake."

"Right now, I'm hoping I never have to set foot in water above my knees ever again."

"Well, we're back in your hands now," Mona said, wringing out her hair. She gestured to the field of rock sloping away from us, lit with the feeble morning light. "What now? How do we get down?"

I drew in a deep breath and exhaled all the fright and confusion of the palace and the river. The sheer cliffs of the Palisades would be nothing compared to what we had just gone through. I reached into my tunic, down where my belt cinched the fabric against my waist, and drew out my compass. Silently, I praised our anonymous benefactor for thinking to return this to me in my prison cell. But when I flipped it open, my heart dropped like a stone.

"No!"

Somewhere in the tumble down the mountainside, the glass face had cracked, and water had filled the cavity. Even as it seeped out, the needle hung limply off its peg, unmoving. Broken.

I cradled it in my hands, this last link to my former life, a little shard of my heart. I ran my thumbs against the etching inside the lid, the faint light glinting on the mirrored surface. Before I could stop myself, I snapped it shut and pressed it to my forehead, mourning the stupid piece of metal like the passing of a close friend.

"What happened?" Mona's voice was dry, unmoved. "Broken?"

I blew out a breath and tucked it back inside my tunic. "Broken, but not useless. It doesn't matter now. I can get us down the Palisades." Reluctantly, I uncurled my legs and stood. "We're at the crest, right before everything drops away. This first bit will be straightforward enough; the cliffs will be where it gets difficult."

"And I don't suppose there will be anything for breakfast . . ." Arlen said.

"I'll look, but I can't promise anything. We're just going to have to push through." I coiled up my wet hair at the back of my head, tying it up with one of the laces I had stripped from my boots. "I have a place in mind that we may be able to camp tonight; it's remote, and far from here, but it'll be sheltered, and we may be able to light a fire. We'll need it without our cloaks."

"We don't have a tinderbox," Arlen pointed out.

I patted my waist, where my compass rested. "I told you. Not useless." I took a few steps down the sloping rock. "Come on, let's go. The Wood Guard won't be wasting any time, and they're going to be hopping mad."

CHAPTER 10

We wound our way down the head of the Palisades, avoiding patches of moss and lichen that might give away our passage. Tussocks of grass clung to the slope, broken here and there by clumps of windblown trees. The Alastaires padded along silently behind me. They were weary, I knew, from the flight from Lampyrinae, but I led them on at a swift speed, anxious to get to the drop-off as soon as possible. Not because our way would get any easier, but because of what I hoped our arrival would do for them. As the pink in the sky was wiped away by a pale blue, we crested the head of the cliffs, and I stepped aside, turning back to watch the siblings as they joined me at the ledge.

It was like watching a sunrise. Mona halted in her tracks, her eyes sweeping the panorama before us. Her fingers clenched on the fabric of her trousers. She drew in a sharp breath. And then she swayed, pressing her palm to her chest. The morning light glanced off the tears in her eyes. Arlen came along beside her and draped his arm around her shoulders, his face split with an almost dreamy grin. I looked eagerly at Colm, who was standing just behind his brother's shoulder. He bore a slight smile, but he wasn't looking at the vast expanse of Lumen Lake spreading out before us. He was watching Mona and Arlen, warmed by their joy. My spirits dipped a little before I silently rebuked myself. Of course—he had told me his feelings about returning to the lake. This was not a relief for him. He flicked his gaze from his siblings to me, and for a brief moment I could read his expression. Gratitude and fulfillment, all shot through with sorrow.

A cloud seemed to pass over Mona's face, and I looked back down at the misty lake. I knew what she was seeing. Even at this early hour, the water was dotted with ships—ships that each bore a patch of russet on their masts. The flag of Alcoro, presiding over the divers working the pearl beds below. Mona dashed her thumbs under her eyes and turned to me with her chin lifted.

"How do we get down?"

"This way."

"As we get closer—won't we run the risk of being seen from the lake?"

"Not if we use the scout paths."

"Along the lake? You have scout paths along the lake?"

I grinned at her surprise. "Didn't know, did you?"

She pursed her lips but waved aside this information. "Won't your folk find it easier to pursue us if we take their path?"

"Yes. But there are several, you see, and we're taking one of the lesser-traveled ones. It bends north, a bit out of the way, but as I said, it will take us to a place we can shelter for the night, and it will allow us a stealthier approach along the lakeshore. Sound reasonable?"

She looked back down at the foreign ships patrolling her country. "Yes, good. I trust you."

I took one step down the slope, but paused as these words registered. I looked back over my shoulder. She shrugged. "I do. You've done a lot for us, Mae, far beyond what you originally agreed to."

"I agreed to get you through the Silverwood." I turned back to our path. "There have just been a few more twists and turns than we expected. Let's hope there aren't any more."

The sun cleared the tops of the mountains as we made our descent, banishing the last of the chill from the river. The mist on the lake burned away, the last shreds clinging stubbornly to the shadows of the islands. From our vantage point, we could see six of the twelve islands rising out of the lake. Mona named them as we worked our way down the path. Grayraen Island, the closest to Blackshell. Fourcolor Island, the largest and most populated, looming like a miniature mountain range. Betwixt Island, teardrop-shaped and sitting in the middle of all the others. Squat little Button Island, presiding over the Pink Beds. Tanglerib and Wilderdrift Islands, disappearing into the mists along the eastern shore.

At first, our path down the Palisades was reasonably wide and solid, worn into natural ledges in the rock as it zigzagged down the mountainside. But before long, it began to narrow and buckle, forcing us to edge sideways with our backs to the cliff, or else leap over empty spaces where the rock had slid away. By midday, the sun was hitting the Palisades in full force, sizzling wherever bare skin touched rock. I was glad I had never been able to buy new boots; the callouses on my feet left over from my worn-out soles were the only things keeping my skin from being rubbed raw.

Many of the creeks and springs that started in the heights of the mountains spilled down over the Palisades, creating strips of moss and grass. These were slippery, and made our way even more treacherous, but we were glad for them; without skins or canteens, we would have fallen prey to dehydration before the day was out if there hadn't been such an abundant supply of water. We slithered carefully across the smaller trickles and took our time traversing the larger cascades, letting the foaming water wash away the sweat clinging to our skin.

"How on earth did our folk manage to move trade goods up this?" Arlen asked after we had edged behind the curtain of a waterfall, the rocks slick with algae.

"There was a road, of course," I said. "Wide enough

for a cart, carved into the stone, connecting Blackshell to Lampyrinae. The monarchs let it fall into disrepair during the Silent War to discourage Lake-folk from assaulting Lampyrinae."

"An unnecessary move," Mona said. "Even with the road intact, we could never have moved any kind of force up the mountains. Your monarchs of the past were overcautious to the point of obsession."

"You built a wall," I pointed out, nodding down to the lake. The settlements scattered across the shore were becoming clearer, surrounding the sprawling wings of the palace, which was closed in by a curved wall.

"I'm thinking of fortifying it, too, if your folk have secret paths I don't know about."

"Well, wait until you're on the right side of it, at least," I said.

One cascade we came upon spilled into a surprise pool, wide and shallow and studded with water grasses. As we skirted around the edge, Arlen pointed out the yellow sunfish drifting among the weeds. I opened up my broken compass, tapped the cracked glass against a rock, and picked the needle out from the shards. Colm raked his fingers through the rich soil along the bank, producing several fat grubs, and using my needle as a hook and my spare bootlace as a line, the siblings set to work fishing the pool. Within fifteen minutes, the bank was lined with twitching sunfish. We strung these up on the bootlace and hung them from Colm's belt. This catch relieved me; it would have been a strain indeed to face a night with no meal after the nonstop events of the past few days. I only hoped I would be able to get a fire going, though I did not discount the option of eating raw fish rather than nothing.

By afternoon, the whisper of a path alternated with a series of hand- and footholds carved into the rock. We inched along these, setting our feet carefully. The cliff slanted back just slightly, so we had some purchase, but the wind was gusting up off the lake, first pressing us into the hot cliffs before drawing back without warning, leaving us clutching the narrow crevices.

"You call this a path?" Arlen howled, hugging the cliff.

"I told you," I called back, easing onto the narrow shelf jutting out of the rock. "We don't use this one much. Don't worry. This is the worst of it."

"It had damn well better be!"

I looked over my shoulder at him. "You jumped off a hundred-foot ledge last night."

"Into *water*!"

He had me there.

After several more precarious traverses, including a tense moment when the foothold Mona had her toe in crumbled away, the slope grew gentler and the path grew wider. We wobbled along, weary from the day of near misses and close calls. The late sun shot straight across the lake, turning the rock and water golden around us. We were picking our way over and through a great many waterfalls now, clambering over some and edging behind others. As we neared my intended campsite for the night, I heard Mona ask, "Colm?"

I turned back. Colm had stopped walking. He had a hand outstretched to the cascade we had just crossed and was letting the water splash against his palm and scatter in the air, catching the light in beads of gold.

"It's funny, don't you think, Mona?" he said quietly. "All our lives we looked up to these cliffs at sunset to see the light hit the waterfalls, and now here we are, among them as it's happening." He turned his palm over. "Seeing the Light from a different angle."

"Oh, wait until you see the cave," I said, beckoning. "Come on, it's best just before sunset."

The path bent around an outcropping and opened onto a crescent set into the cliff. A few gnarled trees guarded the fringes, and a waterfall curtained the far end, catching the sinking sunlight and scattering it throughout the cave in rainbow ribbons. The water itself glowed golden in the light.

I let the siblings stand and watch the spectacle as I gathered up a handful of twigs and grasses from around the roots of the trees. I shredded these into as fine a pile as I could and pulled my compass out of my tunic again. I flipped open the lid and positioned the mirrored surface over the ball of tinder, reflecting the sun's last light into the heart of the pile. The light was rapidly dying, and for a moment I worried it would be too weak to set the tinder alight, but after a minute of concentrating, a finger of smoke wound out of the dry grass. I blew gently, coaxing the meekest flame into existence, and then snatched my hand away as fire gobbled up the fuel. I fed it a handful of twigs before getting to my feet and gathering larger wood.

Colm saw what I was doing and came to help, sharpening a stick with a stone and spearing our catch of sunfish along the length. He propped it over the flames, and finally we sat along the cave ledge, our feet dangling over the sheer drop to the lakeshore, breathing easier than we had in days. Even King Valien's sharpest scouts would be hesitant to attempt the route we had traveled after nightfall. We were safe here. We had a fire going. We had a meal cooking. We had fuel and water to last us through the night. And so we sat, watching the melting sun turn the sky orange and pink and purple, the colors magnified in the waterfall streaming over the mouth of the cave.

As Colm reached over to turn the fish, he glanced up at the cave ceiling.

"What are *those*?" he asked.

I followed his gaze. "Oh, right. Sorry, I had forgotten, with everything else. Petroglyphs. Folk call this Scribble Cave."

Mona and Arlen turned, too, looking at the swath of cyphers carved into the slanted stone ceiling. In the flickering firelight, they seemed to waver, dancing first one way and then the other.

"What script is that?" Mona asked.

"No idea," I said. "They don't belong to our folk. I've heard they're similar to the ones in Alcoro that the

Prism carved. That's one of the reasons I decided to travel south when I was kicked out. I had this vague curiosity to see if it was true. Of course, I never made it to Callais, so I can't say whether they're similar. Hard to think how they could be, though, this being so far away, and so hard to get to."

Mona stood, craning her head in the firelight. "There are pictures, too."

"I know. Sort of a person, and something like the sun. Maybe someone wanted to say they came up here to watch the sunset, like we did."

"Seems like an awful lot of effort to say you watched a sunset," Arlen remarked. "Especially after making this climb."

Mona looked at the cyphers, her brow furrowed. A last finger of sunlight shot out over the far peaks, striking the waterfall in a blaze of red. She moved to the water and held her hand under it as Colm had done earlier, watching the light jump off her palm.

"Do you know what the hillwoman said to me that morning we woke up in her barn?" she asked.

We all looked up at her. I had to wrack my brain. Our journey through the hills of Winder seemed years ago.

"You mean Halle? With the lamb in the kitchen?" I strained my memory. "When did she speak to you?"

"You saw us by the stream house in the morning, remember? She came out to get milk while I was washing my hair in the creek. She saw my pearl pendant." She plucked the front of her shirt, frowning at its absence. "She guessed more than her husband did. Our colors, our route, and then a pearl—she knew we were heading to the lake."

"What did she say to you?"

"She said the Light is more than just how people revere it. It's more than a full moon, or a reflection on a waterfall. It exists beyond how we perceive it, and beyond how folk act on it." She flicked the water, sending droplets of light flying over the cliff. "In essence, she said not to let the actions of Alcoro rob me of my reverence for the Light. If I let that happen, she said, then I was only furthering their quest for dominance. I was letting them take something else away from me."

"And?" I said. "What was your reply?"

The sun slipped at last behind the distant peaks, and the waterfall lost its glow. She wiped her hand on her trousers. "I didn't have one, really. What could I say? That I deeply, vehemently, do not want anything to do with the Light, now or ever again? That it's an accident of our brains that we even acknowledge it as something divine?"

"A little heavy for a morning conversation," I said.

"Yes." She came back to the fire, settling down beside it. "Especially as half of it is just bluster, and the other half is stubbornness."

"You still feel drawn to the Light?" I asked, surprised.

"Of course I do. I can't get it to go away. Believe me, I've tried." She prodded the coals with a stick. "Round and round I go, wondering—do I believe what I feel, or believe what I think?"

I looked back out at the lake. The first stars were peeping down from the heavens. Fireflies. Some sadness stirred inside me, that this quiet divinity was such a sticking point for Mona. It must be hard, I thought, to be so unsure, especially for someone so confident in everything else. I gave a small sigh. "I don't know that anyone can answer that but you, Mona."

"No, you're right. In fact, I doubt whether I'll ever reach a point where I don't struggle with it anymore." She sighed and waved to the sizzling fish. "At least, not any time soon, and certainly not on an empty stomach. Are we ready to eat?"

Colm took the spit out of the flames and passed it around to the rest of us. We sat in silence for a moment, eating with great satisfaction, burning our fingers on smoky flakes of fish.

"Proof," Mona declared, "that the best meal is the one you have to work for."

"I don't know," I said. "I'm ready to have a meal I didn't scrounge up myself."

"We were served a meal in prison," Colm pointed out.

A laugh burst from me. "That's true." I remember the fried egg fondly. "A rare luxury."

Arlen sighed, picking a bone out of his teeth. "When everything is all settled, I'm going to spend a day lying in a real bed, eating handfuls of fried shiners."

"Is this before or after you win back Sorcha?" I asked.

He frowned. "I guess it should be after. Or during."

"I'm going to brush my hair," said Mona.

I snorted. "And what a relief that will be for the rest of us. It's offensive."

"I agree. If only I could disguise it as a bird's nest, like yours." She flicked a fishbone at me. "What are your grand plans, Mae, if it's not seeing to your personal hygiene?"

"I haven't decided yet," I said, brushing the bone over the cliff. "Maybe I'll go to Matariki and sail away south to Samna."

"Will you?" she asked, surprised.

"Well, I certainly can't go back to the Silverwood," I said. "Disregarding the fact that I'd be hanged on sight, I can't imagine I have many friends left anymore. Assaulting a scouting party, starting a rockslide, breaking three enemies of the country out of prison and rousing the entire Guard in the dead of night . . . I haven't exactly endeared myself to anyone."

"What about the man you were going to marry?" Colm asked.

"Marry?" Mona looked from him to me. "Someone was going to marry you?"

"Surprised, Mona?"

"I suppose that came out wrong." She even had the decency to flush slightly. "I mean to say, you mentioned a sweetheart once when we were in Poak, but you never said anything about being engaged . . ."

"No," I said. "Because it hasn't mattered. I told you before, that all got swept away with everything else."

"He could leave the mountains and join you," said Colm.

I gave a hollow laugh. "No."

"No? Why not?"

"Because he couldn't, that's why. He's got his own life in the mountains. A job to do, people who depend on him."

"You don't think he might find you more important?" he asked.

"No."

When the silence had gotten too thick, I glanced up to find him frowning at me. I waved a hand. "Look, it doesn't matter. It's over, it's done. If anything, our trip through the mountains made me realize that I can't keep holding on to my old life. I can't keep hoping I'll somehow magically be able to pick it all back up again. I can leave; I can go away and create something new somewhere else."

"You could stay in Lumen," said Mona.

I flicked a few fish scales off the rocks. "Right, and tiptoe around the water's edge in the shadow of the mountains?"

"We'll teach you how to swim," she said.

"Thank you, but no. We agreed on a payment, and that's all I need from you." I prodded the fire. "And anyway, if you're going to try to avoid confrontation with the Silverwood, harboring me won't do you any favors."

Stars were winking behind the clouds, glittering in the surface of the lake. I yawned and stretched out my sore limbs. "I don't know about you, but I'm going to sleep. I'm dead tired, and I didn't even do any swimming last night."

Mona sighed, her eyes on the lakeshore below. "Yes, I suppose we won't have a chance to rest again for a while."

We built up the fire, illuminating the petroglyphs carved into the stone, before settling down on the softest patches of rock we could find. I shifted against the layers of ache in my body, rolling from one side to the other. Finally, I curled up facing the fire before realizing that Colm was on the other side, staring absently at the flames. I realized we hadn't asked him what his first act would be upon freeing the lake. He looked past the fire to me, his eyes flickering in the light. The corner of his mouth twitched in a resigned smile. I gave what I hoped was an expression of kindness in return before rolling back to my other side. The shell of my compass slid inside my tunic, pressing into my skin, so I took it out. It rested wearily in my hand, empty of everything it used to hold.

With no direct sunlight and our fire burned down to ashes, the following morning was watery and cold. We had very little to do—no gear to pack, no breakfast to eat, no skins to fill—so we took turns washing up in the curtain of water spilling over the edge of the cave.

As I sat next to the waterfall, rinsing off the tender spots on my feet, I heard Colm call, "Shall we keep these, Mae?"

I turned to see him holding up the bootlace and bent compass needle we had used to catch the sunfish. I went back to my feet. "Might as well. I'll put them in my compass." I checked over several suspect hot spots on the pads of my toes, hoping they wouldn't blister before the day was out, and laved my face and neck before tying back my hair.

"Where on the lakeshore does your path bring us?" Mona asked, her gaze on the lake. Below us, the Alcoran ships had already taken to the water. At this distance, we could see the individual pinpoints of divers breaking the surface with their catches.

I joined her at the ledge and pointed. "A little ways outside the outer settlement. It won't take us long to get to the first houses once we reach the shore. At least, as long we don't have to hide from Alcorans."

"I doubt they'll have much presence on the eastern shore," she said grimly. "There's no path away from the lake that way. I imagine they'll have concentrated most of their forces around the mouth of the river, to block off any attempted escapes down the waterways."

"All the better for us," I said, scattering the remnants of our fire and picking up my compass. "As long as nothing unexpected happens, we should make it down before dusk. Are we ready to go? Where's Colm?"

Arlen jerked his thumb to the far side of the ledge. "Around the corner."

We waited a moment, but when Colm didn't reappear, I made my way around the outcropping of rock that walled off the cave.

"Colm," I called. "Are you decent?"

There was no answer. I stuck my head around the bend. Colm was leaning against the rock face, staring up the path we had come down the day before with a furrowed brow. His arms were crossed over his chest, and he had the knuckles of one hand pressed against his lips.

"Colm? What's wrong?"

With no real urgency, he pushed himself away from the wall. Without meeting my eyes, he swerved around me, making back for the ledge to join the others. "I'm not sure yet, Mae."

I stood for a moment, bewildered. What had just happened? Was this part of his reluctance to return to the lake? Today was the day we would rejoin his folk, after all. Had the reality finally hit him? Or was there something else bothering him? He seemed perfectly fine just a few minutes ago.

"Mae?" Mona called.

Confused, I headed back around the outcropping. She was standing expectantly at the far end of the ledge. Colm stood at the lip, gazing out at the lake. I hurried past him and took my place in front of the others, leading the way down the rocky path.

For most of the day, we didn't have much opportunity to speak. While the way was less precarious than the day before, the wind swirled up from the lake, filling our ears with white noise and tugging at our feet as we set them carefully along the path. The rock grew sandier, sometimes crumbling away if we stepped too close to the edge. But we made steady progress, and by midday, the slope had taken on a gentler grade. Trees sprung up along the path. In the afternoon, we came upon a wide patch of woodland strawberries, and we spent fifteen minutes on the ground eating handfuls of the jewel-bright fruits. Colm didn't speak during this time, nor did he catch my eye, so it was impossible for me to determine what was truly bothering him.

I admit it set me a bit on edge.

In the rich light of afternoon, we emerged at last from the shadowy trees to see Lumen Lake spreading away before us. From this low vantage point, the islands soared into the sky, mirroring the mountains slopes we had just descended. Mona drew in a slow breath and walked to the water's edge, crouched down, and sank her hands beneath the surface. She raised them, dripping, and pressed them to her face. As we joined her, she did something wholly unexpected. Slowly, she stood and turned to me. For a wild moment, I thought she was going to embrace me, but instead she placed her hands on my shoulders. Her eyes were a good eight inches above mine.

"Thank you, Mae," she said as I jerked backward in surprise. "I admit it was desperate, the hope I placed in you. There were times I questioned whether or not I had made the right decision. But you've done it, despite everything we encountered. I am so grateful to you."

I flapped my hands, trying to wave her away. "It . . . it was nothing, Mona . . ."

"It was not nothing," she said.

I slouched out of her grip. "We made an agreement, that's all. I'm just glad we're all still alive." I glanced at Colm with a half-grin. "Although you certainly put me to the test."

He didn't return my smile, nor did he share his siblings' easy peace. He cleared his throat. "Perhaps you should go now, Mae."

For a brief moment, the only sound was the water lapping softly at the shore. My heartbeat doubled, but I couldn't think of what to say. I couldn't leave now. Things weren't finished. What did he know that I was missing?

Mona saved me, turning to him with her eyebrows raised. "Don't be silly. She can't go back through the Silverwood with Lampyrinae in an uproar, and she won't be able to make her way south until Alcoro is driven out. And anyway, we still have to pay her. Don't worry, Colm. She'll be safe."

But as she turned away to start down the lakeshore, I caught the expression on Colm's face, and I got the feeling that my safety was not exactly what was on his mind.

There was, in fact, an Alcoran presence in the eastern settlement, but it was sparse, and focused inward, not out along the lakeshore. Under the cover of darkness, we slipped by the occasional sentry, weaving carefully among the sturdy stone houses. The bark of a dog made us screech to a halt, but he was tethered outside a chicken coop, not trotting by an Alcoran's side, and he quieted after we hurried past him. Mona seemed to have a destination in mind, leading us purposefully down the silent roadways. As we skirted around the common green, Arlen grasped Mona by the elbow, stopping her in her tracks.

"Look," he whispered, nodding to the green.

The faint moonlight shone down on a thick pole set into the ground. A whipping post. Mona seethed through her teeth. "If I never meet King Celeno face to face, he will be undeservedly lucky."

We snuck through the town toward the lakeshore. "Folk get quiet early, do they?" I whispered. Flickers of light shone through the cracks in some windows, but there was no noise, no murmuring voices or easy laughter.

"I expect they're under a curfew," Mona said.

We passed what must have been a tavern, its windows boarded up. Beyond this lay a house butting right up against the water. Scattered about the yard were the ribs of half-built boats and piles of wooden planks. A workshop near the water housed shadowy bundles of tools and hardware. We waited a moment in the shadow of the tavern to be sure there was no one about, and then we slunk forward, stepping carefully over the work spread across the yard. We piled onto the doorstep. I edged behind Colm and Arlen, letting them take their places behind their sister. Mona drew herself up to her full height, lifted her hand, and rapped softly on the door.

There was a scrape from inside, as if someone had pushed a chair back, and a murmur of voices, followed by the creak and snap of a door. After a few seconds of silence, footsteps approached the front door. The handle turned. A warm slit of light appeared as the door was cracked open.

"Yes?" asked a hoarse voice.

"Good evening, Cavan," said Mona.

There was a pause, and then the door opened wide, silhouetting a stoop-shouldered man. His eyes swept over the three Alastaires, ragged, dirty, and cloakless, packed onto his threshold.

"Great blessed Light," he whispered.

CHAPTER 11

He hurried us inside, closing the door and snapping the bolt into place as soon as I passed over the threshold. And then he turned, gripping his chest, his eyes wide.

"Great blessed Light," he said again.

"Thank you, Cavan," said Mona.

He dropped to his knees at her feet. He reached forward for her cloak hem, but finding none, he pressed his own fingers to his lips instead. "My queen." His voice was thick with emotion, and he looked up first to her and then her brothers. "My lord Colm . . . Lord Arlen."

"Please get up," said Mona gently. "We need your help, and we have very little time."

He rose slowly to his feet, his astonished gaze sweeping back and forth between the three of them. I stayed pressed into the stone wall in the lee of Arlen's shadow, feeling out of place. I glanced around the room in an effort to occupy my eyes. Above me, the rafters rose in pleasant arches to support a rush roof. A string of mussel shells gleamed in the window, their pearly insides reflecting the firelight. Sitting in front of the fireplace was a knotty wooden table bearing the signs of after-dinner routine: a slate with wobbly letters written out in chalk, three mugs half-filled with tea, and a smattering of boat plans sketched out in charcoal.

There was the faintest creak, and through a far door, I saw a small red head peep into the room before a hand jumped out and dragged him back. Cavan turned to the door, dashing his thumbs below his eyes. "Come out, Ena. Come out, Brieg." He pushed the door open to reveal a young boy being clutched by his mother.

"The queen has returned to us, Ena. The rumors were true all along. The Alastaires did escape."

"Great Light . . ." The woman strode forward, clutching her son's hand, and dropped at Mona's feet as her husband had done. "I knew it, Lady Queen, I knew it wasn't you they killed that day. I was there on the terrace at Blackshell." She clasped Mona's hand in her own, her eyes shining. "Oh, thank goodness. You do not know what this means."

Colm was standing rigid with his back to me; I touched his elbow gently. He drew it away and moved aside. I was washed suddenly in candlelight.

"A mossgrubber, Mama," said the boy, pointing at me.

His parents' eyes fell on me with surprise, and his mother's hand jumped to cover his mouth. Before they could decide how most politely to inquire what I was doing in the present company, Mona drew me forward. "This is Mae, our guide. She has led us from the eastern coast through the Silverwood Mountains in safety." She glanced sidelong at me with a hint of a smile. "Mostly in safety. We've had a few close calls. It has not been the easiest of journeys."

"Sit, sit, sit," said Ena, sweeping the table clear. "Brieg, fill the kettle, love."

"Where is Ula, Cavan?" asked Mona as she took a seat at the table.

A shadow passed over his face. "Alive," he said, pulling a heavy wooden chest alongside the table to serve as an extra chair. "She's out on Button Island. The Alcorans have reconfigured all the settlements on the lakeshore and the islands. They split up families by ability, you see. Most of the craftsmen and laborers are here, along the shore. All the best divers are kept out on the islands, except for the few kept on shore to dive the Moon Beds. Ula was taken out when she turned fourteen to dive the Pink Beds."

"Have you seen her since then?" Mona asked, her eyes sharp in the candlelight.

"The Alcorans allow us three visits a year," he said heavily. "It's how they keep most of us in line. Each family has a different date, so we're not all mingling together at the same time. That's what Betwixt Island is used for these days. A meeting place for families. If we get unruly, they begin taking away our visits. It's been quite effective," he said, glancing to be sure that Brieg was fetching water and out of earshot. "They haven't had to beat anyone for quite some time. At least not in this village. I suppose it could be much worse."

Mona closed her fist on the table. "Well, it's over now. Tomorrow we're going to drive the Alcorans out."

"Tomorrow?"

"It has to be tomorrow," she said. "There's a fleet of ships heading for the lake with news of our return, and they could very well be here the day after tomorrow. We must act while we have the chance."

"How?" asked Ena, setting the kettle Brieg handed her over the fire. "The Alcorans are scattered throughout the islands and the lakeshore. Their captain is based in Blackshell, and he keeps the wall well-guarded. They've taken our bows and swords. I doubt we could create an uprising they couldn't stamp out."

"I have a feeling we can," she said. "But we don't have time to explain our plan many times over. Who can we gather here, right now, who can help us? We need several swift swimmers, and any other boatmen within reach."

Cavan rose from the table. "I'll go to Doane's house, just up the track, and have him send his sons out to the right families. We can probably convene here in an hour or so."

"I don't want to put you at risk," Mona said, watching him fetch his cloak.

"The Alcorans don't usually patrol for very long. They like their rest, and we have become a very docile people."

In the time that Cavan was gone, Ena filled the Alastaires in on the changes that had taken place in Lumen, all the while throwing her cupboards wide and preparing nearly every item she pulled out. In between plates of biscuits, jars of apple butter, wheels of cheese, and about a dozen varieties of fish, she informed Mona that singing had been banned on the lake. The Alcorans, she told us, were concerned that folk might use their age-old tradition of spreading song across the water to communicate and unite. Which was nonsense, of course, she said, but it had served to isolate folk even further. As she chopped handfuls of scallions to add to a simmering pot, she described the schedule of a typical day. Folk were expected to have finished their breakfasts and be at their work by the time the sun cleared the tops of the mountains. The divers were taken out onto the lake in one of the nine ships that patrolled the channels, and they stayed out on the lake until close to sundown.

"There's no joy in it anymore," Ena said, throwing a handful of carrots into the soup pot. Mona had already assured her that she didn't need to prepare any more food, but I got the feeling it was helping her channel her nervous energy. "There's no camaraderie in it, no beauty in the process. It's all about quantity. Especially prolific folk might earn an extra visit with their families. Slower folk may lose a day, or get removed from the islands altogether and placed in another trade. Woe be to us who are not among the most skilled; we aren't allowed to dive at all. But, as Cavan said, I suppose it could be worse. They're not especially cruel, the Alcorans, not after those first few months. There were beatings, and a handful of executions, but only as many as were needed to tamp down an uprising. The need for violence mostly dissipated once they scattered us throughout the islands."

"What about overharvesting?" asked Arlen. "Surely the Alcorans don't know how to manage the beds, if they're making folk dive for quantity."

"Oh, no. They've been extremely strategic about this whole thing. This invasion wasn't some lark the Alcoran king decided on one day—they had been planning this for years. They kept all the old advisors to manage the beds. Several of them refused to cooperate, of course, but after the captain executed the lead advisor, they became more compliant."

"They executed Cora?" Mona said sharply.

"They did. She held out to the very end—absolutely refused to cooperate with them. It was inspiring, but ultimately . . ." She gave a sad shrug. "People have families. Nobody wants to lose their life. And if we had let them ravage our beds, what would we do then? We can't make our livelihoods with any of our other resources. In the end, it made more sense to cooperate."

Mona started to ask another question, but she

was interrupted by a sharp series of footsteps on the stoop. The door flew with a clatter. We tensed, but it wasn't an Alcoran watchman on the step. In rushed a strawberry-haired girl, her round face streaked with tears.

"Oh!" she cried, flinging herself toward the table. We jerked out of her way as she fell at Arlen's feet. "Oh, oh, oh!" she gasped, clasping his hands against her heaving chest. "Oh, my lord Arlen!" She clambered up his tunic, clutched his collar, and crushed her lips against his.

Mona pressed her palms over her mouth as if trying to forcibly hold in her laughter. I met her eyes across the table and mouthed, *Sorcha?* She nodded, shaking with suppressed mirth. Arlen, eyes wide, face pale under his freckles, was leaning so far back in his chair that Colm's hand on the back was the only thing keeping him from toppling over.

"We counted you as dead!" Sorcha cried, hanging off his neck. "Oh, how we mourned you!"

He might have given some croak of a response, but it was difficult to tell under her sobbing. Colm glanced at Mona, his face edged with the faintest smile. When he saw me fighting my own grin, though, he looked quickly back to the line of people now filing into the room.

The Lake-folk greeted their queen with deferred astonishment. Some kissed her hand, others knelt at her knee. Colm stood to return his own greetings, clasping the forearms of some and holding the hands of others as they knelt before him. Some turned to greet Arlen, but he couldn't seem to disentangle himself from Sorcha's keening, his arms held up in the air as if trying to avoid touching a hot skillet.

Cavan returned not long afterward with several more folk in tow. It was a constant stream of greetings and tears, and I had to admire Mona's perseverance. She held herself with stately poise, listening intently to each and every person, a gentle smile on her face. After another wave of newcomers squeezed into Cavan's home, I gave up my seat on the chest, retreating to sit on the windowsill near the corner. Several people did double-takes when they saw me, but if anyone had questions, they kept them to themselves.

An hour after Cavan left to spread the word of our arrival, every corner of his home was packed with people. The fire had been doused in an attempt to keep down the heat in the room since we didn't dare open the windows. Every flat surface was serving as a chair, and folk were squeezed into doorframes and stacked on the ladder leaning against the rafters. Cavan laid several wooden planks across crates of potatoes to create a row of makeshift benches. Sorcha was kneeling at Arlen's side, stroking his hand while he stared ahead with a bewildered, unfocused gaze.

"Well," said Mona, looking around the room. "Here we are. Thank you all for coming here. I know it's a risk for you and your families, but if we're fortunate, by this time tomorrow, you won't have to worry about the Alcorans any longer."

"Hear, hear," someone called from the hearth.

"I regret that it took us this long to return to you," she said. "We escaped down the southern waterways after the initial invasion but found we couldn't make our way back through the Silverwood. We were at a loss until we met Mae Hawkmoth, a former citizen of the Silverwood and opponent of the monarchy of Lampyrinae." She gestured to me in the corner, and every eye turned my way. I gave a miniscule wave, my cheeks hot. "She guided us through the Silverwood at great risk to herself and brought us to the lakeshore in safety this very day.

"But the details of our journey don't matter for the moment. All that matters now are the next twenty-four hours. Who can tell me what the security is like on the islands?"

"The divers live in common houses," said one woman next to the fireplace. "The entrances to those are watched through the night. But there are no sentries on the shores themselves."

"Is there a way an outsider could communicate with those inside?" Mona asked.

"Perhaps through a window," said an older man. "I used to dive until they decided I was too slow. When I lived there, the windows were barred, and the Alcorans checked them regularly to be sure no one was working on filing through them. But the shutters open. A careful person might be able to talk to someone inside without having to get near the sentries."

"It's doable," said a man squeezed in one of the

doorways. "That's how my wife and I said our marriage vows."

"But, my queen," said the first woman hesitantly. "I doubt we can get to all of them in the same night. There are at least a dozen on Fourcolor alone, and there's even one all the way out in Glider's Bay . . ."

"We don't need to get to all of them," said Mona. "We only need to get to nine of them—one for each Alcoran ship. I'm trusting the word will spread among our folk if we can get it to the right people first. But tell me." She looked at Cavan. "There are no boatmen on the islands? No dockbuilders?"

"No," said Cavan. "They bring us over to do repairs as needed."

"Do you bring your tools with you?"

"Oh, no. There are supply sheds with lumber and tools so the jobs go quickly. They don't like us lingering away from our assigned settlements for long. Harder to keep track of us."

"Excellent. Now, the lakeshore. What's the security like here?"

"Here in the outer settlements, it's not so tight," said Ena. "But Blackshell is the hub for everything. They receive reports on all the activity on the lake and the shore throughout the day. If anything seems amiss, they're quick to investigate it. One time a handful of divers started brawling with the Alcoran shipmen, and the whole lot of them were cuffed and brought to different whipping posts within a half an hour."

Mona frowned. "That's no good. We can't have them catching on too quickly to what's happening."

No, indeed, I thought.

"So we need some kind of distraction," said Cavan. "Something to occupy the captain and his soldiers in Blackshell."

"We could stir up some kind of trouble," said a boy perched on the top of the ladder. "Pick a fight, or start a fire or something."

"That wouldn't distract the captain, though," said Cavan. "He would just send out a few of his officers. We need something out of the ordinary. Something he'll think is worth his own time."

Throughout the conversation, I'd been examining my own plans in my head—plans that had seemed so straightforward in the tavern in Tiktika. If Mona's strategy failed, my own aspirations wouldn't be worth a pile of dust. All my efforts over the past few weeks would be for nothing.

I wasn't quite done with the Alastaires.

"What about an ambassador from the Silverwood?" I asked from the corner.

The room went dead quiet. Every head once again turned toward me. Colm met my eyes in full for the first time that day, his brow furrowed. I tried to speak around the dryness in my throat. "Someone he thinks has come to parley with him?"

Mona pursed her lips, but it wasn't in disapproval. "Helping us carry out our plan was never part of your original agreement, Mae. I hesitate to ask you to enter a fight that's not your own. But I won't deny that it may be exactly what we need for this to succeed."

"I beg your pardon," said Ena carefully, addressing me as if I was one of the royals, "but you don't quite look the part."

"No," I admitted, glancing down at my scuffed feet. "I'll need a change of clothes and a cloak. Green would be best."

"But even then, you'll look more like a civilian than one of Valien's officials," Arlen said.

"I think I can get around that," I said. "Does anyone have some kind of fancy jeweled piece? A signet ring, or an heirloom cloak pin? Something that could be counted as a royal token?"

"The Alcorans stripped us of most of our personal pearls," said Ena, rising from the table. "But some of us managed to hide a few oddments." She disappeared into one of the back rooms, squeezing past the press of people in the doorway.

"Mae."

It was the first time since the lakeshore Colm had spoken to me. He was frowning at me, but it was more in puzzlement than anger.

"Why are you doing this?" he finally asked.

I shrugged. "I told you before. I want new boots."

"Even with a green cloak and some kind of token," Mona said quietly, "this is still a huge risk for you to undertake. What if the Alcorans see through you, and hand you over to Valien?"

"Come now, Mona," I said with mock bravado. "Where's all that faith in my skills you had a little while ago?"

"Dodging scouts and saving lives, yes. Lying convincingly in a room full of hostile officials . . ."

"I'll give it my best shot," I assured her.

The group in Cavan's house dispersed in the darkest part of the night. Each person slipped off to see to their own appointed task, even if that was simply going back to sleep and pretending nothing out of the ordinary was taking place. Sorcha lingered at Arlen's side with pretty tears in her eyes, pleading for him to stay safe.

I made my own departure clothed in a jumble of strangers' garments. Ena's heirloom ring, set with a rich brown pearl, clicked against the inside of my compass. Mona had wanted to embroider the emblem of Lampyrinae on the heavy cloak around my shoulders, but there hadn't been time. As I stepped across the boatyard, a figure melted out of the darkness of the workshop. It was Colm, checking the warp on an atlatl he had unearthed. He stopped when he saw me.

"Good luck, Colm," I said.

"Thank you," he replied.

I swallowed and turned away from the workshop, picking across the yard. I made it to the main track before he spoke again.

"You, too."

The Alcoran sentries on the Blackshell wall were blind as moles and dumber than a box of rocks. I practically had to stomp right up to the gate before they noticed me. It was only then, with a clatter of crossbows and swords, they scrambled from their posts and shouted for me to halt in the name of King Celeno Tezozomoc of Alcoro. Before I had time to bluster about being a messenger from Valien, they crushed my arms in their fists and dragged me through the gates. The hard-soled boots I had borrowed from Cavan's daughter Ula were too tight and inflexible as stone, weighing down my feet. I stumbled along between the sentries as they directed me without mercy into the arched halls of Blackshell.

Ambassador. I'm an ambassador.

"Excuse me!" I spluttered, trying to muster a dignified tone. What would Mona say? "Unhand me at once!"

Clearly I didn't have the same effect. They ignored me, although they did allow me to at least get my feet under myself.

Despite my anxiety, I managed a few glances around Blackshell Palace as we moved down the halls. It was not nearly as lofty as Lampyrinae, but it was built from lighter-colored fieldstone and lined with of mother-of-pearl tiles on the walls and floors, their iridescent sheen reflecting the afternoon light. Being tucked down out of gusting mountain winds, it could allow more extravagant windows, affording views of the lake at every turn. At the moment, the few visible ships out on the water were drifting peacefully, with no sign of any disturbance. I glanced at the sun, hoping my timing was right.

"This way." The Alcoran to my left steered me through a wide passage that ended in a set of double doors, blocked by two more sentries. They stared at me as their comrades led me to the door. Cavan's forest green tunic was too long for me, hastily hemmed and taken in by Ena and a few others swift with a needle and thread. Mona had smoothed my hair and plaited it into a neat braid—more official, she said, than my usual "shapeless nest." But despite all this, I knew I still looked like a simple wanderer. It wasn't helping my nerves—so much was riding on this exchange. I lifted my chin and returned the sentries' gaze, hoping I looked as though I knew exactly what I was doing.

One of my escorts rapped on the doors. At a vague word from inside, she pushed it open and dragged me over the threshold.

The captain glanced up from a table spread with documents, pausing his quill midword. Beyond him was a curved wall of windows opening out onto the lake. Below this was a wide terrace running down to the water. The place, I could only assume, where Alcoro had announced their sovereignty by executing Colm's wife. I worked to keep my eyes on the captain.

The point of the quarrel loaded into the crossbow at my back nudged me forward. I took a few steps into the room, rubbing the place where the sentries had gripped me. The captain set his quill carefully in the inkwell and straightened.

"What do we have here?"

"A spy, Captain," said the woman to my right. "A Silvern, sneaking around the periphery of our battlements."

"I'm not a spy," I said. *Ambassador.* I drew myself up. "And I certainly wasn't sneaking. I was seeking a way in, to find someone of office to whom I could give my news."

He towered over me like a turret, his mouth framed by a dark goatee and mustache. "And what news is that?"

"An arrangement. A treaty," I said, "from King Valien of Lampyrinae."

There were a few seconds of silence. He regarded me, his gaze openly skeptical. "You are not dressed like an official messenger from the king."

"No," I agreed. "We thought it too risky for me to appear in uniform. If things had already gone ill for you here, our hope was that I could appear to the Lumeni citizens as merely a wayward Silvern, and not the king's emissary. But I do have this token." I held out my silver compass. He eyed it, uncomprehending. I clicked the latch and it flipped open, revealing Ena's ring.

He frowned at me, almost quirking an eyebrow in disbelief. "This isn't a token. This could be anything."

"But it's not." I positioned my compass so the light fell across the words engraved inside the mirrored lid.

Valien Redhand, son of Vandalen Warbird, Crown of Lampyrinae

The captain squinted at it, as if trying to detect a forgery. I kept my hand as steady as I could; I wasn't sure if he was aware of our naming customs and would know that the prince had taken a new name upon his coronation. After a few moments, he looked back up at me. "Why did you think things might be going ill for us, and what does it matter to your king? We haven't heard from the Silverwood since Vandalen tried and failed to overthrow us last year. What could his son possibly want?"

I moved to the lakeside windows with as much authority as I could. I heard the sentries twitch, but they didn't jump to restrain me. "It's quite an impressive operation you have here, Captain," I said, gazing out at the water. "How many ships in your fleet? How many soldiers on each to control the Lake-folk?"

He moved to the wall and jerked on the curtain pull, swinging the drapes closed and shrouding the view of the lake. "I will not have you spying on my methods and reporting them back to your king. You claim to have a message from the Silverwood. Are you here with a purpose, or not?"

I turned to him, regarding him with surprise. "Haven't you heard the news?"

"What news?"

"The news of the monarchy of Lumen Lake. Queen Mona Alastaire and her brothers. They've been found.

They're alive. And they're returning here to reclaim their throne."

At this, the captain's eyebrows snapped down like a trap closing on a mouse. "What nonsense is this? The Alastaires were killed in our victory three years ago."

I shook my head. "We thought so, too. Everyone did. No one had any doubts. King Vandalen would not have attempted his assault if he thought there might be a chance of their survival. He would have sought them out and used them to barter with you. But we've all been fooled. The Alastaires escaped on the day of your victory."

"We captured and killed the queen. We executed her here on this very terrace. Lake-folk were present; they watched, they cried out. They recognized her."

"They recognized her, but she wasn't their queen. I imagine they cried out because you were murdering one of their own, and because you were in the process of taking more lives up and down the lakeshore. But they weren't mourning the queen. Besides that, did you never stop to wonder what had become of the two men? The queen's brothers—you didn't capture them that day."

"The queen—the woman we executed—told us we had killed them," said the captain with some aggravation. "She was distraught over their deaths. When they were not counted among the living, we assumed she had told the truth."

From beyond the door filtered the sound of hurried footsteps, followed by a wave of anxious voices. I jumped to assuage his doubt.

"You've been tricked, Captain. The Lumenis may be a quiet people, but they're not simple. Of course they wouldn't reveal to you that the woman you killed wasn't their queen."

The captain waved his hand. "This is utter foolishness. What proof do you have that they're alive?"

Someone pounded on the door, his shout muffled by the thick wood. The captain turned in that direction.

"The proof of our own eyes and a good measure of common sense, Captain," I said quickly. "Three travelers were intercepted in the Silverwood two nights past. Three Lake-folk—a woman with long, golden hair, and two men, one bearded, one with a curved scar under his eye. The woman bore a large pearl pendant. The youngest, a finely made atlatl."

He halted his progress to the door and turned to regard me. The sentries with us in the room shifted, giving each other sidelong glances. The pounding continued from outside.

"You're lying," he said finally. "This is a lie concocted by your folk to continue Vandalen's effort to destabilize us."

"And how would we follow through with this lie, Captain? I assure you, King Valien would only risk sending an ambassador if he was sure you'd believe him."

"Then prove it. Where are they? Locked up, I hope?"

"Ah." I shifted and rubbed the back of my neck. "Unfortunately not. I regret to say they managed to escape the mountains."

"*What?*"

"They'd been following a watercourse that flowed from the high ridge. When our scouts surrounded them, they escaped into the river. All the waterways in the mountains are treacherous, and we couldn't follow them that way. They, perhaps, are cunning enough water-folk to survive that route, but we're not, and we were forced to follow on foot."

His brows knit together. "Then they could already be here." After voicing this thought, his head swiveled back to the door. The person on the far side was still shouting.

"Perhaps," I said. "In which case, we both must make some hefty decisions very quickly. I'm here to tell you that King Valien has decided to diverge from his father's failed conquest. He knows there's more to gain from an alliance with Alcoro, both for your folk and ours. If we open up our tradeways to you once again, you'll be able to spread your influence along the eastern coast, which, if I'm not mistaken, King Celeno has been itching to do for some time. But if Mona retakes the crown, you can be sure she won't trade with either of us."

"She'll have to trade with someone."

"It's my king's assumption that she'll trade with Cyprien. She'll undermine your presence there until you're driven out, and she'll make that nation great once again by allowing them to channel Lumen's wealth to Matariki and beyond. The Silverwood and Alcoro will never see another pearl again. Where will that leave your Seventh King, Captain, if he can't uphold the prophecy of your Prism?"

"She can't overthrow us," he argued. "What power does she have to do so? She has no army. We've stripped the Lake-folk of their weaponry. We've separated and scattered the few warriors among them. We would crush her attempt before it could begin." He waved his hand in disgust. "And anyway, you're still offering me no proof your story is true. The Alastaires escaped your folk, you say? How convenient!"

The handle rattled and the door was thrown open. *"Captain,"* gasped a sentry, striding unbidden into the room. He rushed to the wall of windows and jerked back the drapes. "The folk of the lake are revolting!"

The captain swiveled his glare not to the window, but to me. I raised an eyebrow. His jaw worked for a moment, and then he stalked to see for himself. I joined him.

The situation on the lake was only just becoming apparent. In fact, at first, there appeared to be nothing wrong. But then, slowly, it became clear—the smooth surface of the lake was rising up against the hulls of the ships scattered across the water. Bit by bit, they slipped down, their masts sinking toward the surface. Tiny, frantic figures ran to and fro on the decks before starting their abandonment. The water was soon full of bobbing heads.

The captain's face was morphing from confusion to horror. "What in the *name of the Light . . .*"

"Didn't I say?" I asked, trying to put a touch of fear in my voice—which wasn't difficult, given my own nervousness. "We discovered the Alastaires in the forest because we heard them talking amongst themselves, discussing their strategy. Augers. They dove under your ships and drilled through the hulls with augers."

"That's not *possible.*" But he didn't need to see me gesture out the window to be assured that it was, in fact, extremely possible.

"I suspect most Lake-folk are skilled woodworkers, with their docks and boats," I said. "They don't have an army, no, but they have a legion of folk who can operate underwater for a staggering amount of time. All they needed was a clever leader to unite them. A nation of quiet, strong, dedicated swimmers, and you, Captain, you and your king have managed to make them very, very angry."

He whirled on his sentry. "What of the other ships?" he demanded. "On the far side of Fourcolor, down by Wilderdrift? Tell me they are sound!"

"I doubt Queen Mona is one to leave things half-done," I said, still trying to sound convincingly anxious. I needed him to trust me enough to be on my side—just for a few minutes. "At least, not if the tales of her reign are true. I would wager your other ships are faring no better than the ones you see here."

His eyes swept back to the spectacle unfolding

before us. Fair heads were popping up out of the water, swimming with strong strokes toward the shore.

"So," I said. "What happens to us now? Your closest warships are days away in the Cypri waterways. By the time they get here, I suspect the Lake-folk will have chained off the mouth of the river. They'll set fire to your ships as they bottle up in the water. I imagine they'll devise some creative death for you, Captain, and they'll adorn their pearl beds with your body as a trophy."

I gestured to the windows as he fixed me with a venomous look. "Unless they're stopped."

Horns were blowing on the shore, but there was nothing the Alcorans could do with the few skiffs they had left in the docks. Several soldiers were already racing up the hillside, preparing to burst into the captain's chamber to beg him for orders.

I made a show of craning my head to peer down the lakeshore. "It appears Queen Mona has already rallied a great deal of her folk from where you've scattered them across the islands, and I expect she herself will come ashore momentarily. One can only guess her next move, but if they choose to storm Blackshell, you're going to be outnumbered."

The captain stared stonily out the windows at the growing chaos below. I pressed on.

"But my king is prepared to come to your aid, Captain. He mobilized his Armed Guard as soon as we realized who the Alastaires were and where they were heading. At this moment, they'll be less an hour's march from your mountainside gates. And if you agree to his terms, I'll open the gates to him, and he'll send his army into the grounds. He'll fight Mona's uprising, and I expect the battle will be short. After that, it's only a matter of settling the most decisive method of execution for the Lumeni monarchy."

The captain dragged his eyes away from the lake. By this point, all that could be seen were masts sticking out of the water like teeth. "In exchange, I suppose, for control of the lake?" he snapped.

"Oh, no. Not control," I said, waving a hand. "You've done an admirable job of that already. For a trade agreement. Seventy-five percent of the wealth of Lumen must be sent through the reestablished tradeways in the Silverwood, to be taxed by the king. And you must agree to a representation of Wood-folk in your governing of the lake."

Folk were starting to come ashore, rising out of the water clutching various tools as weaponry. Many had antique atlatls—as we watched, one chubby woman flung a dart at an Alcoran hurriedly loading his crossbow. He crumpled to the ground. The captain ground his teeth, clenching his white-knuckled hands by his sides.

"Time grows short, Captain," I said with an edge of panic in my voice. "Think. Think of your prophecy. Prosperity and wealth for the nation of Alcoro. Perhaps the words of your Prism are simply playing out differently than you anticipated."

His eyes bored into mine, creased in outrage. "We send thirty percent of our wealth through the mountains."

"Seventy."

"Thirty-five."

"Sixty-five."

"Forty."

"Sixty, and no lower," I said firmly. "Remember, King Valien is being generous in allowing your flag to continue flying. He could instead sweep in and kill every one of you, Lumen and Alcoro combined."

His jaw worked. Lake-folk were striding out of the water in droves.

"Fine," he spat. "Fine, very well. In this hour, yes, I concede—though you may expect to hear from King Celeno. He will be furious."

"King Valien welcomes his discourse," I said.

"I suppose we shall draft some agreement?" he asked.

"Yes. When the job is done, he'll sign and seal the document. Now, though, I don't think we have time for such niceties." I waved hurriedly to the window. "We need to open the gates and signal my king—and quickly, before the Lake-folk have time to organize themselves." I gestured to one of the guards who had brought me in, standing baffled and slack-jawed by the door. "If you give me your key, it will look less suspicious."

It was a blatant lie, and I worried someone would surely see through it. But I seemed to have overwhelmed the captain enough for him to suspend his scrutiny. He waved his hand to the guard in a short, aggrieved movement. The guard obediently unhooked his keys from his belt and handed them to me, thunderstruck.

"You are a skillful wordsmith," the captain said viciously. "Your king chose a cunning pawn."

"A talent that has served me well." I held up my palm in thanks. "I thank you, Captain. I'll return soon with the Royal Guard behind me. In the meantime, if I were you, I'd acquiesce to Queen Mona, assuming you don't want to be publicly executed."

I turned and made for the door under the captain's furious glare. I walked steadily past his guards and out into the corridor. I held my head high until I turned the corner, and then I stuffed the keys in my pocket.

I ran.

CHAPTER 12

I ran down the staircase leading out to the terrace, pounding across the flagstones with my heart in my throat. Up and down the shore, Lake-folk were emerging from the water, soaking wet and fierce in victory. Many were towing half-drowned Alcorans, bound at the wrists, but as I looked out at the surface of the lake, I knew many more had been left to thrash in the water, not nearly adept enough to swim the distance to the shore. My stomach gave an unexpected churn; I knew the helpless terror of drowning, and no skilled water-folk would be coming to the aid of the Alcorans now panicking in the water. I swallowed down the sudden wave of nausea and looked among the fair heads for Mona's.

She was striding purposefully up the bank, shedding water and clutching an auger in her hand. Her face blazed with ferocity. "Well?" she said breathlessly.

I looked over my shoulder; we were hidden from the captain's bank of windows by the growing crowd. "It worked," I said, turning back to her. "He listened. I think I've convinced him to surrender for the moment."

" 'For the moment'?"

"At least until you can get his stragglers bound," I said. "Though if he suspects a double-cross, he may begin to fight back."

"Then we must move swiftly." She pointed to a handful of sinewy divers. Some clutched augers, others had atlatls. One had a grain sickle. "Bring the captain and his men to me. Bind their hands and take any weapons they have."

"And your work?" I said as the divers ran to do her bidding. I gazed out at the nubs of masts sticking out of the water. "It looks like everything went as planned?"

"Nearly. One of Doane's sons was caught on Wilderdrift as he tried to relay his message to the divers in the common houses. He pretended he was just trying to visit a lover, but they bound him and took him away. Regardless, enough people got the word in time. We put twelve holes in each ship more or less simultaneously. Folk drilled in pairs to keep it constant. I think one crew noticed what was happening early on, but they were around the bend of Betwixt Island and couldn't signal to anyone else. And there's not much one can do to stop a drill from the outside when you're on the inside. Good luck is with us today."

Her eyes narrowed as she spoke, her gaze over my shoulder. The divers she had sent appeared on the staircase to the terrace restraining the captain and his soldiers. As she strode to meet them, Arlen appeared at my side, clutching an Alcoran sword in one hand. He was grinning.

"Put their tails between their legs, did you, Mae?" he said.

"I hope so. Where's Colm?"

"Lining up the captives." He nodded across the terrace, where Colm and several others were securing the Alcorans who had been dragged from the water.

The divers reached Mona with the bound captain and kicked at the back of his knees to make him kneel. He stared up at her with a face lined with resentment. Lake-folk were swarming up onto the grounds of Blackshell. Somewhere in the crowd, someone lifted her voice in song, and without warning, a hundred other voices joined hers. Some folk wept, embracing family and friends they had been sundered from for years. Others cheered, lifting children up on shoulders. Only those of us close enough to the terrace could hear what Mona was saying to the captain.

"Do you know what you did here?" she asked him dangerously. "Do you know what you did here at my lake, and here on this terrace?"

"You don't know what authority you're challenging," the captain replied forcefully. "You think this feeble show will halt the prophecy of the Seventh King?"

"I recognize no authority before me," she said. "You and your folk are misguided, a nation of fools, and your king is chief among them. You have no divine mission. You are base, and cruel, and corrupt. I should do to you what you did to one of my folk here on this terrace, and I should let her husband do it to you." She straightened, her mouth twisted in rage. "But I don't think I will. You have suffered a great deal of loss in a very short time. Half your folk have already lost their lives to the lake you tried to steal from me. I think I shall send you back to your king with the responsibility for this day resting squarely on your shoulders. I sincerely hope the rumors of his temper are true."

The captain found my face in the crowd, and I could see the gears turning in his head, slowly coming to the conclusion that he had been double-crossed. I tried not to grin. His eyes kindled with fury.

At that moment, a shout rang out, and a quarrel struck the ground near Mona's feet, shattering on the flagstones. Arlen leaped forward and dragged Mona away as another quarrel sliced through the air.

"No . . ."

Too late, I realized the handful of Alcoran sentries who had been brought out with the captain were not all that had been in the palace. They had taken up positions in the windows of Blackshell, their crossbows resting on the sills. In the sudden threat, people began shouting; folk surged this way and that, unsure of which direction led to safety. Several more quarrels whistled through the air. Someone screamed in pain.

As panic flared, the Alcoran captain lunged forward, slamming bodily into Arlen. The sword he had been holding clanged to the ground, and the captain fell on it, drawing the bindings on his wrists along the blade. Over his shoulder, I could see one of the sentries hurrying among her now abandoned folk, cutting their ropes as well. Things began tilting toward chaos.

Mona did not succumb to it.

She shouted for order among her divers, rallying them together and sending them back among the captives, halting the efforts to liberate them. Colm streaked for the palace, atlatl in hand, calling a handful of his folk to join him in taking down the crossbowmen in the windows. Arlen dove forward and wrestled the captain away from the sword, landing several solid punches on the man's jaw.

But before the battle could gain any direction, a distinct shout broke through the mess of noise. Cavan and several other Lake-folk were struggling through the surging crowds, their faces lit with alarm.

"My queen!" he yelled to Mona. He staggered through a swirling knot of his own folk. "My queen!" He flung out his arm, pointing toward the mountains. "Coming out of the woods . . . Wood-folk. The Silverwood army. Swordsmen and archers, and their king at the head!"

Mona's face visibly paled as she turned toward the wall. "The gate . . ."

"Locked. But if they scale it . . ."

"They will not!" she snarled. She raised her voice into the din. "Atlatls to me! Atlatls to the wall!" She turned and streaked away up the grounds, and a string of her folk disentangled themselves from the fray. I followed, dodging the masses of Lake-folk running haphazardly across the grounds, either heading to join the fight or retreating to seek safety. I thundered across the footbridge leading to the wall, my hard soles driving each impact up my spine. Mona was running for the track leading to the main gate, her swath of makeshift archers following at her heels. She turned to direct them into formation, and seeing me in their wake, she stopped and called out.

"Mae, tell me! Your folk—will they attempt to scale the gate or break it down?"

My heart raged in my chest as I ran toward her. She watched my approach, waiting for my response. But instead of joining her, I swerved around her.

"Mae?"

I didn't check my speed; I didn't turn to face her. I put my head down and bolted for the gate. My heart was in my throat—everything was falling apart, right now at the moment of truth.

"*Mae!*" she screamed.

There was no time to explain—things were moving too fast, much faster than I had anticipated. I lunged for the set of locks, fumbling for the keys the Alcoran guard had given me. I thrust them into the keyholes, turning them one by one, and then hauled at the beam laying across the doors. It rolled to the ground, nearly smashing my toes. I grabbed the iron handle and dragged at the massive gate.

The gates swung open and over the threshold strode

King Valien, his sword drawn and blazing in the dying afternoon sun. Mona was roaring for reformation of her warriors, but before they could find new positions, the scene was laid bare before her: wave upon wave of the Armed Guard poured through the gates with swords drawn. Behind them came the Wood Guard, their arrows nocked to their strings. I scrambled out of their way.

Over the heads of my folk, I could see Mona flying back toward the palace with her flimsy front of warriors, desperately searching for better ground. Valien's soldiers began fanning out; the Lake-folk fled at their approach, streaming back to the lake. But the throngs of Lumeni citizens closer to the water were confused, calling for family members, rushing this way and that, obstructing each other's retreat.

A shout rose from the terrace, and I saw the Alcoran captain on his feet. He drew a sword and rushed in among the terrified Lake-folk. My stomach turned over. What had happened to Arlen? I looked up at the windows of the palace. What had happened to Colm? Too fast—things were happening too fast. The confusion turned to panic; screams swirled into the sky. The freed Alcoran captives were spreading out along the lakeshore to prevent Mona's folk from escaping into the water. I streaked back across the footbridge, toward the shoreline, following the rush of my folk as they bore down on the lake.

Oh Light, oh Light, oh Light. . .

It wasn't supposed to happen this way.

The first wave of Silverwood soldiers broke upon the surging masses of Lake-folk. The screams doubled; folk scattered like dust to all corners of the palace grounds, dragging loved ones, clutching children. The high walls circling Blackshell cut off their retreat, but Valien's forces didn't pursue them, heading only for the great terrace. By that point I could see little else, so frenzied was the crush of bodies around me, the scores of soldiers pressing the embroilment toward the lake.

I did not know which way to turn, did not even know which way was up, until the crowd began to split, to fall away. Valien's forces had reached Mona, and they were ringing her with weapons drawn, pressing back the crowds of citizens. She looked like a cornered wildcat, bent in a half-crouch as she cradled Arlen, his face covered in blood. Her eyes whipped around the ring of her enemies, her face black with rage, until she lighted on me. She seethed with fury.

"Planned this from the get-go, have you?" she asked acidly.

Before I could answer, a scuffle broke through to my left. A cluster of Valien's swordsmen were grappling with the Alcoran captain, who was still shouting orders to his soldiers up until the moment the Wood-folk forced him to his knees, his arms behind his back. He looked around with wild eyes.

I was standing just inside the ring of the Royal Guard. I hadn't meant to be there, in that empty space, surrounded on all sides by stares both hostile and surprised. I thought perhaps I could back away, edge out of this mess, but just as I started to shift my feet, a ripple parted the crowd directly behind Mona and Arlen. There were a few hoarse shouts, a flurry of re-organization, and then a quick, decisive movement. The red sun flashed off the dart as it flew through the air. I was nothing more than a dangerous target at that point. A threat. A bear, bluffing.

It was a good hit, considering the distance and press of soldiers, driving into my collarbone as the barbed head found its mark. He had probably been hoping for a true shot, through the chest and slightly to the left, but the crush of people had thrown off his aim. I stumbled backward, more in surprise than from the force, and sat down hard in the dirt. Across the ring, Silverwood soldiers wrestled Colm to the ground, flat on his face, his arms bent behind his back.

I reached up vaguely and touched my chest, the pain beginning to register as blood spilled freely down my tunic. As my heart pounded, the sensation grew from a sting to a hot, wrenching burn, spreading like flames licking parchment; my head throbbed with dizziness. I looked up at the ring of hostile faces, three nations present, three monarchies represented. Dozens upon dozens of people, their eyes bearing down on me like wolves around a kill. In that moment, I could only assume that every single one of them counted me their enemy.

All except one.

I crumpled backward but didn't hit the dirt. An arm wound around my back, keeping me from falling. The

Silverwood king's face swam over my own, his mossy eyes wide.

"Sorry, Val," I said. "I think I made a mess."

He was pressing a cloth to my collar, trying to staunch the bleeding. My blood trickled over the scars on his hand. "You were fantastic, Ellamae," he said firmly. "You were great."

"There wasn't supposed to be a battle."

"I have a mind to keep it going, if you're going to be killed by a Lumeni prince."

I fluttered a hand. "Don't be an idiot. Earth and sky, just finish it."

He took my hand and clamped it firmly over the cloth at my collar. "Don't you dare bleed out." He beckoned to someone behind me, and another set of arms took his place. As he got to his feet, I looked down at the hands holding me.

"Hi, Jenë."

"I can't *believe* you two, Ellamae."

King Valien strode across the ring, his sword bare in his hand. Mona watched his approach with a face like thunder. Arlen's head lolled against her shoulder, staining her sleeve with blood. Colm's face was pressed into the packed dirt, his broad shoulders held down by six Royal Guardsmen.

"Going to kill me yourself, Valien?" Mona asked loudly. "Not going to have your serpent do it for you, like everything else?"

The king didn't answer right away. He lifted his sword, placed the blade in his palm, and then lowered it to the ground, sinking to one knee in the process. His head level with Mona's, he pushed his sword toward her, out of his own reach.

"Let it be known to the citizens of Alcoro, Lumen Lake, and the Silverwood that I pledge my sword in alliance between the monarchies of the lake and the mountains." His voice was steady, strong enough to carry into the perplexed crowd. He reached into his collar and pulled out a chain, lifting it over his head. "And I make a vow of goodwill, in recompense for the years of animosity between our two nations." He rested Mona's royal pearl pendant on top of his sword.

Her eyes flicked between the two items at her knees and his face, and I knew her mind was whirling, trying to detect the hidden motive, the newest double-cross. Arlen gave a groan, and King Valien beckoned at his ranks of soldiers. "Medic."

Someone scurried forward with a kit, producing a clean cloth and salve, and busied herself in front of Arlen. Mona still didn't take her eyes off of Valien.

"And let him up," the king said, nodding to his Guardsmen holding Colm down. Then he looked toward the knot of soldiers holding the Alcoran captain. "Have you bound his hands?"

"Yes, my king."

"Good." He turned back to Mona, still on bended knee. "I offer you a representation of my Guardsmen to assist you in escorting the Alcoran presence out of Lumen, if you desire it. I also offer you the support of my banner should they attempt retaliation for the reclamation of your throne."

She regarded him, her eyes narrowed. Beside her, Colm picked himself up off the ground, his cheek and nose roughed and dirty. He didn't get to his feet, but rather sat down facing Mona, his gaze fixed on her, intensely ignoring every other facet of the present scenario. It was an odd sight; four royals crouched on the ground, ringed by a throng all trying to peek over each other's shoulders to get a better look.

"In exchange for what?" Mona finally asked icily.

"In exchange for your alliance, and for your assistance in planning and rebuilding the tradeways through the Silverwood. Queen Mona, let us become the crowned heads who bring back prosperity to our nations and the eastern ports. Let us be the ones who lift our countries out of the shadow of war that has settled among us.

"Let us outshine the false glare of the Alcoran prophecy."

They were good words. He had always been good with words. The crowd was silent and still, even the Alcoran captain, who seemed to be processing what exactly had gone wrong for him. Mona was rigid, her arms around Arlen, her head crowned with her shining hair. She looked past Valien to me, and I was not surprised at all to feel her anger still radiating in my direction. Finally, she turned to Colm. A moment of silence passed between them, some nonverbal debate, and then he looked away. I couldn't see the expression on his face. In truth, I was starting to have trouble seeing anything at all. My hand was cramping on the cloth at my collar, now saturated and seeping blood down my front.

In a slow movement, Mona faced Valien once more.

"I accept," she said.

The tension in the crowd seemed to relax, and a flurry of whispers took to the air like butterflies as word passed back through the throng.

She pointed at the Alcoran captain. "Get him and his folk out of my country."

Valien rose to his feet. The captain began to shout protests, but I couldn't quite understand what he was saying. I settled back against Jenë—she was talking, too, everyone seemed to be talking, why on earth was everyone talking? What did it matter? The faces in the crowd blurred together, and the last thing I saw was Val half-turning in my direction before I sighed in irritation and gave in to the empty light pressing down on me.

CHAPTER 13

*"**M**y king, the royals of Lumen Lake are not dead as we assumed. And it's only a matter of time before our enemies find out as well."*

Normally when Val and I met during my exile, we spent our precious days out in the hills, hidden from prying eyes. But on that late winter night, sleet drove from the sky in sheets, forcing us into a seedy tavern in Rósmarie. Val was tense, drumming his fingers against the table, a nervous habit he had never been able to break. I hated doing this to him—it wasn't often we were able to meet like this, and our time together was always too short. No doubt he had been hoping to find some solace away from a court still reeling from Vandalen's death. And here I was, dumping this monumental news into his lap. But it couldn't be helped. Mona's reappearance could change everything—for good or bad.

Val regained some measure of control over his hand, tightening it into a fist. "Well," he said. "We must do something about it." Unable to help himself, he rapped his knuckles on the table. "And stop saying *my king.*"

I smiled under my hood. "But you are. Finally."

"Officially, no, I'm not. You're still banished. And I spent the whole journey here determined to bring you back home."

"You can't. Not now."

"I'm the damn king, I can do whatever I want." His voice was bleak under its bluster.

"Val, if you reinstate me, the council will be at your throat. They know you never supported your father's agenda. They'll be looking for any excuse to supplant you with someone more willing to follow their lead. You need time. You need to assert your position over them. You need the Royal Guard back on your side."

"Bringing you back will do that, Ellamae."

"Not if the council still has the power to exile folk who disagree with them. The Guard won't know who to be loyal to."

He pressed his palms to his face. "And I suppose Queen Mona Alastaire will fix that."

"I haven't worked out all the details," I said. "But if you help her retake her throne, you'll forge an alliance even the council wouldn't dare challenge. If you can open trade through the mountains again, trade we can regulate and monitor, you'll turn the Wood Guard back into what they're meant to be—stewards of the mountains, not armed infantry. You'll secure your place over the council *and* unite the Guard."

He pinched the bridge of his blunt nose. "Not if I have to spend the lives of my soldiers to help Mona overthrow King Celeno."

"I don't think you'll have to, Val. I heard her laying into her younger brother in Sunmarten after he shouted out their identities. She was railing about how they'll never get back to the lake if people suspect who they are, how everything they've worked for won't matter. They *want* to go back, they're *trying* to go back. They must have some kind of plan."

He blew out a breath and lowered his hands to the table. "So, what, I send a delegation to Sunmarten to formally approach her? Offer to escort her through the mountains and help her retake her throne?"

I raised my eyebrow at him.

"No," he agreed. "That's a stupid idea. The council would have me ousted by breakfast."

"And she would never trust you," I said. "Lumen Lake and the Silverwood have been enemies for almost two centuries. She'll know your father was killed trying to wrest her country from the Alcorans—the news was all over Sunmarten. She'll never believe you suddenly want to help her, rather than use her as some kind of leverage."

He held his scarred palm over the burning stub of a candle beside us. "So . . . what? If we can't approach her, and we can't let the council catch on . . . what, we have to somehow get her and her brothers through the mountains in secret? I can't order the Wood Guard to turn a blind eye to them bungling their way through."

"No," I said. "They'd have to stay hidden from the scouts."

He snorted. "Ellamae, you're insulting your own office. You're the sharpest Woodwalker since old Nell Foxtail; do you really think . . ." He stopped midword. He stared at me. His palm drifted down toward the candle flame, close enough to be scorched by its heat.

"Stop that," I said, flicking his hand away from the flame.

"You can't," he said. "Great Light, Ellamae, I won't let you."

"Like I'll let you let me."

"I'm . . . the king."

I dropped my chin onto my fist, smirking. "Not my king."

He mouthed wordlessly for a moment and then grasped my free hand in both of his. "You'll be caught! What if you're caught?"

"You just said I was the sharpest Woodwalker since Foxtail."

"Dragging a couple of water-brained divers through the mountains—an uppity queen, no less! You think the scouts would miss your passage? You'll be caught and brought in front of the council, and what will I do then?"

I shrugged. "Dunno. Improvise?"

"They'll execute you!"

"Then I'll fulfill a lifelong dream, and punch Hellebore in the face while they get the rope ready."

I shouldn't have been teasing him; I could tell he was ready to fly apart with anxiety. He lifted my hand and lowered his forehead against it. The pearl on my ring pressed into his skin. I shifted, sliding my fingers from his grip, and cupped his face.

"Val, listen to me. I haven't seen my family in five years. I miss my friends. I miss the mountains. I miss dancing, and the fireflies, and stupid things, like my old boots. I miss you. Great Light, Val, I miss you so much." I swallowed. "I want to come home. But I can't until your council stops tearing apart the Royal Guard and respects you as their king. And now that we have the chance to make that happen . . . I can't just sit by and let that chance disappear." I ran my thumb over his cheek. "Let me help make you my king."

He closed his gray-green eyes, resting his hand over mine on his cheek. He blew out a long breath. "I don't like it."

"I'm not asking you to like it."

He leaned his cheek into the press of my hand. "How will you do it? Mona won't trust you if she thinks you're loyal to me."

"Well, for starters . . ." I drew my hand away from his face and slid the ring off my finger. "Probably not a good idea to be wearing an heirloom of the Silverwood monarchy." I placed it in his scarred palm.

He stared at it, dejected.

"What?" I asked.

He ran his thumb over the pearl. "I'm just worried you won't want me to give it back."

"Don't be dramatic."

"Ellamae, this, all of this . . ." He gestured from my ragged cloak to my worn-out shoes. "This is my fault. And now you're having to risk even more for my sake."

"Excuse you," I said. "Don't be so pompous. This isn't your fault. I shouted down your father, and it was because he was destroying the Silverwood, not because he wouldn't let us get married." I closed his hand over my ring. "I promise you can give it back when this is all over."

He sighed. "It still doesn't solve the problem. How will you get Mona to trust you?"

"I don't know. Throw myself in the ocean?"

"Don't joke about it."

"Sorry." I squeezed his hand. "I'll think of something. Don't worry."

He blew an uneasy puff of air at the candle, making the flame jump. "Oh, Ellamae. If only."

The healers must have had me on something, some sedative or soporific—I was too fuzzy-headed to fathom what—because the memory of my meeting with Valien in Rósmarie was as vivid as the night it happened. Other distant memories slipped in among it, with flickers of Mona and her brothers peppered throughout in places they shouldn't be—Arlen handing me bandages as I dressed Val's burned palm, Mona standing matter-of-factly over Val's shoulder as he asked me, stupidly, foolishly, to marry him. Colm, watching impassively from the courtyard while Vandalen and his council reduced me to nothing.

Every now and again, a murmur of voices trickled through my head, prodding at my consciousness. I didn't have the presence of mind to know if this was part of my drugged dreams or not. I didn't fully surface back to reality until a thin shred of pain accompanied the sounds of conversation. By the time I latched on to lucidity, the voices had died away. But the other sensations didn't. The scent of lavender. The soft weight of a blanket. The press of light behind my eyelids. And weaving throughout it all, the sharp sizzle at my collarbone.

I opened a groggy eye, shifting slightly. Light pierced my skull, driving away the last wisps of my dreams. It took me a moment to blink the tears away and make sense of the mash of colors and shapes. Too late, I noticed there was a person in the room with me. I snapped my eyes shut.

"I saw that. Don't you pretend like you're still asleep."

I heaved a great sigh and opened them again, taking a closer look at my surroundings. I was lying in bed in a room with a window facing west, opened up to the lake.

"Still in Lumen," I said out loud.

"Oh, yes," said the voice. "Still here."

Reluctantly, I turned to face Mona. She sat a few paces away, and she looked like a painting. Her fine hair hung down her back, bedecked at last with her real crown of pearls. I could see what she meant now, when she was describing it on the bridge over the ravine; the silver was twined into a peak like a wave lapping at the shore. Her royal pendant rested against a rich gown the color of the deeps of the lake, belted with a string of lustrous mother-of-pearl beads. But the real regality, as usual, did not come from what she was wearing, but from the authority in her face as she stared me down like a hawk on prey.

"I wasn't going to let you creep away that easily," she said. "I have things to say to you." And then, reluctantly, she added, "And you've got a broken collarbone."

I shifted, my left arm immobilized in a sling against my chest. A great deal of linen was wound over my shoulder.

"You'll have a scar," she said. "They had to cut the barb out."

That accounted for the sedative. "Where's Val?" I asked.

"You just missed him. He and I have been in almost constant council for the last two days." She held up the document she had been annotating in her lap—a draft of an alliance between our two countries. "At the moment, he's directing his guardsmen in sending the Alcorans back to their king. But he'll be back shortly. He's spent every spare moment at your bedside."

A moment of silence hung between us. I flicked my gaze around the room to avoid meeting her accusing stare, but it turned out she wasn't going to wait for me to make eye contact.

"You," she said, "are a vicious liar."

I picked at the coverlet. "I didn't actually tell you that many lies, Mona."

"No? How about the most significant one? *'He's not my king'?*"

"Well, he isn't. I really am exiled. I was only ever a subject of his father, not him."

"I still count it as a lie."

"Well, it was one of the few."

"And how about the way we met? All the nonsense with drowning?"

"Oh, no," I said. "I really can't swim. Not at all."

"So did you really fall off the pier? Or did you jump into the ocean on purpose?"

"Both. I sort of seized the moment. I didn't mean to hit my head. But I suppose it added to the authenticity."

"And you were just assuming one of us would save you?"

"I admit it was a little rash," I said. "But I was running out of time. I'd been tracking you down for nearly three months, after I heard Arlen's proclamation in Sunmarten at midwinter."

She closed her eyes. "Sunmarten. You were there?"

"I was. I had been for several months. Easier to weather the winter on the coast than in the hills. I was at the midwinter festival like the rest of the town.

Arlen was . . . well, you know. He was loud. A lot of folk heard him."

"Apparently." She set her parchment and quill down on the table next to her. "So you brought the news to Valien. He told me how you used to meet in Rósmarie."

"When we could manage it. It wasn't easy, but that time, it worked out for us. We spent several days devising our plan, and then I returned to Sunmarten only to find you gone. The news was starting to spread around—you were smart to run when you did. But it threw me for a loop. Val was counting on me, and when I finally found you in Tiktika, I didn't want to waste any more time."

"So you got desperate."

"I did. But it worked well—I had to make you think it was your idea, that I owed you a debt. You saving my life accomplished that."

She was silent a moment, gazing at me. Then she said, quietly, "You could have just told me."

"Would you have believed me?" I asked. "If I had walked up to you and told you I could lead you through the Silverwood back to Lumen, that King Valien wanted to help you drive out Alcoro—would you honestly have believed me?"

"I might have, Mae."

"Well, I couldn't take that chance. Not with so much riding on the outcome."

"So I've been told. Overthrowing a king, uniting a few enemy countries, destabilizing a corrupt council . . ." She stared shrewdly at me. "Or perhaps you were talking about something else?"

"I just wanted to go home," I said wearily. "It's not my fault I had to shift a couple of countries to do it."

"That was a dangerous game you played in the council chamber at Lampyrinae."

I rubbed my face with my free hand. "A memory that will haunt me forever. That never should have happened. Val was cleverer than me at that point, distracting them from who you really were."

She watched me silently for a moment, her mouth set in a thin line. "So what else didn't go according to your plan?"

"Besides being captured? All the fighting here at Blackshell, for one. No one was supposed to get hurt. Val meant to show his allegiance by helping you escort Alcoro out of Lumen. He only swept in with his soldiers to stall the growing battle." The last of the cobwebs cleared from my brain, and I turned my head sharply to her. "How's Arlen?"

Her gaze didn't leave mine, but a shadow flickered across her face.

"He lost an eye."

I pushed myself forward with my free arm amid a blaze of pain. "*What?*"

She gestured in a tight, succinct motion. "His left. Can't see out of it. Struck by the captain's sword."

I clenched my hand on the bedding, my stomach in knots. "No . . ."

"It could have been worse."

"How is he?"

"He's lying in bed, eating fried shiners." The corner of her mouth twitched. "He'll survive, and with a handsome scar, too. He's already wondering if he can get a patch inlaid with pearl. Sorcha is sitting by his bedside."

My arm began to tremble under the exertion of sitting up, and I collapsed back onto the pillow, pinching the bridge of my nose. She waited, letting me ask my next question without prompting me. I blew out a breath. "And Colm?"

She paused. She folded her hands in her lap, choosing her words.

"He'll come around," she said finally.

"Will he ever forgive me?" I asked.

"Well, he does feel a little guilty." She gestured to my shoulder. "He'd have killed you, you know, given the chance, and being that angry . . . I think it frightened him."

"I didn't mean . . . I had hoped . . ."

"I know," she said. "But he was facing that moment all over again, watching Ama be executed. He doesn't like being tricked." She cocked her head slightly. "He was right, you know, in Tiktika. I was being too quick to trust you. He didn't let the urge to return to the lake blind him like it did me."

"He was beginning to see through me up in Scribble Cave."

"Yes. He saw the inside of your compass." She gestured to my bedside table, where Valien's battered compass lay. I had come to this realization too late, in Cavan's house when I had opened the compass to stow Ena's ring and found the few sorry trinkets inside. Colm had asked me about them—the needle, the shoelaces—in the cave. *I'll put them in my compass,* I had told him. Of course he would have gone to do it himself.

"He didn't know what it meant," she said. "And we still needed you to lead us down the Palisades, so he couldn't confront you about it there. He wanted to trust you, but he couldn't think why you would have Valien's compass. If it was something you had stolen upon your exile, you would have said so early on." She reached out and plucked the compass off the bedside table, clicking it open. "But it's not, is it? What would you call it? A lover's token?"

"It wasn't intended to be. It was one of the only things Val could smuggle to my prison cell after his father sentenced me."

She ran her thumb over the lid. "And this name? Redhand?"

"Ah. Yes. The name he chose when he turned thirteen. His father wanted him to take something more in line with the family tradition, but of course Val didn't want to. He didn't hold much to the principles of the previous monarchs."

"Tell me, how did a young prince stray so far from the convictions of his predecessors?"

I shifted. "Well, the short answer is that Vandalen was the worst kind of father. The long answer is that he loved his wife."

"He loved his wife?"

"Queen Sacie. Valien's mother. They fell in love, got married, a few years passed, and she got pregnant with an heir. But something went wrong. She got sick. A month before her due date, it looked like both she and the baby would die, so the healers cut the baby out. Val was born much too early, but worse than that, his mother was too sick to recover from the surgery. She died in quite a bit of pain."

Mona gave a small, resigned sigh. "I see. And Vandalen . . . ?"

"A good father might have embraced his son in honor of the queen's sacrifice. But he wasn't an especially nurturing man, and his mourning made things worse. He left Val to the care of a nurse for most of his childhood. Later on, Vandalen wasn't subtle about insinuating that Val was the reason the king had no wife and the country had no queen. Val grew up under the impression that his father's antagonism was his own fault. And it wasn't long before the king took out his temper in worse ways."

"How horrible."

"Well, the good news is that it made Val a better man than he would have been otherwise. He sought out other mentors to teach him how to ride and hunt and track. In essence, he was raised by his subjects. They helped him create his own morals, and to come to his senses early on. He knew his folk better than his father did before he was ten years old."

"Which Vandalen didn't appreciate, I imagine?"

"Not at all. Things came to a head near Val's thirteenth birthday. Val planned to take an epithet that would undermine his father's royal eagle, but of course Vandalen wouldn't stand for that. There was a tremendous fight. Vandalen took a swing at Val with a candlestick. He missed, but as Val dodged the blow, he fell and landed with his right hand in the fire grate."

She winced. "The scars on his palm . . ."

"It was a bad burn. To this day he can't feel anything with that palm. I found him by accident in the Guard supply room a few hours after it happened, trying to dress the wounds with his other hand. I had only just met him at that point, so I didn't ask what had happened, but he let me clean and dress the burns. Over the years, he trained himself to hold a sword and arrow with his left hand, and he's gotten pretty good at being ambidextrous. Eventually, he and I grew close enough for him to tell me what happened. I disliked Vandalen before that, but to abuse his son . . ." I blew out a breath. "I could never be loyal to that kind of man."

"And Vandalen didn't object to Valien taking the name Redhand?"

"Of course he did. Vehemently. There were a few more confrontations after that. But Val was past caring at that point. He severed what little allegiance he had left and focused instead on training with us in the Guard."

Mona looked back down at the compass. "But he changed his name upon his coronation. Bluesmoke. What was that supposed to mean?"

I fiddled with the linen over my shoulder. "Folk use the term *blue smoke* to describe the morning mist on the mountains. It burns off as the day goes on. It doesn't last. He picked a name that wasn't supposed to last."

"Yes, of course. Because he plans on marrying you."

I cleared my throat and picked at the coverlet again. After a brief moment of silence, she ducked her head to try to catch my eye. "That is the plan, isn't it?"

The coverlet had an embroidered border of blue fish and white seed pearl bubbles. One of the bubbles was loose. I rolled it in my fingers.

"Mae?"

"Yes, yes. I mean, it is."

"Do you want to marry Valien?"

"Yes." I tugged on the pearl. "Yes, I do."

"But?"

I cleared my throat again. "Well, but. Val's kind of the king now."

"Surely you thought of this before you were banished," she said with dry amusement. "His father wasn't going to live forever."

"And bless the Light for that." I twisted the pearl on its thread. "I guess I've just . . . gotten a new perspective after five years of wandering. Before, I felt like I was standing up to Vandalen in a way, sneaking around with Val. When he found out Val had proposed to me, he raged and fumed and ordered me never to so much as look at the prince again. So that very night, midsummer, I got all dressed up and danced with Val until morning." I tugged at the pearl again. "The next day, Vandalen called me up before his council, gave me corrupt orders, let me shout a little, and then *sst*! Out of the country I went."

"So, you've won the ultimate victory," Mona said. "You're going back to your country, marrying Valien, and undoing everything Vandalen stood for. Stop unraveling my embroidery."

I smoothed the pearl back down with the others. "But that's what I mean, Mona. I'm not out for petty revenge anymore. I don't want to become queen just to get the final word. The Silverwood needs somebody who's right for the part."

"Remind me," Mona said with aggravating surety. "What's that pledge you take as a Woodwalker? Colm mentioned part of it in Tiktika. Something about integrity?"

"My might is in my diligence. My honor is in my loyalty. My strength is in my integrity."

"Mm. Diligence, loyalty, integrity." She leaned back in her chair. "That's a better foundation than a lot of monarchs start off with. Hush, don't talk. Listen, Mae. I know you think you've done all you need to do, that everything is all over now, but it's not." She gestured toward the window. "King Celeno isn't going to let me get away with reclaiming my throne, and now he's going to be howling for your king's blood, too. Valien doesn't need a savvy aristocrat on the throne next to him; he needs someone practical and straightforward with a hefty dose of integrity. And so do I."

She narrowed her eyes at me. "I'm not saying I've completely forgiven you. You told me a lot of half-truths, and I'd be lying if I said I didn't feel a little betrayed. But I'm trying to look past that. Ultimately, you did what you promised me you'd do, and you've given me a powerful ally. You risked your life for ours many times. I am truly grateful for that. And I'll be even more grateful if you stand by me, and finish what you started." She spread her hands. "I'm not asking you to marry Valien if you don't want to. But don't turn him down in the fear that you won't be a good queen. You will be."

A week ago, I would have refused to believe any words of Mona's could elicit such flustered gratitude inside me. But the height of this praise was not lost on me. If there was one thing Mona knew about, it was being a queen.

I cleared my throat again. "I'll try."

"Good." She twitched the document on the desk beside her. "You should look over this before we write out the final draft."

"Ah." I stretched my good arm exaggeratedly. "I would, but . . . the sedative, you know." I waved to my head. "Still a little fuzzy."

"I'm sure." She stood and set the document on my bedside table, planting Val's compass firmly on top. "You rest, then. Get well, so I can send you back to the mountains, where you belong. I'll tell Valien you're awake." She gave me a pat on the shoulder on her way out the door. I winced at the flash of pain this brought, knowing full well it was intentional.

The door closed behind her, leaving me in silence. I glanced at the document. I didn't feel like sleeping, but I didn't feel like reading, either. I looked up to the window. The curtains rustled in a slight breeze, and with the breath of fresh air came a faint tinge of smoke.

Gingerly, I peeled back the embroidered coverlet and planted my bare feet on the floor. I was wobbly and sore, but I crossed the room and gripped the window frame, peering out at the lake. The shore bowed outward to my left, affording a distant view of the grand terrace. Folk were moving about, throwing bundles of cloth into the heart of a bonfire.

There was a door next to my window that opened out onto a patio; I unlatched it and went to the rail. The breeze picked up, and one of the bundles of cloth unfurled as it was tossed onto the flames. A prism, surrounded by seven turquoise stars, set on a field of russet. The Lake-folk were burning the Alcoran flags.

Colm was there. I could see him picking through raw materials his folk were bringing him, sorting out things to be salvaged and things to be burned. I half-hoped he might turn around and see me standing across the water. But I wasn't ready to face him yet, and I doubted he wanted to speak to me.

I turned, suddenly finding I didn't want to look at the panorama of Lumen Lake spreading away before me. The walls of Blackshell rose far over my head, blocking the view to the east. The roof swept down to meet the edge of the patio, and I edged toward its lowest point. Ignoring my aches and pains and the last dregs of the sedative, I wriggled awkwardly until I was sitting on the railing. Steadying my bare feet, I stood up and grasped the roof with my good arm. With a heave that sent a thrum of pain through my shoulder, I hoisted myself onto the shingles and crabbed my way up the pitch.

The palace roof rose in three tiers, but fortunately I didn't have to climb past the gable over my room. As I clambered onto the ridge, I looked up to find the mountains soaring away above me, the Palisades white in the midday sun. I scooted until I reached the chimney and rested against it, breathing sharply. I braced my feet against the warm shingles and drank in the sight of my home like a tonic.

"Ellamae?"

I heard the alarm in the voice as it filtered up through the chimney.

"I'm out here, Val," I called.

The door to the patio creaked open.

"What . . . Ellamae, where are you?"

"Up here."

"Up . . . great Light!" His stricken face appeared down at the railing. "Ellamae . . . come down! No wait, don't move. Earth and sky, you're supposed to be resting!"

"I am resting." I gestured to the mountains. "Come and see. I think I can pick out the waterfall over Scribble Cave."

He hesitated, but eventually he decided it was better to monitor my recklessness up close. A string of mild curses escaped him as he clambered onto the shingles. He crawled up the roof to join me, awkwardly, I realized, because he had something clamped under his arm. He threw his leg over the ridge, the fringe on his boots swinging.

"For some reason I thought once you woke I could be done worrying about you," he said. But as he settled down beside me, he reached carefully around my bandaged arm and pulled me into an embrace. "Oh, Ellamae. How do you feel?"

"Like a fish that got hooked and thrown back in the water," I said, pressing my face into his shoulder. I felt his grip tighten slightly, and I leaned back to find his brows knitted together. I took his hand in mine. "Don't think badly of Colm, Val."

He frowned at our intertwined fingers. "I might," he said finally, "if I hadn't seen him save your life. If you had died going over the Firefall . . ."

"I didn't. And I'm not dead now."

"No. And you can't imagine how relieved I am."

"I can imagine it. It's the same relief I feel that everything somehow worked out the way we planned—even when the plan stopped working a few times." I gestured to the bundle under his arm. "What's that?"

He laid the cloth in his lap and unwrapped it. "I had Jenë bring them on the march down from Lampyrinae."

It was stupid, the strength of the emotion that welled up inside me at the sight of my old boots lying in his lap. But they weren't the boots I wore with my civilian clothes; they were part of my uniform, with the double-banded fringe of a Woodwalker. I took them from him, working the supple leather through my fingers.

I swallowed. "Thank you." I drew up one of my knees, trying to pull the boot on one-handed. "Did Jenë not think it odd, that you had her bring them down the mountains?"

"Oh, she knew by that point." He took the boot from me and slid it onto my foot. "They all knew. I gave myself away at the Firefall." He looked up at me, his hands on my calf. "That was terrifying, watching you go over the edge. I . . . well, one might say I lost my head."

"That's not like you."

"Well, you weren't there the day my father kicked you out, were you? I said and did a fair number of wild things then, too." He rested his chin on my knee, moss green eyes on mine. "I'm not always . . . completely rational where you're concerned, Ellamae, if you haven't noticed. And seeing you disappear into those rapids, knowing full well I might have just killed you right then and there . . . I gave everything away. I whirled on our guardsmen and shouted for them to form their ranks and prepare to march down the Palisades, and I couldn't for the life of me figure out why they were all gawking at me. So I had to tell them we were going to drive out Alcoro and restore the Lumeni queen. Turns out I didn't have to worry about word getting back to the councilors—we were gone before they woke up."

"How did they take it? The Guard, I mean." I gave him my other foot. "How did they react?"

"Admirably, all things considered. A handful of them were angry, at first, for all the confusion over the past few months. But it didn't take them long to move past that. They were ready to march in record time. I think most of them were relieved to have a clear objective that didn't involve usurping a country." He slipped on my other boot. "It helped that I made it clear you were to be reinstated to your office. You still have a lot of friends."

"One of them sprung us from prison," I said, wiggling my toes in my boots. "Do you know who it was? It wasn't Jenë."

"It was me."

"It was *you?*"

"Of course it was me. I sent Jenë away to the ridge—I knew she would try to help you, and I didn't want her getting in trouble. I sent every guardsman I could to the prison yard to build the scaffold, to clear the palace. I slipped poppy into the prison guard's drink so he wouldn't come under suspicion." He raised an eyebrow at my alarm. "I thought you would guess. I gave you back my compass with the key."

"I thought that was because I *needed* it," I said sharply. "Great Light, Val, if someone had seen you . . ."

"I spent six years tiptoeing after you on scout missions," he said with a half-smile. "You used to scold me for making too much noise. Nobody saw me."

I shifted on the shingles, slowly, because the pain in my shoulder was beginning to spike. "You saw us, though, in the corridors near the council chamber. When you sent your guardsmen running back to the armory."

"I thought I saw you. I wasn't sure. I was trying to clear the way to the wagoner's courtyard. I thought you could get out that way."

I leaned my head against the cool brick of the chimney. "I'll add it to the list of things I bungled up."

He took my hand in his. "Oh, Ellamae. Listen to yourself. I have never in my life been more grateful or more indebted to anyone. You did the impossible."

"I did the inadvisable, perhaps." I sighed and closed my eyes. "Not that that's particularly new, I suppose." I brushed the fringe on my boots again. "By the way, don't you have something else that belongs to me?"

He hesitated. "I was going to wait until you felt a little better. I feel like I've put you through a fair amount already."

I wiggled my left hand where it rested in the sling. "I want it back. Unless you've changed your mind. You are asking me to be queen now."

He reached into his pocket and drew out my silver ring. "As if I haven't taken that into consideration from day one." He slid the ring onto my finger, kissed my fingertips, and tucked my hand back into the sling. It was awkward, the angle between us, but I kissed him anyway, pressing my free hand against the back of his head. I buried my fingers in his hair, black and glossy as a crow's wing. Oh, how I had missed the simple comfort of a gentle touch. His touch.

My shoulder throbbed, and I broke away and settled back against him, squeezing his fingers against the pain. Fatigue from the overwhelming events of the past few days—no, the past few weeks, years—washed over me. Weary, I rested my head on his shoulder, grateful to have the opportunity to do so once again.

But a thread of unease still flickered at the edge of my relief. I hoped Arlen was all right. I wondered if he was angry with me. I knew Colm was. I wondered if either of them would consider me their friend ever again. And then, softly, a breath of laughter escaped me.

"What?"

"Ever since that night in Rósmarie, for some stupid reason, I thought this was going to end everything. That we'd rebuild the alliance with Lumen, and everything would be finished. I didn't even stop to think of what we might begin by making Alcoro our enemy." I opened my eyes. "What are we going to do, Val?"

He leaned his head against mine, his eyes, like mine, on the mountains. "It's like you always say, Ellamae." He squeezed my hand. "We're just going to have to take things one crisis at a time."

One crisis at a time. One at a time. Only, I had trouble calling to mind what the next crisis might be. Maybe it was a result of the sedative. Maybe it was the warm press of his arm around me. Maybe it was the sight of the mountains soaring into the sky, the Palisades gleaming in the sun. Maybe it was the relief of my new reality—the one that was slowly becoming a tangible realization.

I was going home.

ACKNOWLEDGMENTS

There are, of course, an outrageous number of people to thank for helping make *Woodwalker* a reality. I am especially grateful to my agent, Valerie Noble of Donaghy Literary, for believing so strongly in this story, and to my editor, David Pomerico at Harper Voyager Impulse, for helping the story achieve its full potential. Thanks to Tom Egner and the art department for working so closely with me to create the cover design, and to Jena Karmali, my copyeditor, for the final polish.

Love always to Caitlin Bellinger, my soul sister and partner-in-crime. Words truly cannot describe what you mean to me. Thanks for supporting all my art and writing, from those first garbled middle school stories to now. Thanks to all my other beta readers, who helped me with everything from building a more believable world to critiquing my query letter—Anne

Marie Martin, Brooke Buffington, and my brother Corey, even though he didn't actually finish the book.

I owe special thanks to Ms. Ila Hatter, an incredible interpretive naturalist and wildcrafter, who answered my questions on the cultural heritage of native Appalachian plants.

Thanks to every teacher and professor I've ever had—*ever*—but especially the ones who have kept a close eye on me over the years. Meghan Chandler, Dana and Todd Howard, Nancy LeMaster—you folks make a difference.

Massive thanks to my parents, for always nurturing my creativity and instilling a love of storytelling in me from day one. Thanks for pulling out the magic in each chapter, and for helping me get my facts straight on entomology and medical procedures. Apologies to entomologists everywhere for the creative liberties I took with the habitat and behaviors of blue ghost fireflies.

Perhaps the biggest thanks go to my husband, Will, my very first reader and believer. Thanks for encouraging me to aim for publication and for letting me keep writing even though the house was dirty and the laundry needed to be folded.

And my girls, Lucy and Amelia—you inspire me.

This book is dedicated to my daughters, in honor of every female staffer—past, present, and future—at Philmont Scout Ranch, and for every male staffer who counts us his equals.

Change lives.

ABOUT THE AUTHOR

Park ranger by summer, stay-at-home mom the rest of the year, **EMILY B. MARTIN** is also a freelance artist and illustrator. She's an avid hiker and explorer, and her experiences as a ranger helped inform the character of Mae and the world of *Woodwalker*. When not patrolling places like Yellowstone, the Great Smoky Mountains, or Philmont Scout Ranch, she lives in South Carolina with her husband, Will, and two daughters, Lucy and Amelia.

Discover great authors, exclusive offers, and more at hc.com.